THE INN AT
HIDDEN RUN

Center Point
Large Print

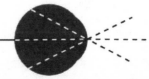

**This Large Print Book carries the
Seal of Approval of N.A.V.H.**

TREE OF LIFE SERIES

THE INN
AT
HIDDEN
RUN

Olivia Newport

CENTER POINT LARGE PRINT
THORNDIKE, MAINE

This Center Point Large Print edition
is published in the year 2019 by arrangement with
Barbour Publishing, Inc.

All scripture quotations are taken from the
King James Version of the Bible.

The text of this Large Print edition is unabridged.
In other aspects, this book may vary
from the original edition.
Printed in the United States of America
on permanent paper.
Set in 16-point Times New Roman type.

ISBN: 978-1-64358-226-9

Library of Congress Cataloging-in-Publication Data

Names: Newport, Olivia, author.
Title: The inn at Hidden Run / Olivia Newport.
Description: Center Point Large Print edition. | Thorndike, Maine :
    Center Point Large Print, 2019. | Series: The Tree of Life Series ;
    book 1
Identifiers: LCCN 2019012501 | ISBN 9781643582269 (hardcover :
    alk. paper)
Subjects: LCSH: Colorado—Fiction. | Large type books.
Classification: LCC PS3614.E686 I575 2019 | DDC 813/.6—dc23
LC record available at https://lccn.loc.gov/2019012501

DEDICATION

Remembering my parents with wonder about the generations that came before and delight in the generations that came after.

CHAPTER ONE

Sad, but true. She would have to procure a new favorite coffee mug. Moving the old one from hand to hand and turning it 180 degrees only confirmed the body of data growing over the last two weeks. The crack down the wide blue stripe would imminently progress to a leak. The wobbly handle was untrustworthy with the weight of the next refill. And the promises of extraordinary adhesive products were not the solution to a receptacle of hot liquids on the way into her throat.

"You're not listening. Jillian Parisi-Duffy, sometimes I wish I could send you to your room like the old days."

"That was twenty years ago." Jillian snatched a tissue from a box on the gray-speckled granite kitchen counter and wiped the bead of brown liquid seeping through the midpoint of one side of the mug and moved to the sink to surrender to reality. The vessel had given her a good run, but it was over. She had thought she could at least finish this cup of coffee. "Besides, I never stayed in my room. You know that. I crept out to the landing and listened to you use the telephone to call your boyfriends."

Nia Dunston, seven years older than Jillian and her former babysitter, swatted her shoulder with the backs of her fingers.

"As if I didn't know that," Nia said. "Sometimes there wasn't even a boy on the other end of the line. It was all show."

"Let's see, there was Ricky and John—and Mario. Then you were over the moon for Jean-Luc."

"In my own defense, I was fifteen, and he was a tall, dark, French foreign exchange student who could already grow a beard," Nia said. "But never mind that. I came to take you for some real coffee."

Jillian pointed to the elaborate café barista-quality espresso and cappuccino system gleaming across the kitchen. Beside it was a single-serve machine with a built-in frother.

"I work at home and look after myself," she said. "I hardly lack for real coffee."

"Real coffee is the kind you have out in the real world with real people," Nia said. "If I didn't show up every now and then to drag you out of this house, you'd never leave."

This was not strictly true. Jillian couldn't rely on her father to buy groceries at appropriate intervals, and she had a weakness for double-dipped, hard-shell chocolate chip cookie dough cones at Ore the Mountain Ice Cream on Main Street. But Nia's assessment was largely true, so Jillian didn't offer a counterargument.

"What's this?" Nia tugged a blue folder from the bottom of a stack of work Jillian had left on the breakfast bar and opened it. She slid out a sheet of paper. "Does your dad know you're taking work from another law firm?"

Jillian lurched across the counter and snatched the folder from Nia. "First, not your business. Second, I have a system, and you're mucking it up."

"Whoa. You seriously need some exposure to the real world."

"Fine. If it will stop you from being so nosy. Let me get my stuff." Jillian picked up the whole stack of folders. She hated carrying a purse, but she wouldn't leave the house without her iPhone. The case held her driver's license, a credit card, and a debit card.

"Run a comb through your hair," Nia said.

"Are you serious?"

"Look in the mirror, girlfriend."

Jillian rolled her eyes but shuffled into the first-floor powder room squeezed between the kitchen and her office in the old Victorian home. Surrounding the green eyes that matched her Irish father's was the mass of black hair that was her Italian mother's legacy, and truth be told, most days Jillian did little to manage it. If she had a video call scheduled with a client, she made sure to tame it and put on a business-appropriate top.

9

Otherwise, she was a wholehearted proponent of working in comfort. Her long-sleeved red T-shirt showed no evidence of breakfast droppings, and her favorite lightweight hooded blue sweater had been through the wash just two days ago, so she deemed herself presentable for an October Thursday. For now, she found a hair band in the cabinet over the sink, gathered her hair at the base of her neck, grabbed her phone and keys off her desk, and returned to the kitchen.

"So you hired her," Jillian said. "That's what you said when you accused me of not listening."

"Well, there you go." Nia's wide-set gray eyes lifted in surprise, and she swung her long brown braid over her shoulder. "I did in fact hire her."

"Even though you know nothing about her."

"I know I need help at the Inn and she needs a job."

"I suppose there's something algebraic about the way that equation settles out." They left through the door on the side of the house that served as its main entrance, and Jillian pulled it shut. Once the home had been a double cottage, two residences sharing a center wall with mirroring floor plans. The other side of the house, just outside Jillian's office, had a similar though less ornate entrance and porch where she sometimes worked while enjoying fresh air and mountain views. A previous owner had opened

10

up the center of the house, making it spacious for one family. Jillian's parents fell in love with the place when she was a toddler, and her mother turned it into a nest of love. For the last fourteen years, only Jillian and her father lived in the nest. She made sure the door locked, just as her mother always had, tugging it toward her twice for good measure.

Anyone who thinks you ever "get over" losing someone you love, or who loves you, from this world—even into the arms of Jesus—is deluded. Jillian had decided that when she was fourteen, and so far nothing had changed her mind.

She glanced over her shoulder at the mountains. Situated nearly at the end of Main Street, before it angled to join the old highway headed west, the house had nearly unimpeded views of the canyon that spoiled her for living anywhere else. The home's gray-blue color, with white trim and rusty red accents, had been her mother's choice, and when it needed repainting a couple of years ago Jillian and her dad didn't even discuss altering the color scheme. They'd never erase this mark of her presence.

Jillian and Nia walked toward downtown Canyon Mines, a community that stretched along the roadway that in its rough form had carried nineteenth-century gold and silver prospectors to the region and now in its modern highway iteration brought tourists, many on their way into the Rockies for skiing, mountain-climbing, hiking, camping, or family day outings.

"You're very analytical, you know that?" Nia set a vigorous clip for someone so short.

Jillian matched Nia's progress with fewer strides of her longer legs and laughed. "I've been told. But I make a decent living because of it."

"You know how much I depended on Carlotta. I hated to lose her, but she had to go look after her mother and she's not coming back."

"You're sure?"

"She called four days ago. The move is permanent."

"I'm sorry to hear that. I didn't get to say goodbye. I'd like to have an address where I can send a note."

"I'll give it to you."

They took a few steps in silence.

"I can't manage on my own," Nia said. "I've tried, with Carlotta gone. I just can't find the rhythms. Leo helps, but when he has a big job of his own, it's hard to juggle everything. I'm exhausted every day."

"The Inn is at capacity every weekend and often during the week," Jillian said. "Obviously you should hire help."

"I haven't even had time to place an ad or ask around town for someone. This young woman shows up inquiring and promising she'll work hard. Providential, don't you think?"

Jillian eyed her friend. "Maybe. What exactly did she tell you about herself?"

"Her name is Meri. M-e-r-i."

"Sounds like it's short for something."

"Probably."

"You didn't ask?"

"You're the genealogist, not me. Meri Davies. She's a graduate of University of the South."

"Sewanee?"

"Is that what they call it?"

"Because it's in Sewanee, Tennessee," Jillian said. "Impressive school."

"She double-majored in biology and chemistry. I did ask that."

"Mmm."

Nia laughed. "You're wondering why she wants a job doing laundry and cleaning up in a bed-and-breakfast with a degree like that from any school. I'm not a complete dolt."

"The question is kind of hanging out there." Jillian's mind drifted to the menu of Ore the Mountain, but she knew Nia's mind was set on coffee and not what she considered the poor substitute served at the ice cream parlor. It was a poor substitute. Nothing to dispute there. She yanked her attention back to Nia.

"I don't know the answer to that question," Nia said. "I realize she won't be at my right hand for six years, like Carlotta was. But I need help, and she needs a job, and it is fairly simple work. So why not?"

"I suppose. When does she start?"

"I left her at the desk when I went to grab you."

"Throwing her in the deep end?"

"Twenty minutes at a time." Nia nodded her head down Double Jack Street. "We'll take a slight detour, check on things, and you can meet her before we hit the coffee shop."

The Inn at Hidden Run Bed-and-Breakfast was the only structure on its block, the second one off Main Street. Another Victorian—most of the structures close to the center of town proudly displayed evidence of the mining era in which the town sprang up—this one was larger and sprawling and painted in natural shades of sand and stone with spots of bright yellow. When Nia and Leo bought it, critics questioned their judgment. But the renovations were splendid, with a veranda encasing the front and two sides of the house, a fascinating web of rooms inside, a partially covered brick patio out back, and a woodworking shop in what had once been a carriage house at the rear of the property where Leo gladly gave demonstrations of his wood-working craft.

They climbed the steps to the shaded veranda, and Jillian quelled a moment of habitual envy, even though she had two perfectly enchanting porches on her own home, and entered through the front door. This was Jillian's favorite way in, the breathtaking view guests saw when they came into the capacious hall at the base of the sweeping oak stairs, with the library that truly was a library to one side with floor-to-ceiling books and a rolling ladder. Across the hall was the parlor with an authentic period piece serving as a reception desk. Behind it sat a young woman with warm bronze skin, blue-tinted black short hair, and studious black-framed glasses on a thin face.

She sprang up.

What a ball of nerves. Jillian hung back.

"Is everything all right?" Nia asked.

Meri nodded. "No one came in." Relief heaved off her words.

"You're doing fine," Nia said. "Remember, Leo is out back."

Meri nodded again.

"I wanted to introduce you to my friend, Jillian. This is Meri."

Jillian stepped forward and offered a hand. "Nice to meet you."

"Thank you."

Was that a tremble in Meri's handshake?

"Jillian and I are going for a quick cup of coffee," Nia said. "We'll be at Canary Cage Coffee, up on Main Street just around the corner. You probably drove past it coming into town. Remember that. It's a great draw for our inn—

just off Main Street and walking distance to many interesting shops."

Meri nodded yet again, this time scribbling notes on a small pad.

"As I mentioned before," Nia continued, "we're fully booked for the next two weeks, so if anyone calls about availability in the short term, the answer is easy. After that, you check the red leather book. I still keep it the old-fashioned way for ambience. I don't like to have a computer out here in the parlor. Even a laptop detracts from the atmosphere guests are paying good money to enjoy in the common rooms, though of course I do the real work in the office. Just open the book and look. The rates are right inside the front cover, if anyone asks about that. If you need Leo, you can push this button on the phone to put a call on hold and use the walkie-talkie to get Leo in the shop. I'll be back soon enough."

Meri pressed her lips together and nodded repeatedly, writing all the while, but to Jillian she looked terrified.

Back on Main Street, Jillian said, "You don't think this is all a bit much for her first half hour on the job?"

"She graduated from Sewanee with a double major. I didn't even ask her to move a load of laundry. Besides, these days most people try booking through our website first. We don't even get that many calls, and no new guests will be checking in for at least two hours."

"You thought this through."

"I'm telling you, I need a break. She practically begged me for the job even though she admitted she has no experience in the industry."

"The industry? She said that?"

"She did. If she wants the job, this is the job. Give me another half hour, and I'll be ready to give her a real orientation. And of course I'd like to figure out how we can help her."

Help her? Jillian cranked her head for a full-on look at her friend.

Nia raised her eyebrows. "You know there's something there."

"Maybe," Jillian said. "What makes you so sure?"

"A person doesn't spend four years as a counselor for at-risk inner-city middle school students without developing an intuition about these things."

"When are you going to take that part-time job with the Canyon Mines School District? They've been after you ever since you came back."

"Jillian. Stay on topic. Helping Meri."

"Nia, I'm a genealogist, as you pointed out."

"So we might need your dad."

"Wrangling a story out of someone definitely is more his style."

They reached Canary Cage Coffee, her father's

favorite spot in Canyon Mines. He could buy anyone a hot beverage and work his magic.

Jillian had her nose within twelve inches of the baked goods case, weighing her options, when an elbow jostled her from behind, forcing her to shift her weight to one foot. She didn't have to turn around.

"Hello, Kristina. You'd better have a waffle cone in your hand."

"Ha. You wish. I just want ten minutes to think about something besides waffle cones and sprinkles and how many customers are going to scowl today when I say yet again that we are out of chocolate chip cookie dough ice cream."

Now Jillian turned around. "You're out of chocolate chip cookie dough?"

"Don't you start," Kris said. "Just for that, you're buying my coffee. I'm going to go grab my couch."

Kris pivoted away from the counter. Jillian didn't mind. She knew what to order.

"Kris Bryant," Nia said, "and now Veronica O'Reilly."

Veronica and her husband, Luke, ran the Victorium Emporium, done up with just enough Victorian charisma to make tourists park their cars, get out, wander through, and then wonder what else might be worth exploring on Main Street. Most of the smaller shops nearby owed their foot traffic to the presence of the Emporium.

"Hail, hail, the gang's all here," Jillian said. "Meet her at the door. I'll get this round and assorted croissants and meet everyone on the couch."

By the time Jillian arrived with espressos, lattes, and enough pastries to allow for extras to take home, the other women were laughing. They all ran businesses and dealt with people face-to-face day in and day out. She had her own business as well, but she was a researcher who prowled depths of the internet most people had no idea existed. Her clients included insurance companies, law firms—her father's, primarily—and individuals who wanted to track missing heirs, sort out unidentified family members, or simply leaf out a family tree as far back as possible. Contacts came from across the country. On her desk were a dozen active cases at various stages of investigation. She had gone from attending genealogy conferences as a participant to presenting at them a couple of times a year, but for many cases she might never meet a client in person, much less have to spend the day disappointing dozens of customers with the lack of chocolate chip cookie dough ice cream.

"These are from Ben Zabel's bakery, you know," Nia said, before biting into a cheese croissant.

Jillian snapped into the present conversation. Everyone knew where the baked goods came from. Ben worked himself to the bone supplying not only his own shop but Canary Cage Coffee, Burgers 'n' More, the Inn, and any other place in town he could think of to keep down the competition by selling them a better baked goods product than they could make themselves and guaranteeing that it would have more tourist-appealing homespun authenticity than anything they could ship in from Denver.

"I hear you have a new Carlotta at the Inn," Veronica said.

Nia coughed brown liquid into her napkin. "That's impossible."

"Then it's true."

"I cannot possibly have a 'new Carlotta,' but yes, I did hire someone this morning. Barely thirty minutes ago. How can you possibly have heard?"

Veronica winked. "I sent Luke over to pick up the latest batch of wooden toy cars Leo had ready. We can't keep those things in the store."

"Well, there you have it."

"Luke stopped in to say hello. He says she's nervous."

"Your husband is enough to make anybody nervous." Nia wadded up her napkin and stuffed it into her empty coffee cup. "I'll thank you all not to scare off my help with your effusion of small-town quirky charm. Come on, Jillian. We'd better get back to Meri."

Jillian stifled a smile and closed the box of

extra pastries. If her father was lucky, there might be one left when he got home from Denver that evening. Or not.

At the corner, Nia hooked a hand through Jillian's elbow. "You're coming with me."

"I should get back to work."

"Just another few minutes. You know what Luke can be like."

"He just likes to kid around."

"He says outrageous things in the process. I might need reinforcements to persuade Meri to stay."

"I doubt it. You said she was desperate."

"But not stupid. Sewanee double major, remember?" Nia began trotting toward the Inn. "Oh no. She's getting in her car."

Jillian trailed a few steps behind.

"Please don't leave!" Nia called out.

Meri, who was leaning into her car, pulled her head out. "Ma'am?"

"Please don't leave!"

They reached the car, a late-model tan Toyota Camry.

"I'm not leaving, ma'am."

"You don't have to 'ma'am' me." Nia braced the back of the car as if she could hold it in place. " 'Nia' is fine. Why are you out here?"

"Your husband said it was all right to get my things. He's at the desk now. You did say room and board came with the position."

"Yes, yes. I'll show you the room right away. There's a place you can park in the back, but you don't have to move your car right now."

Breath whooshed out of Nia's lungs so fast Jillian had to suck in her lips to stifle a laugh. Jillian stepped forward. "What can I help you carry?"

"Thanks. I don't have too much," Meri said. "Just the things in the backseat."

Jillian opened a rear door. The backseat held only a large duffel and midsize rolling pilot case. Meri already had a student-style messenger bag strapped across her torso.

"I'll take the suitcase." Nia grabbed the handle as soon as Jillian had the case out of the car, racing off as if she still feared Meri might change her mind. That left Jillian with the duffel. She closed the back door and started for the house behind Nia.

When the sound of the car's front door closing as well didn't come as quickly as she expected, Jillian squinted back. Meri hunched over a cell phone for a few seconds before throwing it onto the front passenger floorboard and slamming the door.

CHAPTER TWO

He could simply come into her office and kiss the top of her head. But no. That was not Nolan Duffy's style—at least not when it came to his daughter, even if she was twenty-eight. His lips found the crown of Jillian's head and buzzed loudly.

"You'd better not be spitting." Jillian didn't flinch.

"Put your hand up there and find out."

"Ew." Her fingers remained on her computer keyboard.

Nolan's hands moved to Jillian's shoulders and began a massage rhythm. "It's almost seven. Why are you still working?"

"I'm on a trail."

"Come in the kitchen and tell me about it while I scrounge us up some dinner."

At the mention of food, Jillian's stomach rumbled agreement. *Woman cannot live on pastry alone.* She could always return to her work later in the evening. After saving the open file on her computer, she picked up a manila folder and pen and followed Nolan into the kitchen.

He opened the pantry doors and then the stainless refrigerator. "I should go grocery shopping."

Jillian guffawed. "Do you even know where the store is anymore? Besides, we have plenty of food."

"I require inspiration." He opened another cabinet.

"They don't sell that at the grocery store."

"Ah." He pulled a box of their favorite fettuccine from the cabinet. "I shall whisk up a creamy Alfredo sauce adorned with fresh spinach. On the side we shall partake of large pitted black olives, crispy strips of fresh red peppers, and the ever-pleasing sugar snap peas."

"Yum."

Nolan rummaged for pots and utensils. "Now what's your new case?"

Sitting at the granite breakfast bar, Jillian opened the folder. "An insurance company. An older man was found deceased in his home by a neighbor. Police know who he is and found some papers with a paid-up hefty insurance policy, but the beneficiary died years ago and the policy was never updated. There's a provision for the benefit to pass to next of kin, but no one knows who that might be."

"No clues in the man's home about his family?"

"The detectives are stumped. They don't even know who to notify about his death. After six weeks, the coroner is still holding the body in the morgue."

"Enter the genealogist."

"I think they have more information than they realize. They just need help interpreting it. I gave them a list of things to scan and send me to start with. How about you?"

Nolan waved a hand holding a wooden spoon while he poured heavy cream into a pan with the other. "Family law is full of drama. My favorite part is not when I win a judgment or get a big settlement but when I get people to listen to each other. It's all in the story, you know."

"So you've been telling me all my life."

"Because it's true."

Jillian planted an elbow on the breakfast bar, set her chin in her hand, and watched her father cook. He hadn't always cooked. When she was young he was on the partner track at his firm in Denver and missed a lot of dinners at home. On the weekends, his briefcase was stuffed with work that leaked out around the house—under a coffee mug on an end table in the cozy part of the elongated living room spanning the front width of the house where the family watched television, or on the piano bench where he paused to tinker with a few chords, Jillian in his lap, or splayed across her parents' bed, or stacked on an ottoman in the more formal part of the living room. Living in a small mountain town thirty miles outside Denver was supposed to help him balance his life, but ultimately balance had come at the cost of something far more valuable than refurbishing an old Victorian.

"It's your fault I'm a genealogist," Jillian said.

Nolan whisked. "I know. I have no regret. Your mother died. We were both lost without her. I had to make sure you found yourself somehow."

"Thank you, Dad."

He turned around, his whisk still, to meet her green eyes with his.

"You sacrificed for me," she said. "You gave up becoming a partner so you could work less. Work from home some of the time. Miss important meetings. Skip wining and dining the high-powered clients that would have meant high billables. Spend time with me. Help me find something to be interested in, nerd that I was. Nerd that I am."

"You're very good at what you do, Jillian. I couldn't be prouder."

"Dad, the sauce."

He spun around to whisk again just in time.

"It's true, Silly Jilly," he said. "I'm proud. And I never thought of it as a sacrifice. Life is good."

"Still. Thanks."

Nolan whisked.

"Working at home tomorrow?"

"Yep."

Nolan's home office was upstairs, just above Jillian's. She scooted off her stool and took dishes out of the cupboard while he pulled pots off the stove. He slid pasta into the lipped plates and poured the sauce before setting out the raw vegetables. They sat side by side at the breakfast bar. The kitchen held a cozy nook table, and around the corner was a full dining room, but this had always been their spot.

"Tomorrow you cook," Nolan said.

"I have a chocolate croissant I might give you if you'll change your mind." Jillian swirled pasta on her fork.

The landline rang, startling both of them.

"Why do we still have that phone?" Jillian said. They both had cell phones never out of reach.

Nolan peered at the phone tucked away in the corner of the counter. "You tell me. The caller ID says your friend is calling." He got up, lifted the phone from its cradle, and handed it to her.

"Nia?" Jillian said.

"Yes, it's me," Nia said. "Is your dad around?"

Jillian glanced at Nolan. "Yes, he's right here."

"Thanks."

"For you." Jillian extended the phone to Nolan.

"Hello, Nia." Nolan juggled the phone and his fork. "Mind if I put you on speaker?" He set the phone on the granite and pushed a button.

"Did Jillian tell you about Meri?" Nia said.

"A young woman she hired today," Jillian explained. "Carlotta's not coming back."

"I'd like you to meet her," Nia said.

27

"I'm sure that would be lovely sometime," Nolan said.

"Tonight," Nia said.

"Whoa." Jillian swallowed a mouthful of pasta. "We're still eating dinner."

"Perfect," Nia said. "That gives me time to organize an impromptu dessert on the patio. Warm raspberry crumb cake with hand-cranked vanilla ice cream Leo made just the other day. Can you happen by in thirty minutes?"

"Sure," Nolan said.

Jillian returned the phone to its cradle. "You didn't have to do that."

"Nia seems to feel some urgency."

"Something must have happened since this afternoon."

"Like what?"

Jillian shrugged. "This is one of those situations where Nia is operating on instincts more than facts."

"So she thinks there's a story."

"And of course you are just the one to get a stranger to talk."

"She did offer raspberry crumb cake and hand-cranked ice cream. What can it hurt to walk down there and give it a try?"

They strolled in light jackets toward the Inn as streetlights brightened on Main Street, turned left on Double Jack Street, and found Nia, Leo, and Meri on the back patio.

Leo, with his glasses parked on top of his close-cropped head, tended flames in the fire pit. He pointed a finger at Nolan. "Where've you been, stranger?"

Nolan shook Leo's hand. "Figured it was time to make sure you were behaving yourself."

"As well as always."

"That's what worries me."

Nia, standing in the dim yellow light of an iron lamp stand, licked ice cream off a spoon. "Come meet the latest member of our household while I fix you some dessert."

"Hi, Meri," Jillian said. "This is my dad, Nolan Duffy."

Meri shifted her dish to her left hand and started to stand.

Nolan lifted a hand in a stop gesture. "Stay comfortable. Mind if I sit right here next to you?"

Meri shook her head, and Nolan dropped into the two-seat swing beside her and set it into a gentle motion. Nia expertly put a bowl of crumble and ice cream in his hands without disturbing the sway.

"Meri, how did your first day go?" Nolan asked.

"All right, I guess." She glanced toward Nia.

"She was fabulous," Nia said. "Checked in our last set of guests all on her own flawlessly."

"Congratulations! I remember my first day in Canyon Mines." Nolan smeared ice cream evenly over his crumble. "It was Jillian's first day too, though I doubt she remembers it."

"I've seen the pictures," Jillian said.

Nolan's eyes brightened in the firelight. "Meri, didn't anyone take your picture on your first day?"

"No, sir," Meri said.

"Dad." Jillian eyed him sideways. This wasn't the first day of kindergarten.

"Well, you're going to love it," Nolan said. "Friendly people. All sorts of recreation, if Nia ever gives you a day off. You have a car?"

"Yes, sir."

"My wife and I came looking for quiet mountain living. What about you?"

Meri tucked one corner of her bottom lip under her top teeth before answering. "Same, I guess."

"Where'd you come from?"

Another beat. "Back East."

"I've never lived in the East. What's it like?" Nolan filled his mouth with dessert, as if settling in to listen intently to a good story.

Meri shrugged. "More humid and buggy than here, so far."

Nolan nodded in the encouraging way that generally produced ongoing speech in other people. Meri simply took another bite of half-melted ice cream. Jillian counted the number of times her father let the swing glide before speaking. Six.

30

"Leo has always known how to build a nice fire," Nolan said. "He roasts a mean marshmallow too. How do you feel about s'mores?"

"I like them all right once in a while," Meri said.

"Jillian always burned her marshmallows at camp."

"I did not!" Jillian's protest was unhindered by a mouth full of food. This dispute had been going on for fifteen years.

Nolan winked. "Did you go to camp as a kid, Meri?"

She bounded out of her seat, shirking off Nolan's attempt to catch her before the forward momentum of the swing might cause her to stumble into the fire pit, and disappeared around an unlit side of the house. Nia cleared her lap of dessert detritus and shot after her. When she returned alone, Leo, Jillian, and Nolan were upright and staggered at erratic intervals on the patio.

"Well, there you have it. She's gone," Nia said. "I didn't see where."

"I didn't hear a car," Leo said.

"She didn't take it. It's still parked out front right where she left it when she arrived this morning."

"I'm sorry," Nolan said. "I did try."

Nia sighed. "Yes, you did."

"I'll try again another day."

"If you get another chance." Nia sank into her chair.

"How far can she go in Canyon Mines?" Leo began separating logs in the fire pit to put out the fire.

"She doesn't know where anything is," Nia said.

"We're right off Main Street. She found us once. She'll find us again. We'll leave all the lights on."

"What if she doesn't come back?"

"Her things are here," Jillian pointed out. "She moved into her room. I doubt she has her keys in her pocket—probably in her bag—and I know she doesn't have her phone."

"How do you know that?"

"I saw her hook her keys in the pocket of her messenger bag when we dropped her things in her room, and she left the phone in her car. She'll be back." Jillian opted to omit the abrupt and purposeful manner in which Meri had abandoned her phone.

"Your eye for noticing detail is a beautiful thing," Nolan said.

"I promised Veronica to finish a wooden buggy for her shop window," Leo said. "I can stay out in the workshop with the door propped open and keep an eye out for her."

Nia pivoted toward Jillian. "Meri Davies. You're probably right that the name is short for something. Let's hope the last name is genuine. I don't have her Social Security number yet because she never gave me her finished paperwork, but if she's telling the truth about Sewanee, that's a place to begin, isn't it? And if she's from back East, maybe she's lived in Tennessee all her life."

Jillian nodded. "I can start there—if we need to."

"Tomorrow's Friday, and I'll be around through the weekend," Nolan said. "Let's give her a chance to tell her story before resorting to drastic measures."

CHAPTER THREE

Memphis, August 1, 1878

M iz Eliza."
The orphan child's faint voice did not alarm Eliza. She had been ill for two weeks, even while lying in bed at Church Home before coming to the hospital for the last few days, and was soft spoken by nature. The doctor assured Eliza only that morning of the ten-year-old's progress. In another day or two, she could go home to the orphanage where she'd lived the last four years.

"I'm here, honey." Eliza folded a hand over the child's open palm.

"I'm so hot. Is my fever back?"

"No, it's just the weather." It was only the first of August. In Memphis, that meant many weeks of oppressive heat still to come before it was reasonable to expect a break in temperatures. The entire summer had been torrid. By the middle of July, Eliza insisted that her parents—who hesitated to face the reality that the term *elderly* would soon be apt—purchase train tickets for a few weeks in the cooler setting of upper Wisconsin on Lake Michigan with her mother's younger sister's family. They were due for an annual holiday, and so were most of the household staff. Two domestics were attending her parents in Wisconsin, while others had their turns for personal leave, rotating to be sure the grounds and garden in Memphis were adequately tended and the house was looked after.

Eliza dipped a cloth in a bowl of water that had once been cool and wiped Penelope's face.

"I'm thirsty. Am I allowed to drink more water?"

The pitcher at the bedside was empty. Eliza picked it up.

"I would think so," she said. "I'll find one of the nurses to be sure."

The hospital rarely had enough nurses, or so it seemed to Eliza. She was not a nurse. She was not even a parent. Her capacity was a caring lifelong Episcopalian. St. Mary's had been her church for twenty years, ever since it opened as a mission congregation and long before it became the bishop's cathedral. Nearing forty, Eliza was a spinster with no regrets. Having no husband and demands of her own household freed her to care for the children in the orphanage as well as offering occasional support to the handful of negro children in Canfield Asylum, who seemed to her to be in even greater need. Becoming a nun had not been her calling, but the children were. Her parents had ceased trying to marry her off and could not counter her arguments for the Christian virtues of giving herself to the care of others as freely as her position allowed. Throughout the congregation, day school for girls, and orphanages, she was "Miz Eliza," and she answered readily to all who called her name.

Eliza walked down the hall, vowing that tomorrow she would reduce one layer of undergarments and thereby the heat that encased her midsection and legs. Surely no one would notice the fashion habits of a spinster. Already she resisted more than one or two new dresses a season when last year's suited just fine.

She found a nurse who, at least for the moment, was not in motion. Miss Glasserman. Eliza had been at the hospital with Penelope enough days to recognize many of the nurses with their hair twisted in buns beneath their caps.

"For Penelope." She raised the pitcher. "I assume there are no orders from the doctor preventing her from drinking water."

"I'll check right now." Miss Glasserman's heels clicked toward a desk, where she consulted a stack of charts and found Penelope's. "No, no special examinations today. In fact, the doctor is encouraging extra hydration as she tolerates it. Small sips. We all hope she will be released soon if she remains comfortable."

Eliza nodded. "I'll work on that. I don't suppose there is any ice."

"You'll have to check with the kitchen. They'll at least be able to give you cool water most recently from the well."

"Of course."

A pair of doors at the end of the hall burst open, and two men hefting a makeshift blanket hammock bearing a third man pushed through.

Miss Glasserman marched toward them, pointing. "Over there. Why did you come in this entrance in the first place?"

"It was the closest," one of the men said. "He's mighty poorly. Burning up."

Eliza hastened after Miss Glasserman by instinct. She was not a trained nurse, but she knew where the supply room was and might be some help. Gasping, she gripped the nurse's arm.

"To my untrained eyes, he appears jaundiced," Eliza said.

"You are not wrong," Miss Glasserman said softly.

"Where do you want him?" the heavier-set man said. The two still dangled the blanket between them.

"Take him through to the admitting area where you should have gone in the first place." Miss Glasserman pointed.

"Nurse," Eliza said.

"It is hospital policy. I will go with them and suggest that the patient be kept apart if possible, but only a doctor can diagnose."

"You will want to send for Dr. Erskine from the Board of Health."

"That will be up to the examining physician."

"But surely."

"Many conditions may cause jaundice and fever."

The men breathed heavily now with their continued effort in the heat, their faces shimmering in sweat.

"Orderly!" Miss Glasserman called in full voice, and a young man came from around a corner, saw the need, ran for a wheeled gurney, and raced toward them with it.

The nurse trotted alongside the gurney toward the admitting area, calling for a doctor.

Eliza stood with the men who had surrendered their charge and now tried to catch their breath.

"I am Eliza," she said.

"Not a nurse?"

"No. I am here with a parishioner." She still held Penelope's water pitcher.

"Hank." The smaller, wiry man pointed to himself. "This here's Robert. We only meant to get him some help. We found him lying there in the alley. Saw he'd been sick. Didn't seem right to leave him there in it. You know. Since . . ."

"Since you were here five years ago," Eliza said. What was the point of being indirect? "And you know what this illness is."

Both men raised palms toward her and launched rapid protests.

"We just unload steamboats."

"We're not doctors."

"If we don't get back to work, we'll lose our jobs."

"I've got little ones to feed."

"You can't go!" Eliza took a tone stricter than she used with rambunctious boys at the orphanage most days. "You were exposed the moment you checked to see if he was all right." No steamboats had been allowed to dock in Memphis proper for days. They couldn't have been unloading anything. Health officials had seen to that.

They shook their heads.

"They'll take care of him," Robert said. "That's what they do here. He'll get better."

"Have you forgotten the last outbreak already?" Eliza took a step forward in challenge. Five years ago, the orphanage had taken in sixty children. Constance, Thecla, and the other Sisters of St. Mary's had barely arrived from New York, expecting to open a school, not an infirmary. They were teachers, not nurses. By God's grace they had managed to nurse all but eight children to health, but the disease had spread its malignant tendrils through Memphis, shooting fear in its path.

Quarantine was the only answer until officials

could be certain these men had not been infected.

"Is this man a steamboat worker?" Eliza said. "Is that how you know him?"

The two exchanged glances, not answering.

"It is of utmost importance that you give the authorities whatever information you have," Eliza said. "Clearly your friend is unconscious and may not rouse. Who is he?"

More silence.

"Tell me." This time she spoke through gritted teeth. "Or go through those doors and tell a doctor."

"Not a friend exactly. Just someone we see." Robert sighed. "William Warren. A deckhand. Sometimes he comes up working a ship from New Orleans. He got in last night."

"I read the *Appeal* every morning. The quarantine notice is widespread," Eliza said. "There have been six yellow fever deaths in New Orleans, and the Memphis Board of Health put a stop to steamers coming from the South. All the boats have been sent to President's Island for quarantine and disinfecting of cargo and crew."

"He had supper in Kate Bionda's restaurant last night." Hank shrugged. "I was there. Saw him myself."

"Then you were exposed last night, rather than today." Eliza swallowed back the scolding burning up in her throat. "How did he get all the way from President's Island?"

Robert raised one shoulder and let it drop. "It's only a few miles. If a man's looking for a good time, he'll find a way off. Even President's Island needs supplies back and forth, especially with all the extra people in quarantine. He didn't mean nothin'."

Tell that to your wife and children if you get sick.

"Why don't you go to the admissions area as well?" Eliza said instead. "They'll appreciate this information. Have a word with Nurse Glasserman. She can explain to the doctor treating Mr. Warren. I'm sure he'll have some advisable precautions to suggest."

"I feel fine," Robert said.

"Me too," Hank said. "We'll just get out of the way so the good doctors and nurses can take care of the sick people who need them."

As one, they turned and strode—nearly ran— toward the door they'd used to enter the building.

"Wait! May I have your full names? The streets where you live?"

But they were gone, the door closed behind them.

"Miz Eliza?"

Eliza turned to the timid voice behind her, a young woman she recognized as an occasional volunteer.

"Penelope is asking for you. If you like, I will fill the water pitcher so you can go to her."

CHAPTER FOUR

"S hall I bring you back a coffee from the Cage?" Nolan gripped the doorframe as he leaned into Jillian's office. No matter how early he was up, she was always at work earlier.

"Like it would still be hot by the time you sauntered back with it after saying good morning to half the town." Jillian moved the orange sticky note she used to keep her place in her notes. "Besides, have you noticed that the only thing missing from our kitchen is a personal barista, a service I am perfectly competent to provide?"

"In other words, you've already had two cups of espresso before seven thirty."

Jillian's voice dropped to a mutter. "I may or may not have." She raised her head. "I may have identified a young woman who will be shocked to discover she is heir to the estate of her father's great-uncle."

"Well done. I never doubted you."

"I've *identified* her genealogically. Now I have to find her physically."

"Can't the detectives do that?"

"I think they're counting on me for the whole package—which I'd like to do. And I've got three other cases I promised results on this week or next."

"You'll get it done."

Nolan had a briefcase full of files to read before the day was over, or at least before Monday when he was due to sit down with two branches of an extended family and mediate their differences in the family business. But first he'd take the long way to Canary Cage Coffee and enjoy some morning sun.

He hadn't forgotten about last night either. He could take his coffee to go and swing by the Inn on the way home and see what happened to Meri. Guarding information happened all the time in his line of work. Sometimes he found himself playing good cop–bad cop with another attorney who preferred to strong-arm information out of a client or opposition counsel suspected of withholding relevant content, but those were not the days Nolan was proud of his work. He didn't go into law to win—at least not in that way.

Clark Addison was behind the counter at the Cage as he always was for the morning rush of Canyon Mines residents grabbing coffee on their way to work or tourists looking for a caffeine lift to start off a day of exploring the area. Nolan never minded standing in line. It meant business was lively for his old friend Clark, and a crowded coffee shop reflected positive economic activity for Canyon Mines in general. Ben Zabel waved on his way out of the shop. Nolan's mouth salivated at the thought that Ben's morning pastries, just delivered, might even still be warm. The line gave him time to contemplate his options—coffee and pastry or a fuller breakfast also available at this early hour.

She slipped in, and he almost missed her. When he caught her eye, she glanced away, pretending she hadn't noticed.

But she had, and Nolan knew it.

He gave up his place in line before she could backtrack and leave the coffee shop.

"Good morning, Meri." Nolan glided to a position between Meri and the door.

She looked around again before visually surrendering. "Hi."

"Have you got time for breakfast? My treat."

Meri's shoulders sank an inch. "Probably. Not sure if I still have a job."

"I take it you haven't talked to Nia this morning."

She shook her head.

"Did you go back to the Inn at all?"

"Late. But I left again early."

"Sounds to me like you could use some fortification." Nolan touched her elbow to guide her toward the ordering line. "You won't see it on the menu, but I can get Clark to make us scrambled eggs and potato cakes. And bacon, if you're not a vegetarian."

"I'm not."

"He'll make any kind of elaborate morning beverage you can dream up." Nolan nudged Meri forward in line. Under other circumstances, he might suggest a companion grab an open table while he placed an order, but he wasn't taking any chances with Meri. While she scanned the posted menu, Nolan slipped his phone from his pocket and sent Jillian a quick text.

I HAVE MERI. TELL NIA. DON'T LET HER COME.

At the counter, Nolan put his forearm down and leaned toward Clark. "We're going to need two of your secret specials."

"Orange juice?" Clark said, his gray hair tied back in a ponytail.

"Of course."

"Coffee?"

Nolan gestured toward Meri. "What do you like?"

"Caramel mocha macchiato?" Meri scrunched up her cheeks.

"Say it with confidence." Clark showed a fist.

She offered a shy smile and repeated, "Caramel mocha macchiato. Whole milk. Extra whipped cream."

"Now you're talking," Clark said. "Your friend here will have a large black coffee. He's a purist with no imagination. Find a place to sit and I'll bring everything out when the food is ready."

Nolan scouted the possibilities farthest from the door. If Meri bolted, he wouldn't tackle her, but he'd like the opportunity to politely stride out with her, not chase her and have the door hit him in the face. He walked past the couch where Jillian sometimes gathered with her friends. Intuition told him that, in addition to the practicality of juggling plates, juice glasses, and coffee, Meri might feel less exposed with a table between the two of them. He found one next to the front window and let her have the seat with the best view of the street and the least sensation of feeling trapped. He hoped.

"I want to apologize," Nolan said.

"About what?"

"Upsetting you last night."

Meri drew a lone finger across the table's edge. "It wasn't you."

Nolan left a silent space, waiting to see if she would meet his gaze. "Something upset you."

Her eyes moved from one side of the table to another but not toward his. "Like I said, it wasn't you."

"I was just being friendly. I'm sorry I made you feel unsafe."

"You didn't."

"You ran away."

"I appreciate breakfast."

"But could I please stop being so nosy?"

She let the answer hang unspoken.

46

A young couple with an infant and a pre-schooler began arranging themselves at the table next to theirs. A booster seat for the pre-schooler—perhaps three years old, with adorable pink glasses strapped to her head. And a bib. And a toy to occupy her while they waited for their food. Adjusting the angle of the stroller for the infant. Making sure the baby didn't need changing and plugging her mouth with a pacifier with a limp giraffe hanging from the end. Giving her another toy to clutch in one hand. Picking it up when she dropped it immediately. Pulling out a disinfectant wipe to clean it.

Nolan caught the eye of the young mother and smiled.

"My wife and I only had Jillian," he said to Meri. "We didn't decide not to have another child. I was just working so much, and commuting to Denver, and we were working on the house here. And we woke up one day and realized we were raising an only child. Jillian wasn't likely to have much in common with a sibling ten years younger than she was without at least one in between."

"I guess not," Meri said.

"That's when we took on the motto 'Make life happen.' We tried to be more intentional about our decisions after that."

"Are you sorry? That you didn't have other children?"

"Sometimes. For Jillian's sake more than my

own. We lost her mother, and now she's stuck with just me."

Meri just nodded slightly.

Clark turned up with their food and set the feast in front of them. Today's version of the secret special included Ben's croissants and melon balls along with the items Nolan had promised.

"How about you?" Nolan asked once Clark withdrew. "Brothers and sisters?"

Meri picked up her fork and nudged her food around for a couple of seconds. "One of each."

"Older? Younger?"

She separated a trio of melon balls. "Older." Her face bore no trace of enthusiasm for the topic.

"I get it." Nolan tore off one end of his croissant, releasing an aroma he craved inhaling. "The sort of siblings who are good at everything, and you come along behind them in school and the teachers remember their perfection."

Her head picked up now, her dark eyes meeting his for the first time in the entire conversation.

"I have two older brothers," he said. "They were always star students, not to mention athletes. It can be a lot of pressure to measure up."

"You're a lawyer," Meri said. "Somehow I don't think you were a slouch in school either."

"Busted." Nolan scooped some eggs into his mouth and considered his approach. "But it would have been nice to have more teachers discover my own aptitudes rather than expect I would be just like my brothers."

Meri chewed eggs while she stabbed a piece of melon with her fork and surveyed the scene on the sidewalk. It was still early. Residents were getting their kids to school and themselves to work. Fall midweek tourists were not great in numbers, but foot traffic in the street might inflate later in the day. If Meri had come from Tennessee, as her alleged alma mater and license plates suggested, she was a long way from home. A long way from the older brother and sister she wasn't eager to discuss.

"You're right," Nolan said. "I am a lawyer. So I'll make you a deal."

Her gaze returned to him, wary. "What kind of deal?"

"I'll go back to the Inn with you so you don't have to talk to Nia alone about—well, about whatever the topic turns out to be in the process of making sure your employment is secure. If that's what you want."

She pushed some more food around on her plate. "I understand in the legal world there's something called 'consideration.' What do you get in exchange?"

Nolan laughed. "Yes. In consideration for what I'm offering, you allow me to be present."

"But that's not really anything."

"Isn't it? It's what I want."

49

Meri pulled her caramel mocha macchiato closer. "This is not some sneaky way of saying I'm hiring you as an attorney, is it? Am I supposed to give you a dollar for a retainer?"

"Of course not. I hope it's a rather direct way of saying that if you want a friend in this town you've come to alone, I'm offering to fill the position. Pro bono."

She sipped on her coffee once and then again.

And then she nodded and slowly let out a long breath.

They watched the young family next to them and the street scene outside and ate their food and drank their coffee without saying much more. Nolan finally crumpled up his paper napkin and dropped it in his plate.

"Well, friend, shall we?"

"Nia will probably tell me to either pay for my room or go," Meri said. "My first full day of work, and I didn't show up."

"I'm pretty sure that's not what will happen, but I'll be there for moral support." Nolan stood and led the way out of the coffee shop. He pointed across the street and two short blocks down. "When you officially get some time off, you have to visit Digger's Delight. The *best* chocolate on the planet."

"Because the owner tempers it all herself every morning," Meri said.

"How did you know that?"

She waved a hand. "These candy shops in small towns are always that way. Why else would the tourists come?"

"Well, be sure to introduce yourself to Carolyn, the owner. She's happy to talk to anyone interested in the process of turning candy by hand."

Walking from the Canary Cage to the Inn could be measured in single-digit minutes. When Meri's pace dragged, Nolan slowed without comment. When she sighed, he did not remark on the tremble of air flowing from her lungs.

"Nia?" Nolan called into the empty rooms of the Inn.

"Back here."

Nia was in the Inn's laundry room, behind the kitchen, folding sheets. She added the one she'd just finished to her stack. The woman could fold fitted sheets with perfect corners. His wife had taught her to do that when she was a teenager, after a babysitting session. Even Jillian had never learned. Certainly Nolan hadn't.

"I'll make tea," Nia said. "We can sit in the kitchen."

"We just had a filling breakfast at the Cage," Nolan said.

"Then we'll just sit in the kitchen and talk."

Meri sat on the edge of her chair, hands tucked under her thighs. "I don't know what came over me. I'm a very responsible person. Really. I'm very sorry. It won't happen again."

51

"I'm here as a character witness," Nolan said. "She means it."

"Nolan," Nia said, "we'll work it out."

"I hope so," Meri said. "I'm genuinely sorry for last night. And this morning. I didn't know how to fix it, so I couldn't face you."

"I was disappointed to find you gone this morning," Nia said. "I will tell you the truth about that. But a rough beginning doesn't mean the end has come already."

"See?" Nolan tapped Meri's shoulder. "What did I tell you?"

"I do want to set a few ground rules," Nia said.

"Of course," Meri said.

"You will have regular time off, and I won't ask questions about where you go when you're off. That's up to you. But I have to know I can depend on you when you are on duty."

"You can. I promise. No more disappearing."

"If a special need arises, just say something. This is not the army. We can adapt. But this is a business, so we have to work together to cover all our bases. It won't be long before the ski season starts, and we'll be busy all the time."

"I understand. You can count on me."

"So you still want the job?"

"Absolutely. If you still want me."

"I will need your paperwork to officially put you on the payroll."

"I'll do it today."

Nolan pushed his chair back. "I'll leave you two to sort things out from here."

Nia was already making a written list of tasks that would form Meri's job description.

At home Nolan stuck his head into Jillian's office again. "You had another cup of coffee, didn't you?"

"I promise, decaf the rest of the day." She tapped a file. "But I closed this project. So what's up with Meri?"

"She has an older brother and sister she doesn't want to talk about."

"That kind of thing is your department."

He nodded. "I'm not giving up. I'm sure either one of us could find out with a phone call whether she really went to Sewanee, and if the answer is yes and her name is real, you could find out who her siblings are without too much trouble. Maybe Sewanee is a family tradition."

"All true," Jillian said. "But I'm used to poking around in people's private business because a client has a justifiable reason to know the information. Doesn't this feel more like an invasion of privacy—privacy she's clearly going out of her way to protect?"

"Valid argument, counselor," Nolan said. "On the other hand, she needs help. So we have to get her on board with letting us help her."

"Which takes us back to your department."

"We're a package deal, Silly Jilly. Deal with it."

CHAPTER FIVE

Ten after three. Jillian rubbed her eyes and ran her hands through her barely brushed hair.

Truth be told, she wasn't sure she had brushed her hair that morning. She showered. She was certain of that. But after toweling out the drippiest weight of moisture from her hair, had she actually picked up the brush on her bathroom sink?

A yawn ensued, and she regretted her promise to switch to decaf. Her to-do list for the day was unforgiving. Mrs. Answald was paying her a ridiculous amount of money to leaf out a family tree in time for a family reunion bringing together a hundred descendants from one married pair six generations back. Jillian had intended to say no, on the simple grounds that the request had come too late for the deadline and the amount of work already on her desk. Somehow she said yes, and she couldn't back out now. Instead, she would just have to pretend she was ten years younger and could get by on coffee instead of sleep.

Except for that promise about decaf.

For now, she wandered into the kitchen, pausing at the coffee station long enough only to pick up the mug she'd used that morning and move it to the sink. It was a squat-shaped thing she'd taken from the cabinet, doubtful it would become her new favorite. The handle wasn't right. But at least she'd given it a fair chance. For now, a cold beverage, even a simple glass of water poured over ice, could help—especially if she threw it straight at her own face.

"You need a break."

Jillian jumped. She hadn't seen her father at the kitchen table.

"You've hardly moved in the last six hours," he said. "I have just the thing."

"I'm allowed coffee after all?"

He shook his head. "Better. Chocolate-covered cherries from Digger's Delight."

"We have some of those?"

"We will, as soon as you walk down and buy them."

"Dad. That's not funny."

"Call Nia and tell her you promised me some cherries for dessert."

"But I haven't."

"Are you saying you don't want me to have my favorite cherries tonight?"

"Don't put words in my mouth."

"Then you do want me to have them. That's as good as a promise, which you are now obligated to fulfill."

"Dad." He was impossible. "I have a pile of work."

"And you haven't seen daylight. It's not healthy."

"And chocolate-covered cherries are?"

"All things in moderation. I believe you'll find a walk and some fresh air will perk you up and give you a second wind for that mound of work. No caffeine required."

Jillian crossed her arms. "Okay, but if I'm providing dessert, then you're cooking dinner again."

"You drive a hard bargain. Deal."

"But why Nia?"

"Oh that. It's the best way to take Meri along."

"This is about Meri?"

"Just take her, all right? Buy the girl some chocolate."

"What if she won't go?"

"That's why you need Nia."

"This is sounding rather circular, Dad."

"Nia invites Meri, and it smooths things over after what happened. Don't let Nia leave Meri behind. They both go with you, and you bring me back some intel."

"Intel? What am I, the CIA? Why don't you just take Meri to the candy store yourself?"

"I bought her breakfast. I can't be her only friend in Canyon Mines. That would be creepy."

"Fine."

"Jilly."

"Yes, Dad?"

"You have your mother's hair."

"Don't worry, I'll brush it." Jillian filled a glass with tap water, downed it, and called Nia.

Meri tried to beg off the excursion. Nolan had been right about that. The depth of her penance did not allow relief from her duties even for thirty minutes once she had finally taken them up for the day.

"It's an order," Nia finally said. "Leo's in the office hanging a couple of shelves for me. He can handle whatever comes through the door in the next half hour."

So they set off down the street.

"Meri has been doing a marvelous job." Nia tapped Meri's shoulder three times. "You would hardly know she started just yesterday."

"That's great." Jillian smiled at Meri, who only shrugged.

"She knows all the guest rooms by their names already, and she's a pro with the electronic washer and dryer. Carlotta was terrified by those machines when I bought them last spring, and I'm not entirely sure I blame her, but not Meri. Bing, bing, bing, all the right buttons the first time around."

"It's not that hard," Meri said. "The instructions are right inside the lid."

"Don't discount yourself," Nia said. "You did a lot today to make things easier for me. You absolutely deserve this little break."

Jillian gently elbowed her friend. *Don't over-compensate.* Meri was an intelligent young woman. She would see through Nia's effort to dredge up every possible compliment after a rough start to the day. Time to change the topic.

"Carolyn's family has been in Canyon Mines since the mining days in the late nineteenth century," Jillian said. "A lot of families around here have long ties to the area. She's been making candy for decades. If you're a history buff at all, you'll find the building interesting."

"It was the old town livery, right?" Meri said. "I do find that very interesting, actually."

Nia glanced at Jillian. "How did you know that, Meri?"

Meri shrugged. "It just popped into my head. I must have read it somewhere. Probably a brochure. I picked up a few when I first came into town yesterday."

Nia shook her head. "I don't think so. I've heard Carolyn mention that fact occasionally, but it's not in the standard tourist materials."

"It could be," Jillian said.

"It's not," Nia insisted. "Running a bed-and-breakfast, I have a vested interest in what the tourist materials look like, not to mention a rack of brochures I'm constantly straightening in the dining room where the guests make a mess of them every morning. None of the brochures say that."

Meri's eyes bulged as her lips pressed closed.

"It's not a secret. A lot of people know," Jillian said. "Does it matter where she heard it?"

"I guess not," Nia said.

Back off, Nia. Don't make her bolt again before we get a chance to help.

"Meri, are you a milk chocolate fan or a dark chocolate fan?" Jillian changed the subject once again. "Or white? Carolyn makes that too, though some people don't consider that real chocolate."

"I guess I'd have to say milk chocolate, when I have the choice," Meri said. "My brother thinks the whole world should be in love with dark chocolate. No matter how many times I say I don't care for it, he sticks it in front of my face anyway."

"Well, nobody is doing that today," Jillian said. "My dad and I are pretty evenly split on these things, so I usually buy a mixture. As long as I go home with something that has cherries in the middle, he's happy."

"Here we are." Nia pulled open the door and let Meri step through.

Jillian hung back long enough to glance at the plaque on the building summarizing its history. It said nothing about the structure ever having been a livery.

So where did Meri pick up that true but obscure-to-newcomers fact?

Inside, Nia introduced Meri to Carolyn, who

asked the innocent question she asked of dozens of people who came into her shop from out of town every day.

"Where are you from?"

Meri examined the crème-filled selections. "Back East. Is it true your family has been here for generations?"

"Since the 1870s. How do you like Canyon Mines?"

Meri smiled at Carolyn. "Have you ever thought of living somewhere else?"

"Never. This is my home. Have you been here before?"

Meri drew a finger along a seam in the glass case. "Did you learn to make chocolate from someone in your family?"

"My mother. What kind of chocolate do you like?"

"Milk chocolate."

"With fillings, or just straight chocolate?"

Meri tilted her head, pushing her jaw forward. "Some of both, I guess."

Jillian listened and observed—intel, after all. Meri often waited a beat before she answered questions, no matter who asked them, or adroitly turned the topic back to the inquirer. Was she making up answers, or was she trying to keep her story straight?

On the top of the glass case were several small plates with bits of chocolate samples. Carolyn urged Meri to try a few while Nia selected an assortment of pieces to use in the parlor for evening guests before foisting a variety on Meri to keep in her room and enjoy as she wished.

Jillian bought some cherries for her father, a couple of marshmallow bars, and two peanut butter cups—one milk chocolate and one dark chocolate. She knew better than to buy too much at one time, because just like Ben's pastries, she would eat uncontrolled quantities of Carolyn's candies at her desk.

They began the stroll back toward the Inn.

"Your brother is wrong," Nia said.

"Excuse me?" Meri said.

"About the chocolate. Milk chocolate is a fine choice, and if it's what you want to choose, then you should be free to choose it."

Meri's eyes moistened instantly, and she deflected her glance.

"Brothers can be such a pain," Nia said. "I have one of my own. But I also wouldn't trade him for the world. What did your family enjoy doing together when you were growing up?"

Meri looked around and said, "This. But I was much younger then. Only eleven."

As puzzlement passed through Nia's face, Jillian gently touched her friend's arm. *Don't say anything.*

Meri cleared her throat. "My parents had very busy jobs. We had a few vacations where we really got away and explored some small towns where nobody knew them. I liked that."

"Makes sense," Jillian said before Nia could jump in. "I remember what it was like before my dad started working from home some of the time. I liked it when I had both my parents to myself at the same time."

Back at the Inn, Meri lunged through the door. "I'll move that load of towels in the washer."

"Thank you," Nia said. But she was talking to Meri's back. She turned to Jillian. "What just happened?"

"I'm not sure, but I think she almost let her guard down."

"So her family has something to do with why she's here."

"Clearly."

"That mean brother of hers."

"We don't know that he's always mean. He may just be thickheaded about chocolate."

"Whatever." Nia moved through the parlor and toward the small office behind it. "Come here."

Jillian followed.

Nia handed her a scrap of paper. "I have her Social Security number now. You can find out stuff with that, right?"

"Some things; yes."

"Then do it."

"We'd be crossing a line here, Nia."

"Call it some kind of employment background check or something."

Jillian sighed. She could find out felonious activity without digging too deep. "Or something. Did you ask her for her actual Social Security card? A lot of employers do that to confirm identity."

"She said she didn't have it."

CHAPTER SIX

Memphis, August 13, 1878

Her mother's telegram was of course meant to taunt Eliza into boarding the next train north.

" 'Refreshing breeze off the lake *Stop,*' " she read aloud. " 'Come *Stop* Callie due for leave *Stop.*' "

"No, ma'am." Callie set Eliza's lunch plate in front of her. Cold ham, cut melon, and a pea salad with a dressing containing a secret ingredient Eliza had been trying to finagle out of Callie for the last six years. "The others have their leave. When dey be back, I go for a week. Dat be how it is. Your mama know."

"You could have your leave now, if you want to." Eliza picked up a fork, spread the pea salad, and sniffed it. "I do not require the tending my mother thinks I need."

She spent most of her days away from the house and could just as well spend more time at the orphanages. With school out of session for the summer, some of the teaching sisters from the day school were on their own break at the Mother House in Peekskill in New York, but the orphans had nowhere to go, and the staff who remained at Church Home appreciated extra hands.

"No, ma'am." Callie wiped both black hands on her crisp white apron. "I be right here, lookin' after you and da house and helpin' you get in your dresses. You just eat da pea salad. No need to bother 'bout what's in it."

"Callie."

"Miz Eliza. Dis be da way it be."

"You could sit down and have your lunch with me."

"No, ma'am."

"We could eat in the kitchen if you're uncomfortable in here."

"Your mama would not abide it."

"My mother is not here."

"No, ma'am."

Callie glided out, leaving Eliza alone at a dining room table that could easily seat twelve for a formal dinner. At least it was the coolest room in the house. Eliza did as she was told and ate her lunch.

Curry, perhaps. Just a pinch. Callie was not live-in help. She left after supper. Before she went to bed, Eliza could check the spice rack in the kitchen and see if it held curry and if it seemed like the tin may have been used recently.

"Miz Eliza." Callie stood in the doorframe, her narrow face squeezed even further.

"What is it?" Eliza pushed her plate away.

"The butcher's boy come with the order. He say Kate Bionda die."

"Oh no." Eliza had dreaded this news—the first death of someone who clearly contracted yellow fever in Memphis rather than carrying it up the Mississippi. It was no surprise when the *Appeal* reported Kate's illness and the others that followed. William Warren had violated the quarantine for his own pleasure. Kate had done nothing but serve him a meal without knowing he was sick.

"I made a lemon custard cake for dessert," Callie said. "Vanilla cream frosting, just the way you like."

Eliza pushed back her chair. "Save it for supper, please."

"You goin' out, ma'am? The orphans?"

Eliza met the servant's dark eyes. "Another errand, I believe."

"Again?"

"There are streets I have not tried."

"Mama not goin' like dis."

"Unless you have taken up writing letters to my mother behind my back, Mama is not going to know." Callie was literate enough to cook and shop, but in all her years working for the family, Eliza had never seen her write a full sentence.

"She have her ways," Callie said. "You know that. You not invisible in those parts of town. People talk. Word get back by da help."

Callie had a point.

"I'll be careful."

"I hope so. I hate to think I waste perfectly good lemons in dat cake if you not here to eat it."

Callie could be cheeky for someone who drew the line at eating with Eliza in the kitchen during the weeks alone in a big house together.

"Perhaps you would do me a favor and go out to the street to wave down a cab while I get my hat and bag."

"Yes, ma'am."

When Eliza exited the house a few minutes later and descended the front steps, Callie was holding the horse's bridle to the consternation of the driver.

"I just makin' sure he wait for you." Callie glared at the driver.

Eliza recognized him. He often drove slowly through her downtown neighborhood trolling for daytime fares.

"Hello, Harry."

"Miz Eliza." He tipped his hat. "I explained to Callie that I can't take you today."

"Do you have another fare waiting?"

"It's where you goin' he don't like," Callie said.

"I haven't said yet where I'm going."

"He know."

"Harry, is this true?"

"Miz Eliza, there's fever over there."

Eliza twisted the handle of her handbag and

sucked in her cheeks. Harry drove an open cab. The risk was low. Besides, how many people did he shuttle around all day? He was hardly insulated from infection.

"Of course I don't want to endanger you, Harry. I'm not asking you to even get down off your driving bench. Just park at the end of the block and wait for me while I knock on a few doors."

"And what if you bring the fever to me?"

"How about this? If I find what I'm looking for and the news is bad, I'll give you a signal, and I won't ask you to bring me home."

"No, ma'am." Callie shook a finger. "No one goin' leave you there if dat happen."

"It's not so far," Eliza said. "I can't expect him to wait for me, in any event. If it happens, when I'm finished I'll walk a few blocks and hail another cab." Or she would walk home. It would not be the end of the world.

"I'm agreeable," Harry said.

"No, ma'am," Callie said.

"Harry, the step please," Eliza said.

Harry pulled down the step while Callie glowered.

"Remember the lemon custard cake," Callie said.

"If I won't be here for supper, I will send word." Eliza gathered her skirts into the open carriage and turned away from Callie's scowl.

Robert and Hank, the two men from that night at the hospital, had never left her mind. She was right about William Warren even before the doctors arrived at the conclusion he carried yellow fever. Dr. Erskine, from the Board of Health, transferred him back to the quarantine hospital on President's Island. She'd tried the very next day to find Robert and Hank, starting with the neighborhood around Kate Bionda's restaurant and gradually moving outward. She didn't know the area well. Four decades living in Memphis, a city of forty-seven thousand people, had afforded her the privilege of choosing her service in the community. She chose the orphans, not the dockworkers. She'd never eaten in Kate Bionda's restaurant or anywhere near it. The goods that came into Memphis on the cargo ships, unloaded by Robert and Hank and their many coworkers, made their way by wagon to the network of shops where her family shopped at their convenience or, more likely, where they sent their servants. This wasn't a part of Memphis she'd needed to know well at any part of her life before this.

But she was getting to know it now.

Kate's restaurant was shuttered, probably for good. Without Kate, would anyone want to operate it? Would anyone want to run a business of any sort in the place where yellow fever had come again to Memphis and taken its first life?

"Miz Eliza?" Harry twisted on his bench. "How many blocks this time?"

Too many and he might turn the horse around before her home was out of sight. Too few and she might come close to answers and never know it.

"Six."

Silence.

"Five, then, but that is firm."

"Yes, ma'am."

"Are you certain you do not know these men?"

"Yes, ma'am."

"I had another driver the other day. I'll have to show you where we left off."

He dropped her, as agreed, at the end of a block, and Eliza knocked on doors asking not only for Robert and Hank but whether anyone inside had symptoms of the fever. She wasn't a nurse. She wouldn't go inside willy-nilly, but if she discovered someone was ill and without care, she could at least gather basic information to alert someone in the medical profession and arrange help. Officially the city was still under quarantine. Surely the Board of Health had some sort of plan for handling the cases that had erupted so far. The papers were vague about opinions of members of the Board of Health. Memphis physicians did not seem to be of uniform mind about the threat of yellow fever, nor appropriate treatment, but surely someone in charge would know how to dispatch help. Eliza strongly suspected Kate Bionda was not the first yellow fever death of a Memphis citizen, despite the official records. Callie was right. The help talked, and they'd been talking about a rash of illnesses on Second Street after a man came by riverboat to visit his wife, a cook in Mr. Turner's home. Two feverish deaths in four days, the visiting man and an innocent child, raised alarms. Eliza blinked away the image in her mind of Callie's disapproval and proceeded with her task.

Knock after knock either brought no one to the door or opened to people, mostly women, shaking their heads at the descriptions of Robert and Hank. One or two seemed to know who she was talking about but hadn't seen them for certain in a couple of weeks—not since the quarantine began—and weren't sure where they lived. As Eliza moved through the blocks, Harry followed in his cab, staying at the end of each street but always within view. Eliza wasn't worried. He wouldn't abandon her. But he would get antsy.

Dock slips had two conditions, those that stood empty because ships had not been permitted to enter the city with their goods, and those that had been full for too long with ships trapped by the quarantine and not permitted to leave—especially now that multiple cases of yellow fever had broken out. Some guarded lengths of the river were more given to recreation, and Eliza knew them better. Boat rides. Views. Pretty sunsets. Private estates. An evening picnic to escape the summer heat with a breeze off the water. But much of the shoreline was devoted to industry and trade, and normally Eliza had little reason to observe it. As she moved closer to the river, water slapped against the piles on a stretch that ought to have been bustling with enough commerce to disguise the subtle sound.

One more house, and then one more, before she was testing Harry's patience. It was as if Hank and Robert had disappeared into thin air. If William Warren could slip through the quarantine to get into Memphis, perhaps they had slipped through to get out.

Eliza went home to her lemon custard cake.

The true exodus began the next day. The commotion in the street woke Eliza even before Callie arrived to cook breakfast, and she leaned out her second-story bedroom window at men loading wagons up and down the street.

Without Callie, she'd never get into her corset, and without a corset her clothes wouldn't fit. Eliza ran to her mother's bedroom and flung open the wardrobe, seeking a more loose-fitting garment to get into without assistance. She piled her mahogany hair under a roomy out-of-fashion hat and went outside.

Callie met her in the street. "Miz Eliza!"

"What's happening?"

"Dey leavin'."

"But the Board of Health has the city under quarantine."

"Dey don't care. Bad enough folks gettin' sick. Now Kate die and the *Appeal* print it. Everybody know."

Eliza hitched her skirt and strode down the street. If the families on her block—households of money and privilege—were leaving, who else was trying to go?

"They have tents now," Eliza said. "The *Appeal* published that too. They're setting up Camp Joe Williams miles away from the infected neighborhoods. The paper said they have a thousand tents. People will be safe there."

"Don't matter. People be leavin'. Dey not tent people."

"Don't they understand? They'll carry the disease wherever they go. They could be infected and not know it yet."

"Yes, ma'am. Don't matter."

"It *does* matter."

"To you, mebbe. But some say it better to get out. Dat way not so many get sick."

Eliza leaned her head into one hand. That theory could work if they could be sure only healthy people left Memphis.

"Besides," Callie said, "people like me got no place to go. No money to go with. But dem folks? Dey can go."

Eliza was nearly jogging down the streets now, and Callie kept up. What Callie said was true. Colored men might be loading the wagons and driving the carriages, but it was the well-to-do white men coming out their front doors and locking up. White shopkeepers hung the CLOSED signs in the windows. White women huddled with their children, leaving the colored housekeepers behind.

The wagons were loaded with trunks packed for long stays away, and every cart for hire in Memphis made one trip after another from affluent homes toward the train depots.

Eliza raised her hand to hail a cab. Four clattered past her, full-up inside and piled high outside. Then she saw Harry among the chaos—and his cab was empty for the moment.

"What are you doing way over here, Miz Eliza?"

"I want to go to the train station."

"Where are your trunks?"

She shook her head. "I don't want to leave. I just want to see for myself what is happening."

"I mean no disrespect, Miz Eliza, but if you not leavin', let me take you home. That be safest."

"Harry be right," Callie said.

"Let me see the depot first." Eliza raised her hem and climbed into the carriage unassisted. "Then I'll decide."

At the station, men jostled each other in line

74

for tickets, at first to their desired locations and then for whatever train they could get a seat on, reasoning they could get another train later from another city to get where they really wanted to go.

Just out of Memphis.

"Now, Miz Eliza?" Harry said.

Defeated, Eliza nodded and got back in the cab.

Carriages lined the streets over the next two days in a steady stream of departures on roads leading north and east. The river cut off travel to the west without requiring unavailable ferries to the Arkansas side, and no one wanted to go south where the fever was already spreading. Horses pulled wagons crammed with beds and small furniture, some men having decided they would not bring their families back to Memphis, at least not anytime soon. Small children were nestled safely among the household goods. Women and older children walked beside the wagons in the unending procession. Eliza wondered where thousands could be going in so few days.

Just out of Memphis. Away from the river. Away from the fever.

"The sad case of Mrs. Bionda," the *Appeal* published, "who left two little children and a grief-stricken husband, does not prove necessarily that others will follow. There is no need of a panic or stampede."

Readers were unconvinced. By Friday the

Board of Health gave up and lifted the quarantine. It had been ineffective anyway, many reasoned. Yellow fever had come and had begun killing, so how could they justify confining healthy people to await a raging epidemic? It probably was better if people left. Trains rolled in empty and rolled out full, regardless of what the Board of Health said.

By Sunday Eliza walked empty streets. Hardly anyone was in church at St. Mary's for the morning services. Few shops would open on Monday. The faces left to meet her eyes and nod somberly at her were dark, or if they were white, they were drawn and Irish poor.

New cases of yellow fever sprang up by the dozens within days.

Callie managed inventive meals even without the shops, thanks largely to the household vegetable garden and root cellar.

"You should stay here," Eliza said one day at lunch. "You'd be safe. Most of the neighbors are gone. There's plenty of space. Just a couple of weeks to ride this thing out."

"Mebbe."

This was frankly more than Eliza had hoped for.

"Bring some of your things tomorrow," she said. "Keep your options open. Choose any room you want."

"I be fine in the old maid's room behind the kitchen."

CHAPTER SEVEN

"I have done the requisite research and have credible information." Nolan drummed his fingers across the top of Jillian's computer screen.

She glanced up. "Meaning?"

"I have conferred with Kris Bryant, and two scoops of chocolate chip cookie dough ice cream in a waffle cone are yours for the taking as long as we get down to Ore the Mountain in the next twenty minutes."

Jillian pushed the papers on her desk to one side. "It is Saturday."

"And a fine weather Saturday. Afternoon tourists will be out in droves just to enjoy the day."

"And *my* ice cream." Jillian picked up her phone and grabbed the sweatshirt off the back of her chair. "What are we waiting for?"

"Indeed. We could drive."

"Too much trouble to park. Just try to keep up, old man."

When Jillian meant business, she could flip the switch from couch potato to former high school track star. Fortunately, Nolan was the one who taught her to run. He kept pace. Fifteen minutes later he caught Kris's eye at the ice cream counter. The shop was packed. The fall day was just sunny enough, and free of breeze, to make ice cream appealing. Children and adults alike hunched against the glass considering the two dozen flavors on offer in cones, dishes, and shakes.

"The cookie dough spot is empty." The lament rose above the buzz.

"I'm afraid so," Kris said. She glanced at Nolan in reassurance. "We'll have more on Monday."

"Come back on Monday and buy a gallon," Nolan said to Jillian. "Forestall emergencies."

"If I do that, I'll have to take up serious jogging."

"Or develop as much self-discipline about ice cream and coffee as you demonstrate in your work."

"I don't *always* work on Saturday," Jillian said. "If you knew what this woman is paying me . . ."

They moved forward in the line.

"We should do something tomorrow after church," Nolan said. "A hike on the glacier, maybe?"

"Maybe."

"Look for fall foliage? Are the Aspens turning yet?"

Jillian laughed. "Dad, I promise not to work tomorrow."

As they approached the counter, Kris slipped

away and left the duties to her two employees. By the time it was Nolan's turn to order, she smoothly handed Jillian two scoops of chocolate chip cookie dough ice cream, dipped in hard-shell chocolate, and seated in a waffle cone as if she had just made up the order. It was the only flavor Jillian ever wanted. Nolan, on the other hand, rotated among his favorites—butter pecan, pralines and cream, and cherry chocolate chip chunk.

Kris eyed him. "I predict pralines and cream today."

Nolan laughed. "Why not?"

"Two scoops in a dish."

"Clearly Jillian and I need some new habits."

"The old ones serve you well." Kris grabbed a to-go dish—they would want to wander down the street with their treats—and started filling it.

Jillian had already bitten through a spot of the hard shell on her cone in exactly the way she always had since she was first old enough to be trusted not to drop a cone and was licking ice cream through the opening. She was nothing if not systematic in the way she consumed her chosen delicacies, just as she approached every-thing else she did. Waving at her friend, her face oozed pleasure and gratitude.

Nolan slipped Kris more bills than needed to cover the cost, grabbed some napkins, and turned toward the door.

They walked more slowly on the way home. The point now was not to race *to* the ice cream but to enjoy every freezing, tingling sensation of it on their tongues.

"Thanks, Dad," Jillian said between careful bites. "This was a good idea."

"Always happy to share my wisdom that the work will always be there later, but the moment is only here now."

"Should I be writing that down?"

"You jest, but you know I'm right."

They paused in front of the Victorium Emporium. Jillian swiped her tongue around her cone to catch a drip. "Too bad Luke and Veronica don't like people eating in their store."

"We could try sneaking in," Nolan said.

"Tried that once. Didn't go well. No exceptions."

Nolan pointed in the window. "Look. Leo's toy wooden cars. And that buggy he was working on."

"Help! Somebody help!"

The cry came from behind them, and they both turned as the congestion on the block parted to reveal a mother with a toddler in her arms.

"That's the woman from the Cage," Nolan said.

"What woman from the Cage?"

"I saw her there yesterday with her husband and another child." Nolan tossed his half-eaten ice cream into a trash can and hustled across the street. It was Jillian's turn to keep up with him.

"It's a seizure," someone said. "Put her down and make her be still."

The young mother knelt on the sidewalk.

"Stay calm," another voice said. It was Meri. Nolan hadn't even noticed she was on the street a few minutes ago, but she may have been in one of the shops. She gestured now for people to clear away and stepped into the scene. Nolan got as close as he could but respected the space Meri created as she took off her own jacket, folded it, and placed it under the child's head. Jillian slipped a hand in his.

"Is it a seizure?" the mother asked.

Meri nodded tentatively. "It looks like it could be."

"Isn't it dangerous?" The woman reverted to trying to still her daughter's trembling limbs.

"Don't try to hold her down," Meri said. "She'll start breathing again as soon as her muscles relax."

Nolan turned his head toward Jillian. "Make sure someone called 911."

"I already did." Behind them, Veronica had wedged her way through the crowd. "They said they had several calls."

"Good."

"Can you believe Meri?" Jillian said.

They inched closer.

"I'm just going to take off her glasses," Meri said, "so they don't get broken or lost." She eased them off the child's moving face and handed them to the woman.

The mother reached for the girl's mouth. "We were just in Digger's Delight. She was eating a piece of candy!" With a finger extended, she grasped her daughter's jaw.

Meri immediately pushed her hand away. "Don't do that."

"But she could choke!"

"There's actually a greater risk of pushing anything in her mouth farther into her throat where we wouldn't be able to get it out."

The woman put her hand over her own mouth. "Where's my husband? He was supposed to change the baby and meet us at the Emporium. We promised she could have that buggy."

Meri put one hand under the girl's back. "It's good she's not wearing anything tight around her neck. I'm going to turn her to one side. We want to keep the airway open."

By the time she finished the explanation, the task was done.

"She knows what she's doing," Jillian whispered into Nolan's ear.

Everyone around them seemed to recognize this as well. No one interfered with conflicting advice or frantic shouting.

"She's been trained," Nolan said.

"First aid?"

"Maybe. But I think it's more than that. She's seen this done, or done it herself—like it's been drilled into her."

"See, she's doing better now," Meri said.

"You're the young woman from the coffee shop yesterday," the mother said.

Meri nodded.

"I can't thank you enough."

"Amelda!" A man with a stroller pushed through into the clearing and knelt on the sidewalk.

"Dustin, where were you?"

Sirens parted the street traffic as the EMTs arrived. Two uniformed EMTs squatted to provide assistance while a third stepped aside for a quiet conversation with Meri.

"I can't hear," Jillian said.

"I don't think we're supposed to," Nolan said.

Meri gestured a few times, looked at her watch, shrugged, pointed, answered questions. Once she'd given her account and was freed up, Veronica broke away and touched her shoulder.

"You look awfully young to be a doctor," Veronica said. Nolan could hear clearly now.

"I'm not a doctor."

"An EMT?"

"No."

"A medical student?"

A beat passed. "No."

"Well, you should be. No telling what would have happened if you weren't here."

"The seizure—if that's what it was—would have passed and the EMTs would have arrived," Meri said. "The episode was short and the response time was fast."

"Don't sell yourself short. You were calm in a crisis. Not everyone can do that. You should think about a medical career."

Meri pivoted and pushed her way through the gawking crowd still watching the EMTs administer care and prepare to transport the child to a hospital.

"There she goes," Nolan said. "I'm not going to lose her this time."

"What do you mean, this time?" Veronica said. "Jillian, what's he talking about?"

"Just let him go," Jillian said.

Nolan didn't jog the way he used to in years past, but he still hiked at high altitudes, and even on the days he worked in Denver he tried to get out of the office for power walks rather than accept a string of power lunches. He would keep up with Meri Davies.

And he would be a friend.

She didn't head straight back to the Inn, which didn't surprise him. Her pace and route said *Get me out of here*. Without a car though, there was only so far she could go. As long as he didn't lose her in the immediate crowd on Main Street or miss seeing her duck into a shop that may have a rear exit, eventually he could give her some space and follow her.

None of his business? One could certainly make a case.

Creepy? Maybe.

Something a friend would do to help? Yes.

Meri trotted the opposite direction from the Inn—if Nia had sent her into town on an errand, she might be wondering what happened—before detouring off Main Street a few blocks down, circling around a few blocks in a manner that suggested that she didn't know what she wanted to do, turning down Placer Street, and finally settling on the cement back steps of the old historic brick school building that now served as a visitors center. If she stayed there too long, an employee would come out the back door and chase her off.

But not if Nolan was sitting beside her.

So he took his spot, wordless for a long time.

"I saw," he said. "I hardly know you, but I was proud that you could do that."

She buzzed her lips. "In my family, that's like getting a participation certificate for being in the first grade."

"Sorry to hear that, because most of the population would find it remarkable."

She said nothing.

"Here's what I think," Nolan said. "I think

you've been to Canyon Mines before, and it was a happy time. I think your relationship with your brother distresses you. And I think talk about medicine *really* distresses you."

Meri leaned her head against the painted metal railing alongside the steps. "You and your daughter have been comparing notes."

Nolan nodded. "We do that, especially about things—or people—we care about."

"Like you said, you barely know me."

"That doesn't mean we don't care."

"Well, that's just swell for your family. That's not the way mine works. So let's just leave it alone."

"We could. But I also think that 'back East' means Tennessee, and I figure that means you're a good twelve hundred miles away from your family, so it's probably safe to tell me just a little bit more about why they make you so unhappy."

Meri sighed heavily. "They have a thing about doctors, and I wish they would just let it go."

"What kind of 'thing'?"

"Everybody has to be one."

"Why?"

"Who knows? It's just always been that way— at least after our people weren't slaves anymore. Forever and ever, amen."

"Mmm. You know Jillian is a genealogist."

"Right."

"Most people think that means she just looks

86

up birth and death dates in some mysterious place the rest of us can't find, but there's really a lot more to it. She's pretty good at interpreting the information she finds, and when she shares it with me, between us we're pretty good at piecing together stories from the past."

"I don't follow."

"Let us help you—not just by being kind, but by being good at what we do. Jillian would just need some basic information about your family to get started."

"Nia is keeping me pretty busy." Meri jumped up and slapped her forehead. "She's going to kill me. I was supposed to be back ages ago, and I haven't even done the errand she sent me out to do."

"Tomorrow, then," Nolan said.

Meri waved a noncommittal hand at him and raced back toward downtown.

CHAPTER EIGHT

W e can't let the grass grow under our feet on this one."

Jillian didn't have to ask what her father was talking about as she buttered her whole-wheat toast and imagined it was one of Ben's buttery, flaky, fruit-filled pastries.

Meri.

"It's Sunday, Dad."

"I know! Perfect, isn't it?"

"Now you've lost me." She chomped into the toast and picked up her coffee. Today's plain gray mug had a sturdy handle that fit her hand perfectly. She wasn't sure about the weight of the cup though.

Nolan straightened the purple-and-silver-striped tie that Jillian had never liked.

"We go to church," he said, "and Meri will be there. She has the afternoon off. You promised you won't work today. I'm not working. I casually invite Meri over for Sunday after-church dinner. I whip up something the three of us can eat and voilà, we're having a nice easy conversation."

"You read too many novels, Dad. It doesn't work that way. You don't know Meri will want to go to any church, much less ours. And Nia might need Meri this afternoon. Weekends are busy at the Inn. We don't know what time-off arrangement they came to. Anyway, what's to say Meri would accept your invitation?"

"I see that when you read fiction, you fixate on the plot complications."

"Just being realistic."

"Well, I'm being possibilistic."

"That's not a word."

"Think what the world could be like if it were." Nolan winked at Jillian over his raised coffee mug, the same green one he used every morning. Somewhere in the cabinets was another just like it. "Plan B is we come home from church by way of the Inn and nab her there."

"Nab her?" Jillian swallowed more coffee. "Okay, let's say you wrangle Meri into coming home with us. Then what?"

"You do your thing, of course. Be a genealogist."

"Dad."

"Are you finished?" He picked up her plate, whether or not she was finished, and put it in the sink. "We don't want to be late for church."

Three hours later, Jillian smiled across the living room at Meri, unsure which of them felt more unsettled.

It wasn't her father. That much was clear. His tenor tone floated from the kitchen. *"Che bella cosa na jurnata 'e sole, n'aria serena doppo na tempest-a!"*

"Does he always do this?" Meri asked.

"Cook Sunday dinner?" Jillian said. "No."

Meri cocked her head to the left, pushing her chin out. "Sing in Italian!"

Nolan stepped out of the kitchen in a white apron and chef's hat, spread his arms wide, and belted out, " *'O sole, 'o sole mio sta 'nfronte a te, sta 'nfronte a te!"*

Then he withdrew.

"I guarantee you that your childhood was very different than mine," Meri said, her mouth not quite closing between sentences. "I don't even know what those words mean."

"Something about a beautiful sunny day that shines in your face," Jillian said. "My mother was from an Italian family. He took up singing in Italian because it made her laugh."

"Is it my ears, or is it possible he does it with an Irish accent?"

Jillian chuckled. "That's what made Mom laugh even harder."

"Sounds sweet."

"It was. He stopped singing for a long time after we lost her. When he started again, I thought it was to embarrass me. I was a teenager, after all. But I finally realized he had found himself again, and he could remember her without cracking into pieces."

"I shouldn't be here." Meri lurched to her feet.

Jillian matched Meri's posture. "Why would you say that?"

"You'd give anything to see your mom again, and I'm running away from mine. I don't belong here."

Jillian closed the few feet between them to put her hands on Meri's shoulders and eased her back into her seat.

"In my line of work, one thing is clear. Families are complicated, but that doesn't mean you don't belong."

Nolan launched into another song. *"La forza che tu dai, e'il desiderio che ognuno trovi amore intorno e dentro se."*

"Puccini," Meri muttered.

"You know this one?"

"It's an actual opera. My mother used to drag me. Culture, you know. She's big on it."

"It's a prayer of sorts," Jillian said, "asking that life be kind and we find another soul to love."

Meri looked up at her. "I guess that part never stuck. I just know my mother loved to hear Pavarotti sing it."

"My dad's favorite too! See, something in common."

"What would poor Luciano think about the Irish spin?" Meri dared a smile.

"I think it would please him to hear someone delighting in the music."

"You're probably right."

They settled back into their chairs, with Nolan's kitchen sounds a backdrop to a period of wordlessness. Jillian was out of her depth. Nothing she thought to say seemed right.

"I know your father brought me here because he wants me to talk to you about my family," Meri said, "but to be honest, I don't see the point."

"I meant what I said," Jillian said. "Families are complicated."

"Don't I know it. Look, your dad seems like a really nice man, and he's in there cooking up who knows what, and I don't want to be rude, but we can just have a nice lunch. We really don't have to do this other stuff."

"Sometimes in order to understand ourselves, we have to understand our families."

"I understand my family plenty."

Jillian nodded. "Of course. We all understand our own experiences of our families in ways no one else can. What I've discovered in my work is that we don't always understand what makes our families function—or not function—the way they do. Sometimes we have to look to the past to find out."

Meri tilted her head again, this time her chin quivering for a second or two. "And you can figure that out?"

"We can try—together. I'm willing if you're willing."

"I don't know how much I can tell you that is any help."

"Probably more than you realize."

Meri shrugged. "Okay then."

"I'll get my laptop."

Jillian paced directly across the living room and through the dining room, pausing at the kitchen threshold to give her father a quick thumbs-up as she ducked across the hall into her office for her computer and returning to Meri before the dinner guest had time to marshal more reasons why this project was untenable.

"I have a form I use to gather basic facts." Jillian dropped into a comfortable chair and propped her feet up. She could have invited Meri into her office, but the more casual she made this process feel, the more likely Meri would stick with it. At least that seemed logical in the moment. She had no chance to check the strategy with her dad. "From there it's easy to import into a family tree or databases that could help us."

"Whatever you say."

"Let's start with your parents' names."

"Michael and Juliette."

"Mother's maiden name."

"Mathers."

"Birthdays?"

Meri supplied them.

"Do you know all your grandparents' names?"

"Richard and Olive Mathers. I think her maiden name was Freeman. But I can't tell you their birth dates. Not the years."

"You're doing great. On the Davies side?"

"Thomas and Rosie. Rosalie McNeal."

"Great-grandparents?"

Meri shrugged. "I never knew them, but my father's Auntie Mo used to tell me some stories."

"Not your father?"

Meri shook her head. "He never had time for things like that. He was too busy being important."

And there was that edge that took the story out of the realm of strict information and put it in Nolan's world. Jillian tried to look busy with her form and waited to see if Meri would provide any names in the Davies lineage tracing further back. It didn't necessarily matter. With her parents' names and her grandparents' names, Jillian could search various databases for the next generation back.

"That's all right," she said. "Most people don't know their great-grandparents. In a lot of families, it only takes two generations before people know almost nothing about more than one branch of the family."

"I'm glad we're normal in at least one way." Meri's laugh rang false.

"Meri, can I ask about the doctors in your family?"

"What is there to ask? There have been a lot."

"Like who?"

"My mother is a thoracic surgeon. My father an oncologist."

"Who else?"

"My dad's sister is in family practice, and his other sister is a physician's assistant. Everyone thinks she didn't work hard enough to be a real doctor. And his brother died in a car accident while he was in medical school."

"That *is* a lot of doctors."

"I'm just getting started. My grandfather was a doctor, and my grandmother was a nurse. In those days it was really hard for a black woman to become a physician, or I'm sure she would have been one too. On my mom's side, her sister is a clinical psychologist, which is practically the same as being a doctor, though not quite the same in the eyes of the *real* doctors in the family, even though she has a PhD."

"What about before your grandfather Davies?"

"My great-grandfather? Yep. Even Auntie Mo was a nurse."

"I'm starting to see what you mean about your family having a 'thing.' Mo sounds like it's short for something."

"Muriel. I think she was fairly accomplished in her profession, but she was one person who talked to me about other stuff, which I was always glad for, so I'm not sure of any details."

"Do you know where any of them worked?"

Meri crossed and uncrossed her legs. "It was a long time ago. Small towns, I guess. It was the South before civil rights. Black folks had to look after their own, and that's what they did."

"Tennessee?"

"Mostly."

"Where else?"

There was that shrug again. "Not sure."

Not sure or not telling?

"Did they move around?"

"I suppose. Don't most people? Through the generations, I mean."

"Depends." Jillian clicked to a different screen in her form. Maybe sibling information in the current generation would be a safer topic for the moment. "Tell me about—"

The crash clattered from the kitchen.

Jillian leaped up. "Dad!"

"Well, isn't that a fret!"

She exhaled and looked at Meri. "He's all right."

"How can you tell?" Meri said.

"That's what he says."

"Maybe you should check."

Jillian nodded.

Nolan appeared. His apron was no longer white, and his chef's hat was cockeyed, but he looked otherwise unharmed.

"All is well," he said.

"I don't think so, Dad." Jillian kept moving toward the kitchen.

He spread his arms. *"Che bella cosa na jurnata 'e sole!"*

"You're not going to sing your way out of this," Jillian said. "Come on, Meri. You can sit in the kitchen while I help clean up and see if there's anything left of our dinner."

"Our Sunday dinner is unscathed, I assure you," Nolan said.

"What exactly were you cooking?"

"Traditional Irish black pudding."

Jillian led Meri into the kitchen. "Not true. That requires pig's blood, and nobody in Canyon Mines sells that." Which he would know if he had a clue about shopping.

"I bought it off the internet."

"Also not true." Jillian glanced in Meri's direction.

"Crubeens."

"Because in the absence of pig's blood you figure pig's feet is the next best thing to make our guest comfortable. Nope." Jillian pointed Meri to the nook and pulled a string of paper towels off the roll to start cleaning up whatever had exploded.

"Cottage pie?" Nolan said.

"Now you are in the realm of believability."

"That doesn't sound Italian," Meri said.

"It's not," Jillian said. "It's Irish."

"But the Italian opera."

"He sings the same thing when he makes Saturday morning pancakes."

Nolan's eyes lit. "You must come for pancakes next Saturday morning!"

"How about we see if Meri survives this meal first?" Jillian said. The noise that had drawn Jillian and Meri in from the other room was accounted for by the set of stainless steel mixing bowls her father had used, probably stacked beside the sink, and managed to knock to the granite tile that made enough noise to wake the dead. The pie itself was safely in the oven. Jillian picked up the bowls and wiped up remains of beef, vegetables, and mashed potatoes from the floor. She would mop properly later.

Nolan wriggled a finger at Meri's grinning face. "I assure you, I am a very good cook."

"I can tell by your hat," Meri said.

Jillian laughed freely. "She's got your number, Dad."

Nolan tossed his hat on the counter. "Aw, sure look it. You know it. I'll go set the table in the other room."

Meri was shaking her head.

"What's the matter?" Jillian said.

"I *so* did not have your childhood."

CHAPTER NINE

Memphis, August 20, 1878

Here's the train now." Sister Hughetta pushed up on her toes as she leaned forward to look down the track.

Sister Frances grabbed her fellow teacher's sleeve and pulled her back from the edge of the platform. Eliza simply exhaled relief that the train was arriving on time. Sister Constance, Mother Superior of the teaching order who ran the Church Home orphanage and St. Mary's day school, was coming home, and Sister Thecla would be with her. Twenty days had passed since William Warren turned up sick and soon died. The panicked city would look far different than what Constance and Thecla left behind for the much-deserved rest they didn't get. Their time at the Mother House had barely begun when they got word of the yellow fever outbreak in Memphis. Immediately they'd begun organizing donations, supplies, and extra nursing help before returning as soon as they could.

Sisters Hughetta and Frances, under the direction of Father George Harris, dean of St. Mary's Cathedral, had been serving capably in their response to the crisis. So far none of the orphans had fallen ill. Mrs. Bullock and Miss Murdock, who both lived at the Sisters House, rose to every task asked of them to serve all who came to the church for help. Eliza had seen all this during her daily ministrations with the children.

But Sister Constance was the one who would truly take charge of the sisters. She had already done so in her organizing from afar.

The numbers of people falling ill were shocking. Every day the tangled snarl of infected neighborhoods distended farther. Even the *Appeal* could no longer editorialize that the threat was insubstantial.

The train lumbered to a stop along the platform. Sister Hughetta, least able to contain her anxiety, trotted alongside the cars looking for the familiar faces and habits of her sisters in the windows. It would not take long. The train obviously had been relieved of much of its usual length. The demand for passenger transportation into Memphis was low, and few who remained in the city now had the means to leave. Eliza had fended off multiple inquiries about why she was still there. Even Callie wondered.

"I will get Ned," Eliza said.

But there was no need. The faithful negro driver who had carried the entourage to the depot in a church-owned carriage was already down from his bench and headed for the baggage car of the train.

Sister Hughetta executed her self-assigned duty and was at the bottom of the steps when Sisters Constance and Thecla descended in their black garb, the only passengers to leave the train in Memphis. Sister Frances held more composure in her steps, but the brightness in her face spoke the joy of the safe return of the weary travelers. Eliza stood back several yards, waiting until Sister Constance caught her eye and gestured wide with one arm.

"How could I ever have left you all?" Sister Constance said. "I have been so unhappy, but I am so happy now."

The five women walked toward the wagon.

"I do not believe I have ever seen a train come into Memphis so empty," Sister Constance said.

"The newspapers estimate less than twenty thousand people remain," Eliza said.

"I hope the freights will run. We still need supplies."

Ned arrived heaving a handcart loaded with two small worn trunks. With him another man wrestled with a stack of large crates. Nuns did not travel with a great deal of personal worldly goods, but Constance had not arrived empty-handed with useful items.

"Tinned meats," she said. "Canned milk. Clean linens and clothing to replace what we burn.

There will be more coming soon, but I knew we would need something immediately and insisted on bringing at least a few crates on the train."

Ned paused to smear perspiration from his forehead onto a handkerchief.

"I'll find some help." Eliza pivoted and scanned the platform in search of a driver to whom she could offer a coin. They would need to hire a cart to follow them back to the cathedral with the extra crates.

With the carriage loaded, Ned assisted the passengers in.

"I see they've begun the lime in the streets," Sister Thecla said.

"Constantly," Eliza said. Moving about the city was like navigating layers of fine flour.

"Oh that our eyes could feast on a vision of streets of gold instead of the white lime of death." Constance's words were soft with yearning. "May the souls of the departed have a brighter visage than we."

It was hard to say whether covering the streets in lime diminished the rate of infection, but the Board of Health was committed to the strategy, along with firing ammunition into the air every night and burning barrels of tar. Late August heat was made all the more complex by the need to avoid breathing the smoky outdoor air meant to kill off the infectious disease.

On one corner a half dozen coffins stood

stacked—empty, Eliza hoped, though it was hard to be sure. A hearse passed them. The undertaker had squeezed in two coffins.

Sister Hughetta spoke up. "Sister Constance?"

"Yes."

"The Citizens Relief Committee is very grateful for any assistance we can offer."

"Of course. That is why Sister Thecla and I have come home."

"They have a proposal I feel you should be aware of at the earliest moment."

"What is it?"

Eliza cocked her head.

Sister Hughetta leaned forward. "I've discussed it with Father Harris and said I was quite sure what your opinion would be."

"The proposal, please, Sister."

"While they are grateful for us to work in town among the sick, in accordance with our calling—adjusted for the circumstances, of course—they wish us to sleep in the country, out of the infected atmosphere."

Eliza gasped.

"It is for our own good, they say."

"We cannot listen to such a plan," Sister Constance said. "If this is the opinion you gave to Father Harris, then you have spoken rightly."

"It was indeed, Sister."

"It would never do." Sister Constance tugged at the front of her habit. "I have been informed daily by telegraph of the numbers of people falling ill. The fever outbreak is already an epidemic, and the need will only increase. We will be nursing day and night. We must be at our posts."

Voices around the carriage murmured agreement.

"I also want to do everything I can to help," Eliza said. "I am at your disposal."

"Thank you, Eliza," Constance said. "There will be a great deal to do. A great deal to organize. I've arranged with the Trinity Infirmary in New York to send us some nurses who are medically trained. Sisters Ruth, Helen, and Clare will arrive soon and stay at the Sisters House with us. We are teachers. That makes us also learners. We must all learn everything we can from them about providing the best nursing care possible."

"Yes, Sister," came the waves of concordance.

They arrived at the Sisters House, the large structure next to the cathedral that also housed the school for girls that the sisters operated for paying students. A buggy ride away was the Church Home orphanage and the school they ran for children in need.

Ned wrestled the crates and trunks into the house. The sisters, Eliza, and Mrs. Bullock sat down together to hear Sister Constance's report from New York and the outline of her plan going forward.

"We have ample space," she said, "especially

with school out of session. Obviously we will not undertake to begin the new school year in the middle of an epidemic. We can clear classrooms to suit the more pressing needs. People in our parish already are accustomed to coming to us when they have a particular need, as they should. I'm sure this has continued in my absence."

"Especially since the shops closed," Eliza said. "Some of the shop owners with fresh goods made some arrangements that items not go to waste, but others simply locked up when they left Memphis. Mercantiles may have needed items, but people cannot lawfully get to them."

"And many lost their employment when those of means departed," Sister Hughetta said. "Even if the shops were open and well supplied, money is in shorter supply than usual."

"We have taken this into account with the types of support Sister Thecla and I have arranged," Sister Constance said. "We have donations to underwrite the purchase of needful goods, and the cost of getting them to Memphis. Unfortunately, what we cannot hasten is time to ship them, and not every shipping company is willing to come here—at least not without considerable upward adjustment in pricing."

Eliza seethed. Must even a tragedy be turned into an opportunity for profit? Where was people's compassion for the sick and dying?

"There are a few freighters and a few

steamers," Sister Constance said. "We will keep the telegraph office busy with constant communication about the urgency of the need."

Mrs. Bullock jumped up. "Telegraph. I almost forgot. I guess I did forget, but now I remember." She reached into her apron pocket and held a telegram out to Eliza. "Your Callie brought this by."

Eliza flinched. "Thank you." She tucked the telegram, unopened, under her bag on the table.

"We will turn the House into a dispensary," Sister Constance said, "of all items we can manage to stock. Tinned foods. Fresh foods, if we can get any. I suspect we'll find quite a few abandoned gardens, and rotted vegetables will have no value if and when the owners return."

"I have a few neighbors with rather large gardens," Eliza said. "I'll ask Callie to help me."

"We might dare to also send with you a couple of the older orphan girls who can be trusted to be strictly obedient to your instructions and not put themselves at risk by unnecessary contact with anyone."

"Penelope," Eliza said. "And Judith."

Constance nodded. "I will post a list of the various items I have arranged to be shipped to us, and we will be unabashed in our prayers that they be delivered. Even if they come one crate at a time, we will give thanks for each clean tunic or bedsheet. Even matches will become dear as we must insist—and assist, if necessary—that members of households that have been infected burn clothing and personal items of anyone who has been ill. Mattresses must, I repeat, must be destroyed. We are nuns who have taken vows and are accustomed to sleeping on wooden planks or at best a bag of straw. A real mattress comes dear for the coloreds and immigrants left in Memphis. I'm doing my best to get some so we have something to give them when we insist that they must burn the old ones."

Eliza mentally counted the number of mattresses in her family's home. She would gladly donate every one of them, including her own, and meet with her mother's ire later.

She slipped open the telegram.

EPIDEMIC ALL OVER PAPERS *Stop* WORRIED *Stop* PLEASE COME IMMEDIATELY *Stop* SEND ARRIVAL TIME WHEN TICKETED *Stop* LOVE MOTHER

Eliza folded the sheet back into its envelope. She would have to tell her mother something, but she was not going to Wisconsin.

"We can become an infirmary," Sister Constance said. "I am not sure where the beds will come from, but we have the space. The relief committee might be able to help with cots. In the meantime, if anyone sees even the least sign of illness in any of the orphans in our care, we must immediately arrange quarantine. Sadly, I believe we must be prepared to receive more children if we discover they have lost their parents. I've asked Sister Frances to oversee this so that we have a few beds ready and if we need to place a child at Church Home there will be no delay. Is this understood?"

Heads nodded around the table.

"We will care for all who come to us or call upon us, especially the children. The Howard Association will help with organizing nurses who can go out into the neighborhoods, but they will rely on us to know which houses to send them to. We must keep impeccable records. Addresses. Family names. Descriptions of how many people are in the households and what conditions we observe."

Eliza scanned the faces at the table, moistening her lips and swallowing the words no one would voice. *And if one of us becomes sick?*

Sister Constance shuffled several pages of notes. "Eliza, do you have any report on the children at Canfield Asylum?"

Eliza straightened in her chair. "Yes. I have been out there several times since the start of the fever, most recently being just two days ago. I am happy to say there has been no sign of illness. They seem to be far enough out of town and self-sufficient with their gardens and chickens to have little reason for contact with people from town."

"This is good news. Thanks be to God. We shall

continue to pray for our children here, those at Canfield, and the many who will find themselves orphaned before this scourge is over."

"Father Harris continues daily services in the cathedral," Sister Hughetta said. "We have been praying for families by names as much as we are able."

"We shall all try to commune daily as much as it is possible without neglecting the sick," Sister Constance said. "It is vital to keep up our spiritual service."

They closed the meeting by reciting together the Lord's Prayer, and Sister Constance began assigning tasks, including reviewing the list of households Sister Hughetta had prepared who should receive visits.

"Shall I go?" Eliza asked. "I want to help."

"We covet your prayers," Sister Constance said.

"Of course I pray," Eliza said. "What can I do with my *hands?* To ease the workload you have just outlined?"

Sister Constance glanced at the telegram envelope. "Your mother has other ideas, doesn't she? Will you not go to her in Wisconsin?"

Eliza could hear the pleading in her mother's voice, see the consternation in her face.

"No, I will not. I must stay and serve."

Sister Constance nodded.

"The pantry then. Start with the crates I brought with me. Keep a close inventory. The families who come to our doors need the same careful attention as those who need us to come to them, and I need someone I can be confident in overseeing the items that come in and go out. And this way you can honestly assure your mother that you are caring for the poor and not nursing the sick. Perhaps that will allow her to rest in your decision to remain in Memphis."

CHAPTER TEN

"Nine o'clock meeting," Nolan said when Jillian put her father's green mug under a spigot at the coffee bar the next morning.

"Then I'll put this in a travel mug." She switched out the cup. "Are you sure I can't fancy it up for you? Steamed frothy milk?"

"I'm a plain soul and I like my coffee to match, don't you know."

Jillian pressed a button for a large serving. "You don't know what you're missing."

Nolan double-checked his briefcase while he bit into a bran muffin. "Did you get anything at all from Meri yesterday? By the time we ate, she seemed more interested in our family than hers."

"A few names and dates." Jillian handed Nolan his coffee. "Enough that public records might get me a bit more. I'll pop info into a family tree, see what else I can scrounge up to add, and make time to wander over to the Inn later today. Usually when people see a tree, they get excited and chattier."

"I shall expect a full report tonight over dinner, then."

"I will make it my top priority." Never mind the pile of paying, contracted work on her desk.

Nolan checked the lid on his coffee, crumbled the last of the bran muffin into his mouth, and left through the back door.

Jillian opened the cabinet and stared at the mug collection for a few seconds, still missing the favorite she'd been forced to discard. None of the remaining options ever had been even a distant contender, but she had to drink from something. She chose one Nia had given her one year for her birthday with the image of a yellow butterfly nestled in the open bloom of an orange daylily. It was on the slender side, but at least it had a good sturdy handle to grip. She pressed several more buttons for her morning libation than she did for her father's and carried it to her office, where she'd already spent a good two hours at her desk.

Her computer chimed with an incoming Skype call, and she checked her calendar. No, she hadn't overlooked a client meeting. At least she wore a decent top that morning and her hair was fastened under control.

She answered the call. "Good morning, Raúl."

"Good morning. I just wanted to check in on your progress locating the mystery heir, now that you've identified her."

"Not quite there." Jillian eyed her coffee, willing it not to get cold while she tried to carry on a professional conversation. "Though I'm tracking three different addresses around St.

Louis. I'm certain I've got it narrowed down to that area."

"And you really don't think she has any idea?"

"She's very young and seems to be on her own. I'm not sure she knew her father, much less that he had a great-uncle."

"You can still pass along the information you dug up and let one of our detectives take it from here."

"If you don't mind, I'd like to finish it," Jillian said. There was something about finding a name from among millions in the bowels of the internet and connecting it to a living, breathing being. Genealogists did a lot of digging into the past. Bringing the past to create a surprising future for someone—she didn't get to do that very often.

"That's all right by me," Raúl said, "but I'm getting some pressure about it. Considering how long the body has been in the morgue, and all that."

"It's not as if she'd be able to identify the body if she never knew him. They already know who he is."

"They will insist on the protocol. It will at least be her prerogative to make the arrangements."

For a perfect stranger? *Hello, you're about to inherit a fortune, as soon as you make the burial arrangements.* She might leave that piece of news to the detectives to deliver.

"I will make it my top priority," Jillian said.

They clicked off the call.

She couldn't really have two top priorities, could she?

Jillian drank coffee and mentally rearranged her day. Putting what she had from Meri into a tree would have to be enough for today. She could do that and shoot over to the Inn at some point in the afternoon for a short—emphasis on short—break and see if she could get anything more from Meri. Otherwise the reality was she owed Raúl her time. He was paying her, after all. And she still had to put the finishing touches on the expansive six-generation family tree for Mrs. Answald's family reunion just around the corner.

Jillian rubbed her eyes, gulped more coffee, and dug in.

At two in the afternoon, she carried a folder with only the most elementary family tree for Meri Davies. All she'd had time to do was put information Meri already knew in the tree. Because of four unexpected phone calls, including two from Mrs. Answald, and a trail that led nowhere for an entire branch of her family tree, exploring public records on Meri's tree—so far—proved beyond Jillian's time capacity. But she'd promised her dad she'd make contact.

She walked around the Inn to the back and entered through the kitchen.

"Knock, knock," she called.

Nia's head leaned around the corner of the

laundry room. "Oh good. I was hoping you'd come by."

"You were?"

Nia glanced around. "Did you run the number?"

"The number?"

"You know. Don't play dumb with me." Nia came into the kitchen with a stack of dish towels and opened a drawer to put them away.

"Oh the *number.* No, I haven't."

"I figured it would be an easy thing for you to do."

"I guess it would be, but honestly, I've been swamped. Just ask my dad."

"I believe you. Yet you're here now."

"I was hoping to talk to Meri. Casual-like. I started a family tree."

"Oh good. Let's see."

"Don't you think Meri is the one who should see it first?"

"You've already seen it." Nia reached for the folder.

"That's different." Jillian pulled the folder out of reach. "Stop being so nosy. Is she here?"

"We're in a bit of a lull until the three o'clock check-ins start. Even then it's Monday. Hardly the busiest day for a small-town B&B."

"So you won't mind if I take some of her time?"

"Not if it will help the greater cause. I'll help you find her."

They walked together through the first-floor

115

rooms—the office, the wide parlor, the library with its floor-to-ceiling shelves and upholstered Victorian chairs, and down the hall to the private quarters where Nia and Leo lived and Meri had a private room and bath separated from them by a small turn in the hall.

"She didn't say anything about going out," Nia said. She led Jillian up the broad staircase that always made guests ooh and aah, and they ducked their heads into the various guest rooms, all empty now and made up in readiness for the next occupants.

But no Meri.

"You don't suppose . . . ," Nia said.

"Suppose what?" Jillian said.

"You know."

"No, I don't."

"That she would leave. I'm going to check for her car." Nia charged back down the stairs, through the Inn, and out the back door toward the parking area.

Jillian followed her and caught her elbow. "She's there. Let me talk to her."

Nia exhaled. "She doesn't look like she packed her bags or anything."

"Why would you think she would?"

Nia twisted her braid. "Sometimes the kids I thought were benefiting the most from school counseling would turn out to be the ones who did something no one ever saw coming. You end up with a very sensitive radar after letting a few fall off."

"This is not that, Nia."

"I have bedding to fold." Nia pivoted and went back into the house.

Jillian, with just the manila folder that held only one sheet of paper, approached Meri, who was foraging around on the passenger side of her car.

"Meri?" Jillian said.

Meri's frame straightened. She had her phone in her hand.

Jillian looked from the phone to Meri's eyes.

Meri shrugged. "I haven't had it on since I got here. Four days. Figured it was time to see just how bad things are."

"Maybe not as bad as you think."

"Probably worse."

"Let's sit on the patio."

Meri nodded, powering up the phone as she turned her steps toward the patio where she had bolted from the swing the last time they were out here together. Jillian chose an adjacent chair alongside the idle fire pit, and the phone came to life as they sat.

Jillian couldn't keep count of the number of dings indicating missed text messages and voice mails now loading in. One after another the noti-fications lit the screen, and Meri's thumb swiped through them as if sifting for hope.

117

Finally Meri set the phone down on the chair beside her. "I'll have to read them all later."

Somehow Jillian doubted she would.

"Besides," Meri said, "I should go back to work. I don't want to get on Nia's bad side again."

"Nia doesn't really have much of a bad side," Jillian said.

"She said there would be rules, and I want to respect that."

"Of course. But she knows I'm here and said it would be all right to talk for a few minutes about your family tree."

"Oh, that. Lunch was nice yesterday. Your dad is a good cook."

"Even if he is a goofball?"

"I like that about him."

"He can be serious when it matters. He's a great lawyer, and an incredible mediator."

"Are there other lawyers in your family?"

"Nope. He's the only one."

"Did you think about being a lawyer?"

"Not really. By the time I was old enough for college, my interest in genealogy was pretty fixed. My dad was the one who steered me that way after my mom died, so I could understand my roots."

"He didn't even strongly suggest what you should study?"

"No. Genealogy is not actually a college major,

but I studied things that would help me learn to research and how to run my own business."

"That must have been nice—not that your mom died, but that your dad cared about what you might be interested in."

Jillian ran her tongue behind her upper lip. Her father would know what to say. Something empathetic. "I gather in your family there's a lot of pressure to be a doctor," Jillian said.

Meri didn't answer. She picked up her phone and looked again at the stream of messages.

"I brought the beginning of your family tree." Jillian offered the folder. "I haven't had time since yesterday to research and try to add to it, but I thought you might like to see the format. Maybe it will trigger some names we can add."

Meri shook her head. "What's the point? I may not know all the names, but I know we're doctors for a hundred years. That's who we are. I can give the spiel about how we take seriously the responsibility that comes with opportunity and never turn our backs on the hard work that will help us help others. That's the Davies way."

"Buried in that speech are some good values."

"You don't get it. With a father like yours, you could never understand one like mine."

Meri was probably right, but Jillian had to come up with something to say. She moved closer to Meri, removed the sheet from the folder, and said, "We can still do the project. Maybe we'll find

119

some answers, or at least the right questions."

"There's no point. I'm not going to be safe here much longer anyway."

What in the world did that mean?

Meri's phone rang in her hand, and she startled. Jillian could see that the caller ID said MOM. Meri immediately tapped the option to decline the call and shut the phone off.

"Meri," Jillian said, "I know things are complicated with your family, but are you afraid of them?"

"You're right. It is complicated." Meri stuffed her phone in a back pocket, but she didn't answer Jillian's question.

"We want to help—Nia, my dad, me."

"No offense, Jillian, but a pretty family tree is not going to fix this."

"It might shed some light on why things are the way they are."

"Doctors for a hundred years. Doctors marrying nurses or other doctors. Like a private club and swearing an oath to a creed. What else is there to say?"

"You're describing *what*," Jillian said. "Aren't you interested in *why?*"

"In my experience, *why* is not a relevant question in the Davies household." Meri stood up. "I really should get back to work. I need this job right now."

Because you don't know how long you'll be

here. Because you don't feel safe. From your own family.

"Sure," Jillian said. "Just take the folder in case you change your mind. We can always work on it later."

Meri took the folder, but she was about as likely to look at the single sheet inside as she was to read four days of messages from her family. Jillian trudged home, trying to formulate what sort of report she would give her father about this debacle of a conversation.

And in the meantime, she still had to find a young woman who seemed to have dropped off the grid in the middle of St. Louis.

CHAPTER ELEVEN

Tuesday's mug looked too lonely. Jillian couldn't even remember how it had come into the household, but it was too beige, too stark.

All these mugs. Why did they even keep them? She and her dad had their favorites—well, she needed a new favorite—and they rarely reached for anything else. Jillian was lining up the ones that failed her trials along the back of the counter on one side of the sink after they were washed. Why not give them to someone who would use them?

Of the three St. Louis addresses she'd been tracing in the last couple of days, phone calls and searches of public records had narrowed it down to one that was the last known record for the young woman she sought. But she'd only been there six months, her neighbors hadn't known her well, and her landlord had encouraged her to look for somewhere else to live because if she was late with her rent one more time, he would be less friendly in his demands.

No forwarding address.

One neighbor said she thought the young woman was a student, though just barely. She'd had to drop down to only one class because she couldn't cover her tuition.

She had a job, but no one Jillian spoke to could tell her where. Food service? Hotel housekeeping? Both? Something like that.

After spending a good chunk of Monday and half of Tuesday morning trying to crack this nut, Jillian was reconsidering her determination not to involve Raúl's detectives. He could at least hire someone to go to St. Louis. But she was so close. Maybe she would go. The expense would be a small bite out of her fee.

The doorbell rang—an unusual occurrence—and Jillian was barely in the hall on her way to respond when Nia burst through the unlocked door.

"Now I've done it." Nia bent her head down into her hands. "Now I've really done it."

"What are you talking about? Did you and Leo have a fight?"

"What?" Nia's head arced upward, still held between her palms. "Leo and I don't fight. I married a saint. You know that."

"Then what?"

"Meri."

"I thought you two had come to an agreement."

"We did. I've went way over a line. Big-time."

Jillian pointed into the living room. "Maybe you'd better sit down and tell me what happened."

"I can't sit down." Nia crossed the room with a

123

nervous hitch in her step, pivoted, and returned.

"Then I'm going to sit down." Jillian chose the comfortable purple chair with the matching ottoman. It was hard to feel distressed slouched in this chair.

"I didn't mean to." Nia zigzagged across the room. She paused long enough to pick up a porcelain carousel that had belonged to Jillian's mother and then immediately set it down. "See that? That's what I did. That's what gets me in trouble."

"I'm not following."

"I pick stuff up. Why do I do that? But now that I know, I can't just ignore it."

"Hold the phone," Jillian said. "You found out something you're not supposed to know?"

Nia blew out her breath and looked at Jillian square on. "I invaded her privacy. Not like asking you to use her Social Security number but actually invading her privacy."

"Maybe you should tell me exactly what happened—without telling me what you shouldn't know, because I shouldn't know it either."

"I went to Meri's room to take her some fresh towels. The door wasn't locked. It wasn't even closed. I thought I would just leave the towels on the bed instead of on the floor outside her room."

"That doesn't seem so bad."

"It wouldn't be, if that's all I'd done. Perfectly

124

innocent. In and out in ten seconds. No harm, no foul."

"I can't believe I'm going to ask this. But . . . ?"

"I knew Meri was away from the Inn. I'd just sent her on an errand—some food shopping that would take her a while. And the letter was right there on the dresser next to the door. How could I not see it?" Nia was on the move again.

Jillian raised both hands, palms up and out. "Whatever it was, keep it to yourself. You shouldn't have seen it, and you certainly shouldn't be telling me."

"But this is big, Jillian. And when I tell you, you'll understand."

"Nia, no. This is not a good idea."

Nia began to pace again. "You know my curiosity gets the best of me. Even when I was your babysitter, I used to come over here and look through the cupboards just to see what your parents kept."

"I'm pretty sure every teenage babysitter on the planet does that."

"And I touch things in museums even though the sign right in front of me says 'Do Not Touch.' It's like I think rules of civility don't apply to me."

Jillian swung her feet off the ottoman, planted them flat on the floor, and leaned forward. "Did you see something that puts Meri in danger?"

"No."

"Harmful to anyone else?"

"No."

"Illegal?"

"Definitely not."

"Touching on legal matters in any way?"

"Not that I can think of."

"Then I think you have to just block it out of your mind."

"But Jillian, if you saw where the envelope was from, you'd be curious too."

Jillian covered her ears. "Lalalalala. I'm not hearing this."

Nia stopped roving long enough to tug at Jillian's arms. "You should. This is why Meri is here."

Jillian considered. Five seconds. Then ten. "Okay. Where was the envelope from?"

"University of Tennessee Health Science Center."

"That sounds suspiciously like it could be related to a medical school."

"That's exactly what it is."

"Okay. So she has an envelope from a medical school. Her family is full of doctors. That's not all that surprising."

Nia swatted Jillian's shoulder. "It's not the envelope that matters. It's the letter."

"Whoa. Are you telling me you opened the envelope?"

"Technically it was already open. It's not as if Meri hadn't already read the letter."

126

Jillian stood up. "But now *you* read it. You read her personal correspondence."

"It's terrible. It's awful." Nia threw herself onto the navy sofa. "I'm a wretched soul, probably beyond redemption. But it explains so much. You'll agree when you hear what it is."

"I can't know this." Jillian pointed a firm index finger at Nia. "I can't be dragged into this. Let it go before we both need to engage legal counsel."

"Meri flunked out of medical school."

"Nia. Nia!"

"I know."

"I said don't tell me."

"But don't you see? This matters. It was a letter from the dean dated about ten days ago."

"It's so early in the academic year," Jillian said. "How is it possible to get a letter like that with this timing?"

"Well, there you go. You're sucked in, just the way I was."

"I still wish you hadn't told me." Jillian dropped one hand on top of her head. "How can I possibly unknow this now?"

"You can't. Not any more than I can. And we can't act like we don't know, not when she shows up on my doorstep acting like a frightened, skittish kitten."

Jillian tilted her head back to stare at the twelve-foot ceiling with its original crown molding.

"Well," she said, "you're right; coming from

a family of doctors, this is no small thing. No wonder she's running away from home." Jillian returned her gaze to Nia. "But you have to come clean with Meri. And you have to do it right away."

"What am I supposed to say to her? I accidentally picked up an envelope, opened it, read your mail, and put everything back, and now I can't behave normally around you?"

"Leave out the 'accidentally' part, and I think you have the basics."

"I'm sorry and not sorry all at the same time," Nia said. "Come on, let's go and get this over with."

Jillian glanced toward her office and the unrelenting stack of work. The family tree for the reunion. The lost young woman in St. Louis. An article to write for a genealogy journal. Deciding whether to accept an invitation to speak at a conference. Three proposals from potential clients she hadn't even had time to read yet, much less prepare quotes for her fee.

"Of course I'll go with you," Jillian said. "Will Meri be back?"

"I think so."

They walked together to the Inn, Nia's stride slower than usual. Jillian adjusted to Nia's speed, wishing her father were the one walking into a situation that would require his mediation skills. Nia and Meri wouldn't be bargaining over compensation or property or custody, but Nolan always said his greatest satisfaction came when he knew that parties across the table had truly listened to each other. All Jillian had was a ten-year-old introduction to psychology college course about which she remembered very little beyond the fact that the professor never wore socks and rooted for Ohio State during football season. Neither of those tidbits was likely to be useful in this situation.

"I got everything," Meri said as soon as they entered the kitchen at the Inn. "Free-range organic eggs, thick-sliced sourdough bread, center-cut bacon. And I made sure the butcher knew it was for you so he wouldn't give me the fatty stuff, just like you said. And pastries from Ben's Bakery—fresh, not day-old."

"Thank you, Meri," Nia said. "It was a tremendous help to be able to send you out for these things and know you would come back with the right stuff and not let anyone push you around just because you're new."

"I got the vegetables too. They didn't have as many orange peppers as you wanted, so I got extra yellow. I hope that's all right."

Meri's face was lit with pleasure. For a couple of hours she had focused on something other than the dread that infused Jillian's conversation with her the day before. For the moment, Jillian put a smile on her own face.

"I'm sure everything will be fine," Nia said. "I'm used to working with whatever ingredients I can find, as long as they are high quality, and I'm sure you did your absolute best to represent the Inn well in your purchases."

"I did try," Meri said. "I'd like to help make tomorrow's breakfast buffet and see what you're going to do with all these scrumptious things."

"I'd be delighted to have your help."

Jillian tilted her head at Nia's falsely bright tone and softly cleared her throat.

"We've had a busy morning," Nia said. "I have some chicken salad and a few of Ben's croissants. Why don't I make us all some sandwiches?"

"I had a bite while I was out," Meri said.

"And I should probably get back to work," Jillian said. "But we could just sit and talk for a few moments."

"I'll get out of your way," Meri said.

"Actually," Jillian said, "we'd like you to sit with us."

"I still need to sweep the upstairs hall and make sure all the wastebaskets got emptied."

"That can wait." Nia's tone gave in to what had to be done. She pulled out a chair and tapped the back of it for Meri to sit down.

"What's going on?" Meri sat and folded her hands on the table. "Have you decided I'm not working out?"

"No!" Nia said. "Nothing like that."

Jillian took the seat opposite Meri and waited for Nia's reluctant compliance. Finally Nia sat.

"I thought you could use some clean towels," Nia said, "and I noticed your door was open, so I went ahead and put them on your bed."

"Thank you." Meri's tone carried more suspicion than gratitude, and the light was flickering out of her eyes.

"On the way out, I couldn't help noticing the letter on your dresser."

Meri's eyes widened.

"My cousin went to medical school in Nashville, so I got curious. I have a terrible, lifelong problem with curiosity. Anyone will tell you that."

Meri said nothing.

"There aren't enough words in the universe to tell you how sorry I am, at least not any of the ones I know. I shouldn't have stopped. I should have just kept walking. But I didn't. I picked up the letter."

Meri scraped back her chair. "You are not about to tell me that you read my personal mail in my private room."

Nia's face was as red as Jillian had ever seen it, redder than that weekend they went over the mountain to Grand Lake and Nia insisted she never got sunburned but of course she fried to a crisp.

"I don't believe this," Meri said. "Here I've

been working so hard the last few days to earn your trust after running away that first night. It never occurred to me that I shouldn't trust you."

"It never occurred to *me* that you shouldn't trust me," Nia said. "I don't know what came over me. I was just going to leave the towels outside your room, and then the door was open, and then . . . well, there are no excuses. It was a complete breach of your privacy and your trust, and I am deeply sorry. I hope you can forgive me."

Meri looked away. "I don't know what I think right now."

"I'm sorry for what I did," Nia said, "but I'm not sorry for what I know. It helps me—us, because I told Jillian—understand something about you. If this is the reason you showed up in Canyon Mines, you should know that you still have friends here. This changes nothing on my end."

"Yes," Jillian said, "it certainly puts some perspective on everything you've been telling me about the doctors in your family. We want to help."

Meri stood up. "Well, my family will know by now. All those messages—it's only a matter of time before they find me here. Nia, if you wouldn't mind paying me for the days I've worked, I'll just leave."

"Leave?" Nia said. "And go where?"

Meri shrugged, as Jillian had come to expect her to do.

"Somewhere else. Find another job. I'll have to get a different phone. A prepaid one. And somehow get a different car. My parents own that too, so I can't sell it. Maybe I can get a bus ticket. Do you think my wages will be enough for a bus ticket somewhere?"

"Meri, let us help you," Nia said.

"Will today count as a full day of work if I finish everything?" Meri said.

"Yes, of course."

"Then I'll go in the morning." Meri left the kitchen, her soft steps taking her through the dining room, into the hall, and up the stairs.

"We can't let that girl leave," Nia said.

"I don't disagree," Jillian said, "but I don't know how to stop her. Gagging and tying her would just make things worse."

"What have I done, what have I done, what have I done?"

"You broke her trust," Jillian said, "but if it's any comfort, I'm pretty sure she was going to leave anyway and you just wouldn't have known why. She doesn't want her family to find her."

"I have to go talk to Leo."

"That's probably a good idea. And I'm going to call my dad."

Nia headed out to Leo's workshop, and Jillian

went out to the Dunston patio and pushed her father's speed dial number, hoping he wasn't in a meeting. She was in over her head with this intuitive and mediative stuff, but she couldn't see how it would be in Meri's best interest to let her abandon her car somewhere and get on a bus to who knows where. Nolan promised to help that evening. If they could just keep Meri close by all day, he would take her out for dessert.

Nia came marching out of the workshop, her demeanor transformed. "I have a plan."

Jillian followed her into the house. "What is it?"

"You'll see."

"What happened to being contrite and remorseful?"

"I am those things, but I am also determined to help Meri out of whatever mess has her hiding on the run. And that means she is staying put."

"How are you going to do that?"

"Just watch."

Nia stood at the base of the stairs and called up for Meri to come down.

Meri came three-quarters of the way down the staircase, broom in one hand and a wastebasket in the other.

"I have quite a list of things I need your help with over the next few days." Nia waved a sheet of paper. "I've written them out, so you can see for yourself that it's far too much for me to

134

handle on my own with an employee leaving without notice."

"What are you getting at?" Meri sat on a step. "I told you I'm leaving in the morning."

"Tomorrow is Wednesday. We agreed that you would be paid on Fridays, at the close of each week. So I will pay you on Friday as we agreed. We also agreed that you would give me a week's notice. Telling me today that you're leaving in the morning is hardly a week's notice."

"I don't believe you," Meri said. "First you invade my privacy, and now you treat me like an indentured servant?"

"This is what we agreed to."

"That was before."

"I apologized profusely," Nia said, "and what I did does not interfere with our ability to perform our respective responsibilities for the term of your employment."

"You are a piece of work, you know that?" Meri stomped up the stairs.

Nia withdrew to the office, and Jillian followed. Nia collapsed into her desk chair.

"You just bought us a week," Jillian said.

"I hope I did," Nia said. "Now you and your dad have to do your part."

"Piece of cake," Jillian said, "especially since now she hates you and hates us by association."

CHAPTER TWELVE

Memphis, August 26, 1878

Callie had taken to feeding Eliza enormous breakfasts. Eliza's mother had always over-seen a genteel vegetable garden but had drawn the line at having clucking chickens on the property. After all, they lived in town, not out in the country. She did not appreciate the less refined households whose roosters announced the dawn. But the clacking and crowing had come closer in the last week. Clearly Callie had rounded up abandoned chickens and sheltered them behind the coach house, where a well-oiled carriage sat idle while the horses were boarded at a livery during the household driver's annual leave— which had been extended by the impossibility that anyone should return to Memphis in the middle of an epidemic. Eliza was always content to hail a cab. It was her mother who wanted the security of her own carriage and a driver she knew. Now though, cabs were becoming scarce. Drivers spent their days hauling wagons loaded with coffins, and still the task was greater than the hours in the day. Eliza walked anywhere she needed to go in town and planned for the extra time that took.

Callie came into the dining room.

Eliza nodded. "I'm finished. Thank you for another breakfast sure to last me all day." Eliza had made herself consume every bite of the scrambled eggs, griddle cakes, bacon, and toast. Whatever food there was at the Sisters House should go to those who lived there or those they served.

"Yes, Miz Eliza. Your mama would want me to make sure you keep up your strength."

"I'm not ill, Callie."

"You tired though."

Eliza offered no dispute. Everyone at the Sisters House was exhausted. The epidemic showed no sign of abating.

"It be rainy again today," Callie said. "Wear your wellies and take the umbrella. Your mama would say."

"Yes, she would." As if August heat were not enough, constant dampness now soaked through every layer Eliza wore, no matter how carefully she selected her wardrobe, and she spent half her time outdoors swatting at mosquitos.

"How are your relatives?" Eliza asked.

"Dey be fine so far." Callie stacked Eliza's dishes. "No fever in da house. Dey say I should stay here and not visit. Look after you because you doing fine work."

"Your sister's little boy?"

"He be just fine. Dey keep him inside. Da girls

137

look after him while da grown-ups go to work."

"If they need something, you let me know."

"Yes, ma'am. But I send messages, and dey say dey be fine."

Eliza sucked in her cheeks and said nothing more. The adults in that house had been born slaves, as had Callie. She hadn't seen where they lived, but she knew enough about the general part of town to know there were probably too many people in too small a space. At least Callie was here now, in a neighborhood not affected by the fever.

Yet.

"We need a cart, Miz Eliza," Callie said. "We have vegetables from da gardens for the Sisters House."

"Yes. I'll see what I can do when I get over there today. We need them. That is certain. If the wagon is free, I'll send someone with it at some point."

"Yes, ma'am."

Eliza pinned on her hat and gathered her bag, the umbrella, and the small notebook she had begun carrying to keep track of what needed to be done in the pantry. She made sure she had a fresh handkerchief. As much as she tried to steel her stomach, at times the stench in the street overtook her and she had to block it from her nostrils as she walked. Death, and the efforts to combat it, hung ugly, blistering, and unmerciful in the air.

She was only four short blocks from the Sisters House, and her mind on the first tasks she must undertake upon arrival, when a man stopped her in the street.

"Are you going to the sisters?"

His garb was worn but had once been a well-tailored suit, though Eliza doubted it had been made for him. It did not fit at all well. Too short in the arms, too long in the legs, too wide in the shoulders. Eliza dragged her mind from these irrelevant details to his face, where pleading, mournful brown eyes filled the round shape.

"Yes, I am," she said.

"Will you take this note? It's urgent." He pressed it into her hand and strode quickly past before she could question or refuse him—not that she would have refused him.

Eliza opened the single sheet. It gave an address on High Street.

Father and mother are lying dead in the house, brother is dying. Send me some help. No money. Sallie U.

High Street was not far from the Sisters House. Eliza hastened her steps.

"Sister Constance?" she called when she pushed through the front door.

Sister Constance's steps answered, and she came into the hall.

"A man gave me this," Eliza said.

Sister Constance read the note. "Another one. Was the man ill?"

Eliza shook her head. "I don't think so."

In a matter of days, since Sisters Constance and Thecla returned from New York, not only had the sisters undertaken the expanded pantry and dispensary, which Eliza helped to run, but they had begun taking patients into an infirmary. It was not enough.

"Do you have a nurse to send?" Eliza said.

"A true nurse? No. Everyone on my list is working herself to the bone as it is."

"When do the nursing sisters from New York arrive?"

"Any day now, I pray."

"Shall I go inquire at the Howard Association?"

"It will do no good," Sister Constance said. "I spoke with the relief committee yesterday. Even the Howard Association no longer has enough nurses—not that they ever did. Doctors and nurses get sick too. And perish, God rest their souls."

And sisters. Eliza offered a silent prayer that the Sisters of St. Mary's would weather this epidemic, that God would reward the selflessness of their service with their own health. God sends rain on the just and the unjust alike, Matthew said in his Gospel, but did he also not say that with God all things are possible?

"We will have to send someone," Sister

Constance said. "I'll have to look at my book and see which of us might be able to squeeze in a visit."

"It sounds urgent."

"As they all are."

"I'll go," Eliza said. "Tell me what to do."

Sister Constance's eyebrows went up. "I believe our bargain is for you to do valuable, needful work here that allows you to keep your mother's mind at rest as much as possible."

Eliza pointed at the note in Sister Constance's hand. "But these people might be dying."

"And so might be family members of everyone who comes to the pantry and dispensary." Sister Constance's face was unyielding. "If you go to High Street, who will open the pantry? There is already a line."

Eliza nodded. She'd seen the line when she came in but blocked its significance because of the urgency of the note.

"I will send Sister Thecla," Sister Constance said.

"Yes, Sister Constance. Oh, will the wagon be free at all today, even for a few minutes?"

"Do you have vegetables?"

Eliza nodded.

"I will make sure it is free, then. We need to be able to offer the best nourishment possible."

"Callie will be ready."

The shops had been closed for nearly two

weeks, ever since Kate Bionda's death of yellow fever frightened half the city's population into dispersing in the space of three days. Some steamers and trains carried in supplies funded by donations, and men hungry for work would unload the cargo, but it was difficult to say what would be available. It might be something useful, or it might be something donors wanted to send regardless of whether it was helpful. Lined winter gloves, for instance, and second-hand embroidered camisoles did little to relieve the needs in Memphis, yet they turned up in the relief barrels. Sister Constance spent long chunks of her days in correspondence trying to arrange for goods that would genuinely bring relief or the funds to purchase what they needed for the growing numbers of people clamoring for help from St. Mary's.

"There are tea and broth in the kitchen," Sister Constance said. "It should be ready before too much longer. I will remind Mrs. Bullock to bring some jars to you as soon as she fills them."

Eliza nodded. She took only a few moments to organize herself in the pantry. She could have used the help of some of the girls from the orphanage, but Sister Constance was emphatic that the children not be exposed to visitors at this stage of the epidemic. Despite precautions, already some were ill, and the number of orphans swelled every day—but not the number of volunteers. Whenever Eliza had a glimpse of Sister Frances, she looked more haggard. For help Eliza relied only on Mrs. Bullock or Miss Murdock, when they could spare a few minutes, or a dwindling number of volunteers from the church.

She glanced through the shelves, fixing in her mind what was available today. It would all have to be rationed, and for each request she would have only seconds to make decisions about what she could give out based only on scant information or her own assessment of the physical condition of the inquirers. Was sanitation adequate? If there was no water, what was the point in offering a bar of soap? How far away was water for any purpose, and was there anyone at home healthy and strong enough to carry it? If she gave clean, uninfected clothing or pillowcases, could the person be relied on to burn the old in order to stop any infection they might contain? Was someone in the home well enough to prepare fresh food before it spoiled, or would it be better to send tins? How many people were in the home, and did they have any food at all on the shelves? Were there any infants who should be a priority for canned milk? Every day, it seemed new situations added to the grid of questions Eliza must quickly run through in her mind as she assessed needs and assembled bundles in response.

She monitored the shelf of canned milk carefully all day, asking questions about the presence of children in the home of everyone who requested some. From the start, it was clear the supply would not last the day. She might or might not have any to begin the day tomorrow. Already, in less than a week running the pantry, she had learned she couldn't harbor for tomorrow what someone needed today, but she could stiffen the standards as the supply tightened.

"Do you have an infant younger than a year old?" she asked a beleaguered father at mid-afternoon who asked for milk.

"He's a year and a half."

"I've got some potted meats that are quite soft," Eliza said, "and a few eggs."

"The wife asked for milk. Hers dried up, and he won't stop crying."

Eliza swallowed hard. Everyone had a story that could crack her resolve if she let it, and the pantry would be empty by eleven in the morning every day.

"I'm sorry. We have to save the milk for the babies. If you need fresh diapers and a clean dressing gown for your son, I can give you those also."

"Diapers?"

"How about half a dozen?"

He nodded. "But we still need milk."

"I'm sorry. He's too old."

"Our neighbors got milk here this morning." His voice filled the room now. "He sent me down here. Their boy just turned two. How can my boy be too old?"

"My baby is only seven months," a woman shouted from down the line. "You can't give him the last of the milk and then tell me you don't have any."

Eliza stared into the man's eyes. "That's why. We have only a few cans left."

"So you are saying if I have a dire need, I should have it early in the day."

"I am saying I cannot give you milk, but I can give you potted meats, eggs, diapers, a clean dressing gown, and tea and broth if anyone in the home is sick."

He huffed but nodded.

Most of the sisters were still out on house calls when she ducked her head into the infirmary at the end of the afternoon.

"Mrs. Bullock has your supper ready," she told Sister Hughetta.

"Please tell her I'll eat it cold later." Sister Hughetta looked up from her desk at the end of the room. "There's no one to keep watch here."

"I'll stay," Eliza said.

"Sister Constance warned us about you."

"*Warned* you?"

"She says you are very eager to help, but we're not to let you take care of the patients."

From the doorway, Eliza scanned the room. "Everyone looks restful at the moment."

"They are. I am listening for changes in breathing that might indicate distress."

"When is the last time you had a good rest, Sister Hughetta?"

The nun did not answer.

Eliza pointed to a hard, straight-back chair. "This is what I propose. You bring that chair over here, to the doorway. I will sit in it very quietly and listen to changes in breathing. You will go eat a hot meal. Then you will go lie down, at least for a couple of hours—longer if you wish. I will remain here until you awaken or until one of the other nurses comes on duty."

"Sister Constance was quite clear."

"I will not approach the patients," Eliza said. "If I hear the slightest change in breathing, I will immediately call for you. Immediately. I will not put anyone at risk with the slightest hesitation. Neither will I doze off in my vigil."

Sister Hughetta scraped her chair back and glanced at one of the orphan girls sick in a bed. "Have you been to Canfield Asylum recently?"

"It is more difficult since I began organizing the pantry."

"I pray the colored orphans are safe away from the city limits."

"I join your prayers."

CHAPTER THIRTEEN

"Dad, I really, *really* have to do some work today."

Nolan handed Jillian a plate of scrambled eggs, but she didn't even sit at the breakfast bar to eat them.

"Raúl is on my back about the St. Louis thing," she said, "and Mrs. Answald calls me three times a day to see if this is the day I'm finally going to FedEx everything she needs for her family tree. My journal article is due in two weeks, and I don't even have an outline yet. And if I don't review those proposals soon, I'm going to miss out on some serious work for the next three months."

"I understand." Nolan nudged a glass of orange juice in her direction. "You've gone over and above the last two days on the Meri front. I know it's been distracting."

"I tried, Dad." Jillian took a fork from the drawer. "I even tried talking to Meri after she blew up at Nia yesterday. It was like being a match in a tinderbox. I'm in over my head with the relational stuff."

"You don't give yourself enough credit."

"Don't sweet-talk me. You're working at home today. Your turn."

Nolan had his own pile of briefs to read to prepare for three meetings tomorrow in Denver. But he had connived far more than Jillian to get involved with Meri. He could hardly play the "too busy" card now.

"I'll do what I can to dampen the tinderbox," he said. "Eat some breakfast. You drink too much coffee and don't eat enough real food."

"Dad."

"I know. Grown-up and all that."

She took her eggs and orange juice into her office, but she'd be back before long for some of her fancy-schmancy coffee in another mug she would ultimately reject as not meeting her specifications.

Nolan slid the rest of the eggs from the skillet onto his own plate, buttered his wheat toast, filled his cup with pure unadulterated coffee, and considered his strategy for the day.

As soon as the clock ticked past eight o'clock, he called Nia. She might be in the middle of the breakfast buffet, but if Jillian's reports of her remorse were accurate, Nia would take his call.

"It was a good strategy," he said.

"Snooping into personal belongings?" Nia said.

"No. Whatever you found by that method would be inadmissible in court."

"Nolan, don't mess with me."

"Fine. But using a technicality to stall was a great strategy. Lawyers do it all the time when we need more time to get a case together. Nothing illegal or unethical about it."

"It was Leo's idea."

"I'd like to think he listens to something I say once in a while, but he probably just watches too many legal dramas on television."

"Nolan, please, get to the point. I'm sorry as all get-out and didn't sleep a wink because of the mess I made. But we know what we know, and we have to help Meri." Nia's desperation left her mouth, bounced off a cell tower somewhere, and landed in Nolan's ear.

"This is what I need," Nolan said. "Carte blanche."

"Whatever you need."

"I have to make some calls that are already on my schedule today, but first chance I get, I'll come to the Inn. I'll invite Meri out—lunch, ice cream, coffee at the Cage, a walk, it doesn't matter what. No matter what's going on at the Inn, you have to say she can leave with me."

"Yes, anything."

Now relief bounced off the cell tower.

The phone calls and making notes took all morning. One of the trade-offs for Nolan's working at home two days a week was functioning without his assistant within voice distance. He called her with a set of instructions and emailed the files she needed so he'd have the documents necessary for tomorrow's meetings.

He hadn't heard a peep out of Jillian all day. Down in the kitchen though, he saw evidence that she had emerged long enough to make a sandwich and carry it back to her office. He glanced at the clock on the wall. The morning had bled into the afternoon, and he'd probably missed his chance to take Meri to lunch.

He stuck his head in Jillian's office, hesitated a moment, and stepped all the way in to massage her hunched shoulders.

"If that's your way of telling me I should sit up straight, I know." She relaxed under his palpating fingers. "That feels great."

"I'm going now," he said. "Is there anything you need first?"

"Six more hours in the day?"

"I will try to perform that miracle as soon as I accomplish the first one I promised for today."

"Thanks, Dad."

"And I'll cook tonight. I can shop on my way back."

"Dad. Do we have to have that conversation every single day?"

"Have you no faith in me at all?"

"Great faith! Just not for shopping."

"Okay then. I'll pick something up and keep things simple for both of us."

"Now that's a plan I can believe."

Nolan rummaged in the fridge for some sliced roasted turkey and pushed it into a folded piece of bread to munch while he walked toward the Inn. By the time he got there, extricated Meri, and walked with her into town, it would be at least two thirty. He should have something in his stomach.

He entered the Inn through the front door. The parlor, with its vintage reception desk, was unattended, but it didn't take long to discern where the activity in the house was. He traversed the front parlors through to the dining room.

"You'll have to do it again," Nia said to Meri.

They stood beside the antique oak sidebar. Nia held out a rag and tin of furniture wax to Meri.

"I already did it exactly the way I've done it two other times since I got here," Meri said. "What you're asking is unreasonable."

"I believe it is my prerogative to determine when a task is completed to satisfaction," Nia said. "This sidebar dates to the original era of the house. It garners a great deal of attention with the guests, and it must be polished impeccably."

"Do you seriously expect me to believe that someone can find fault with the way I've polished a hundred-year-old piece of furniture?" Meri's voice rose. "I don't think that's why people come to Canyon Mines."

"Please do as I ask."

Meri snatched the rag and wax. "You're punishing me."

Nolan couldn't be sure whether Nia was still in

her bad cop mode—if she was, she was going too far—but nothing was manufactured about Meri's anger. Misplaced, perhaps. Nia was the most recent offender and was holding Meri's paycheck hostage, but the greatest irritation was that she was the closest target for Meri's pent-up distress and anxiety.

"Hello," Nolan said.

Nia and Meri snapped apart.

"Hello, Nolan," Nia said. "What brings you by?"

"Oh, please," Meri said. "You can all stop treating me like an idiot."

"Meri, that's uncalled for," Nia said.

"I don't think you get to tell me what's uncalled for."

Whoa. Tinderbox may have been a mild description.

"I was in the mood for some ice cream and thought Meri might like to go with me."

"Sure!" Nia took the rag and wax back from Meri. "It's a beautiful day, and on a Wednesday, Kris's shop won't be crowded. Take your time."

"Excuse me," Meri said. "Don't I get a vote? Have the two of you decided the entire rest of my life or only the remainder of my captivity?"

Nolan turned his palms up. "It was only a suggestion."

Nia held the rag and wax toward Meri. "Of course you don't have to go."

Meri looked from Nolan to Nia and back again. "Ice cream sounds fine. Let me get my sweater."

They were hardly off the front porch of the Inn before Meri scowled.

"I know they sent you to make nice, and I like you fine. But under the circumstances, I know whose side you're on."

"Side?"

"You're here to smooth over what Nia did yesterday."

"I'm here to see what I can do to help."

"Help who? That's the key question."

"Help you, Meri," Nolan said.

They walked half a block without speaking.

"I'm not really in the mood for ice cream," Meri said. "I just had to get out of there. She's been riding me all day—like I was the one who stepped over the line yesterday."

Nolan waited a few yards before speaking. "Well, considering that we're practically at the ice cream shop, what do you say we go in anyway? If you look around and still don't feel in the mood, we'll wander the Emporium or take a walk down to the park or whatever you want to do to have some space from Nia."

"I don't need you for that."

"Except that's what she thinks you're doing, so why make trust issues worse by ditching me now?"

"I'd call it getting even."

"You can get even with ice cream in your stomach." Nolan held open the door to Ore the Mountain.

Meri stepped inside—barely. Nolan stood beside her, prepared to go at her pace. She tilted her head and took in the decor. Gradually fury slipped off her shoulders. How could anyone stay angry in the presence of ice cream?

"I like it," she said. "The mining picks, the old photos, the maps. It makes me feel like I could go digging for an undiscovered flavor."

"Now you're talking," Nolan said. "I think that's just what Kris is after when she's constantly concocting new combinations. If you've got a creative inspiration, I'm sure she'd love to hear it."

"I'll think about it."

"Shall we?" Nolan gestured toward the counter. Meri shuffled forward.

Kris waved. "I'll have that cherry chocolate chip chunk right up for you. And what does your friend want?"

"This is Meri Davies," Nolan said. "She works at the Inn for Nia." *Hopefully that statement will still be true tomorrow and the day after.*

"Welcome to Canyon Mines," Kris said. "What would you like?"

"How did you know what Nolan wanted?" Meri asked.

"We go back a long way," Kris said.

"Do you use real strawberries?"

"We use real everything."

"Then I'd like a strawberry cream shake, please."

They took their ice cream to a table. The only other customers in the place were a middle-aged couple Nolan recognized as fairly recent residents to Canyon Mines.

He sucked ice cream off the end of a spoon and let Meri slurp her shake.

"I'll bet it's been a long time since you've had ice cream this good."

She nodded, not taking her mouth off the straw.

"So the story I got," Nolan said, "is that you ran into some trouble with medical school."

"They told you."

"You were right earlier. We are all on the same side," Nolan said, "but that side is Team Meri."

She looked away.

"No one thinks any less of you for having a rough patch."

"Except if you're related to me."

"Is that why you don't want Jillian to work on your family tree?"

Meri scratched her forehead above her glasses, right at the scalp line. "It's more complicated than you could know."

Her voice wavered as her words took on a dagger shape that cut into him, making her pain his.

"Tell me," he said softly.

Meri sucked up some more of her shake.

Nolan waited.

"I was salutatorian in my exclusive private high school class. Why wasn't I first? my father wanted to know. I missed it by three-tenths of a percent. Then I double-majored at Sewanee in biology and chemistry."

"No slouch there."

"Summa cum laude. But I came in second in my class again. Why wasn't I first?"

"I'm sorry your parents didn't recognize your stellar accomplishments."

Liquid glimmering lines slithered across the bottoms of her eyes. "I was supposed to redeem myself in med school. I didn't get into Harvard, like my brother, but it was going to be okay because my family has a tradition in southern medical schools, and he had turned his nose up at that."

"And then you got the letter."

"My parents know now."

"Did you tell them?"

"Of course not. I don't have to. The dean is an old friend."

Double major at Sewanee in two sciences. Salutatorian. Summa cum laude. How would someone with those credentials fail a few weeks into her second year of med school?

Unless she didn't want to be there in the first place.

"You didn't want to go to medical school, did you, Meri?"

She slurped strawberry cream shake and shrugged. "That's irrelevant."

"It's not irrelevant to me."

Now her eyes overfilled, their deep brown color clouded. "Please don't say things like that."

"Why not?"

"Because. That's not my life."

"But it's why you're in Canyon Mines, and it's why you don't feel you can stay here."

Eventually she nodded.

"We want to help," Nolan said. "What Nia did was wrong, and she knows it. We don't want to see you run away from your own life. Nia cares. She did from the first day. We all do."

"You haven't even known me for a week. How can you possibly care that much?"

"Because we do. Can you trust us?"

Meri pushed away her unfinished shake. "Strangers and a family tree can't fix this."

CHAPTER FOURTEEN

Jillian had ducked Mrs. Answald's calls twice already that day, and if she didn't pick up this time, the voice mail would be noticeably terser than the last one.

She picked up. Yes, she was almost finished. Just a few more finishing touches.

Yes, she could FedEx tomorrow, the next day at the very latest, in time for delivery on Saturday morning. A printout on regular-size sheets for her review but also a thumb drive with a large file Mrs. Answald could take straight to any print-and-copy center for a full-color, high-quality, large-size printout worthy of display at the reunion event.

Absolutely it would be finished on time.

Jillian clicked off the call. The young woman in St. Louis would remain lost for another day and she would have to think of something to tell Raúl, but she could check Mrs. Answald off her list before she laid her head on her pillow tonight—save the trip to FedEx in the morning.

The back door opened, and her dad's keys clinked into the copper bowl on the kitchen counter where he'd been keeping them as long as she could remember. He never lost his keys, which was more than she could say.

Jillian leaned forward for one final cross-referencing and proofreading of every entry in the six-generation family tree, comparing the data in her research with what showed on her printout and what she saw on the screen.

"Change of plans," Nolan said from the doorway.

Jillian stuck a finger on a sheet of paper to keep her place and looked up at him. "What happened?"

"I almost made Meri cry."

"Actually, I think that might have been good for her."

"Me too. So I invited her to dinner."

Jillian dropped her chin and stared at him out of the tops of her eyes. "To try again to make her cry?"

"That is not my precise goal, but it might be a collateral event. She trusts no one. She will find no healing for what wounds her if she cannot trust at least one person. Right now, it can't hurt for her to work enough to earn her wage, but otherwise what she really needs is to truly believe she has people on her team."

Jillian didn't disagree. But two more substantial queries for her services had come in today, and she hadn't even yet fairly reviewed the ones already on her desk. She had planned to spend the evening looking at neglected proposals so she could start putting together quotes to ensure her work flow for the next few months. If she wanted out-of-control interruptions, she'd get a job in an office.

"I'll still keep it simple," Nolan said. "I need to work a couple more hours myself this afternoon. Then I'll call in an order for Chinese, drive over to pick it up, and swing by to collect Meri. We'll just eat in the kitchen. I promise it won't be a late evening."

"Thanks for understanding."

"I only need one thing from you before supper."

Jillian restrained the little girl pouty face of displeasure she wanted to give her daddy in that moment.

"This isn't just about keeping Meri and Nia apart," Nolan said. "I already called Nia and suggested she back down from her mean boss posturing. She made her point by stating the rules. Wouldn't it also be useful if we got some information about Meri's family that you could use?"

"I guess." When she could work on Meri's tree was the big question. The hours from two to six in the morning yawned open.

Jillian listened to her father's explanation of Meri's academic merits and the theory that flunking out of medical school was no accident, despite her anxiety about her family's response.

"Did you ever find out her siblings' names?" he asked.

"No, but I have her parents' names, so that wouldn't be hard. I just genuinely haven't had time."

"I know. Until yesterday, none of us knew there was a timeline."

"But now there is."

Nolan nodded. "Think about what would be helpful. Something she might not be so guarded about. Something that would untangle why there's so much pressure on her to become a doctor."

"It doesn't seem like she's much in the mood to cooperate, Dad."

"Give me some pointers, and I'll try to steer the conversation."

Jill pushed a fist into the opposite palm.

"You do that when you're thinking hard," Nolan said.

"Are you sure we can't do this tomorrow?"

"I have to be in Denver tomorrow—unless you want to try on your own."

Jillian shook her head. "She won't talk to me without you. I think we've established that. How about Friday?"

"She could be gone as soon as she gets that paycheck."

"She's not supposed to leave until Tuesday," Jillian said. "One week's notice. That's what Nia said they agreed to."

Nolan shrugged one shoulder. "Meri's not interested in the agreement. She's interested in the paycheck."

"I'm just so swamped."

"Just two or three items," Nolan said.

"Are you going to write them on your hand so you won't forget them?"

"Oh ye of little faith."

"Okay. But you might consider a sticky note."

"Thank you." Nolan buzz-kissed the top of her head. "No computer. No papers. Just a casual takeout dinner where she talks about things she doesn't realize she knows."

Kung pao chicken. Beef and snow peas. Sweet-and-sour pork. Cashew chicken. Vegetable spring rolls. Wonton soup. White rice. Fried rice.

Nolan had it all covered. As he unpacked the options with considerable cheer, Jillian offered Meri a smile and set out the largest-size plates the household offered and some bowls that resembled the size Chinese restaurants used for soup. Nolan would want some of everything. Jillian hoped at least one dish would appeal to Meri. Nolan added pitchers of cucumber water and raspberry lemonade to the nook of a table and declared the feast prepared. The three of them scooted into their seats.

Nolan offered his hands to both young women. When Jillian laid hers in one of his open palms, Meri followed her lead.

"May you always find nourishment for your body at the table," he said. "May sustenance for your spirit rise and fill you with each dawn. And may life always feed you with the light of joy along the way."

"Is that a traditional Irish blessing?" Meri asked when Nolan released her hand.

"My ma used to say it to me," Nolan said. "I have a feeling her ma made it up."

"And he has said it to me all my life," Jillian said, "so that makes it traditional. Four generations. What sustenance can we offer you tonight?"

"I haven't had sweet-and-sour pork in a long time."

"Then sweet-and-sour pork it is." Nolan passed the dish. "I recommend the beef and snow peas. And the cashew chicken—though it does have a little zing."

Meri gave a half smile. "Okay. A little of everything."

Nolan pushed every dish in Meri's direction before serving himself.

"So Jillian's great-grandmother made up that blessing?"

"That's right," Jillian said. "At least that's the family legend."

"Did you know her?"

"No, but I wish I had. I've never come across that particular Irish blessing anywhere else in all my research. I'd love to have the chance to know what else was in her mind."

"How much do you know about her?" Meri passed the fried rice back to Nolan.

"My dad has some memories and old family photos, but I've discovered some other things through my genealogical research."

"Like what?"

"She knew the Unsinkable Molly Brown, for one thing."

"I've heard of her."

"She lived a colorful life, including surviving the *Titanic*. Her home in Denver is a museum now, and I like going there and thinking about how my great-grandmother was once in that place. She was a maid there for a few months, but I've uncovered notes that suggest Mrs. Brown rather liked her, perhaps because they both came from Irish immigrant families."

"How did you find out something from so long ago?"

"It takes digging, but it can be done. My great-grandmother's family came from Ireland like so many others during the late nineteenth century and ended up in Colorado to work the mines. But by the time she was sixteen, she was orphaned. So she went into domestic service. She moved from Leadville to Denver and married a man who worked in a small newspaper office. Their daughter married a Duffy."

"And the rest is history, as they say." Meri forked a chunk of breaded pork. "My great-aunt once told me a story about how my father's grandparents got married in Atlanta. It almost didn't happen. They had a certain window of time when both their families could come, or they were going to have to wait for months. I don't know why. But there was a terrible rainstorm that washed out a bridge. My great-grandfather wanted to get married even if no one could be there but the preacher, but my great-grandmother was having none of that. At least that's how the story goes."

"But it worked out?" Nolan's plate was loaded by now and his fork ready.

"At the last minute. Apparently there was a lot of mud involved, but they got married."

Jillian laughed. "I love these stories."

"That was the original Canfield Davies," Meri said.

"Original?" Jillian said. "How many have there been?"

"At least one in every generation since, as far as I know," Meri said. "I haven't kept track of all the cousin lines. My dad is one."

"I thought you said his name was Michael."

"He goes by C. Michael. Canfield Michael. But he's always been Michael in the family."

"And in your generation?"

"My brother, Canny."

"Canny?"

"He hates it. He spends his life explaining it's not Manny or Danny. But he can hardly shorten it to Can. Too many mean childhood jokes there. In the family he's still Canny. Professionally, as an adult, he tries to be Canfield, but then everyone thinks that's his last name."

"What about his middle name?" Nolan said. "Couldn't he do what your father has done?"

Meri shook her head. "Canfield Mathers. My mother's family name."

"Wow. He's in a jam, for sure," Nolan said.

"A Canfield in every generation for the boys, and an Eliza in every generation for the girls." Meri pointed at herself. "Meriwether Eliza."

"And do those names go back just as far?" Jillian said. "Pardon me, my genealogist badge is showing."

"It's all right. I have no clue."

"Meriwether," Jillian said. "That must have significance."

Meri shrugged. "When I was little and asked why I had such a hard name to spell, they said I should be grateful to have a name that meant something happy to my father."

"It does have sort of a cheery sound to it," Jillian said.

"People always think of Meriwether Lewis, but I doubt that's it," Meri said. "I'd like another spring roll, if no one else wants that last one."

"Of course." Jillian passed it to her. "You

know, you have a very interesting family—from a genealogical point of view."

"Yeah. As long as you're not living on the inside of it, I guess you might see it that way."

"You've had a rough week," Nolan said. "A rough couple of weeks, getting yourself all the way out here from Tennessee. But we really do want to help."

"My dad does mediation work professionally," Jillian said. "He can help you talk to your parents about how you really feel about medical school."

Meri dropped the spring roll onto her plate. "You just don't get it. There is no talking. There never is."

"The offer is open," Nolan said. "In the meantime, I have an apple caramel pie from Ben's Bakery."

"I didn't save any room for that," Meri said. Her interest in the abandoned spring roll had faded as well. "I should get back. I promised Nia I would wipe down the kitchen before I went to bed."

"I'll walk you home." Nolan caught Jillian's eye and stood up. "It's dark."

He could have offered to drive her the few blocks to the Inn. The walk, Jillian knew, would give him the chance to take Meri's emotional pulse even if they didn't speak for the whole ten minutes it took to escort her.

While they were gone, she cleared up the

leftovers, put dishes in the dishwasher, and went into her office.

Nolan was back in twenty minutes. "What did we get?"

"Canfield," Jillian said. "I knew it as soon as she said it."

"A family name that her father and brother prefer not to use?"

"Eliza will be harder to figure out, because it's just a common female name. Meriwether is a place—a town or a county or something like that. I'll have to hunt it down and connect it to the family. But Canfield is the big one."

Nolan dropped into a chair across from Jillian's desk. "I have a feeling I'm about to get a history lesson."

"A brief one. It's a genealogical hazard. During the Civil War, Colonel Herman Canfield led a volunteer infantry regiment in Ohio into the Battle of Shiloh, where he was killed by Confederate fire. He was a known abolitionist, and he left a wife and several children. Martha Canfield was not one to abandon the cause, and she went south to Memphis, where she helped gain medical supplies and food for Union bases. Memphis had fallen to the Union in a battle of just a few hours' duration early in the war and was not particularly dangerous. After the war, she opened an orphanage for black children. Canfield Asylum."

Jillian met her father's widened eyes, one brow arched. How did he do that?

"This could be what we're looking for," he said.

"Genealogically speaking, yes. But Dad, we're talking about the 1870s. Who knows what records were like? The orphanage was closed by 1900. Whether I can tie Meri's family to it is one question, and what that has to do with this business with all the doctors is another."

"But it's a start. And you have the Meriwether clue."

"I do."

"I'd say the price of the Chinese food was money well spent."

"The family definitely enshrines the past—for generations. But why?"

"My question," Nolan said, "is that if Meri can't tell us why, then how many generations back would we have to go to find someone who could?"

"Bingo."

"In the meantime, Meri is calmer. My read is that she is not going to bolt. Not before Friday, and hopefully not before Tuesday. She even told me that she agreed to go antiquing with Nia tomorrow."

"Do you think that's a good idea? The two of them together alone all day?"

"I think it's Nia making a good faith effort

to repair the relationship, and I'll have a word with her about it before I turn in to set some boundaries. But we have to stay on this. And we can't break her trust again."

Jillian glanced at the clock. "Okay then. I've got work to do."

CHAPTER FIFTEEN

Memphis, August 29, 1878

If Eliza put her mind to it, she could learn to drive a wagon. It would make her so much more useful. Ned could teach her. That's all there was to it. On the way back into town, Eliza would persuade Sister Constance there was time for a driving lesson by presenting a case for how much more she could do during the duration of the epidemic if she were permitted to drive a team of horses. She was a quick learner at everything she undertook. Why should driving be any different?

The carriage carried precious cargo, not only supplies of food and clothing for the asylum, but children.

Stunned children still absorbing the reality of their new status as orphans.

Sister Constance had no choice but to allow the driver to slow the carriage despite the distance that still lay between them and Canfield Asylum. Men lined the road, some with rifles, some with heavy sticks.

Inside the carriage with the children, Eliza raised a single finger to her lips and met the eyes of every child. The youngest was on her lap. She cradled his head with the most confident comfort she could conjure. He must not squawk. Not now.

"Gentlemen." Sister Constance leaned out and met the eyes of the men. "I beg your indulgence to clear the way, please."

"You are not passing with those children," one man said.

Sister Constance leaned against the door to open it and stepped out of the carriage. "Mr. Morris, isn't it?"

"Sister."

"Consider the children, please. They've lost their parents."

"I'm considering the children—my children, and the children of every man here. We've had no fever out here in the countryside. Now you want to bring children straight from houses where people have died. We won't have it."

"We don't propose to place them in your homes, Mr. Morris," Sister Constance said. "These children are healthy, and we're going directly to the asylum where they can stay that way."

"You have no right."

"Ah, but we do, and I suspect you know that. The relief committee asked the Sisters of St. Mary's to take over managing Canfield Asylum to care for orphans whose families have been lost to the epidemic, regardless of race or religious affiliation, and we have accepted this grave responsibility. We have telegraphed to the

172

Mother House for additional help from our own community. More sisters are on the way."

A man shouldered his rifle.

Eliza squeezed the baby in her lap to her chest with one arm and gathered the hands of two tiny children with the other.

"My good sir!" Sister Constance angled herself between the man and the carriage, her arms open wide. "Will you threaten innocent orphans with a weapon of war in the middle of a public thoroughfare?"

"We have to protect ourselves." The growled response was unmoved.

"Then I suggest you return to your homes where you will continue to be miles away from any infected individuals. Tonight as you hear the bedtime prayers of your own children, teach them to pray for those less fortunate."

A child whimpered in the carriage.

"Look what you've done," Sister Constance said. "Are you so heartless that you cannot think of the good of another man's child when he is no longer here to speak for her?"

"If we don't speak for our own families, then who will?" Mr. Morris moved forward out of the clump of men, shaking his fist. "This is our land out here. We decide what happens on it."

"Would you like to take that up with the Board of Health and the Citizens Relief Committee?" Sister Constance said. "How about the City of Memphis? I'm quite sure these various authorities would point out that the road on which you stand does not belong to any of you, and Canfield Asylum certainly does not. No one is asking you to go to Canfield or to attend to the children there—none of whom is ill in any manner, certainly not with yellow jack."

Mr. Morris pointed at the wagon. "You're starting with half a dozen. How many do you intend to transport?"

"As many as need be, and we will gladly report the numbers to the relief committee. If you would like to go into town and consult with them, I'm sure they would be happy to speak with you."

"We're not going into that disease-infested town."

"Good. I do not advise it." Sister Constance took her seat in the carriage again, pulled the door shut with a daring thud, and motioned for Ned to take up the reins. Her modulation softened as she surveyed the group of men. "Would you have us refuse to these children the very protection you have obtained for your own? We do not propose to make a hospital of the asylum. If any of the children are taken ill with the fever, they shall be carried immediately to our infirmary at Church Home or the Sisters House."

"You turn that wagon around and go back where you came from."

"We will not." Even with an attempt to mollify her vocal approach, Sister Constance's disposition was unyielding.

"Children," Eliza said, "lie down on the floor. Cover your eyes. Right now."

They burrowed among the sacks of flour and cornmeal and the baskets of squash and beans Callie had harvested.

"Are you not willing to trust the sisters?" Eliza called out. "Women who have sacrificed their lives to do God's work?"

Silence.

Then one man cracked. "I am."

Others followed. "We are."

Eyes forward, Sister Constance urged Ned to proceed. Eliza, however, turned her head with deliberation from side to side, taking in the faces of every man. If there were violence and any harm came to even a hair on the head of one of the children in the carriage, she would be ready with a description of the man or men who inflicted it. For now the police were overwhelmed with keeping order, their own ranks decimated with illness. But the day would come that city officials would once again be operating at full capacity, and she would personally lead a crusade of justice for children. She burned the features into her memory while Sister Constance dared any to further impede their progress.

At Canfield, Eliza was on familiar ground. She

knew the colored couple who cared for the half dozen children who lived there and the arrangement of rooms. Within minutes she could suggest how they might make space for the children from the carriage—and more. For surely there would be many more.

"The relief committee has promised mattresses," Sister Constance said. "Dozens. But many of the children will have to double up."

"We'll start with the little ones," Eliza said. "And siblings who will want to be together anyway. What about bedding?"

"Promised as well. I'm not sure where they are getting it, but they assure me it will be new and uninfected."

They settled the children. The husband who lived at Canfield agreed to feed all the additional mouths to come—with provisions the nuns would supply—and the wife would look after the extra children until Sister Constance could send one of her new nurses from New York to take charge—only a day or so.

They unloaded supplies.

They prepared food.

They sketched out schedules for the sisters coming from the Mother House and volunteers who would be glad to come and serve at Canfield, away from the infectious tendrils of the disease, in a place where it was safe to stand outside and breathe the air.

The next day another twenty orphans found a temporary home at Canfield.

Over the next four days Eliza did indeed learn to drive a team pulling a wagon, and a total of fifty orphans traveled the miles from dense Memphis neighborhoods, where they survived the plague that captured their parents, to the building that would be their home for the duration of the epidemic and until some arrangement could be made for determining their future. By then Sister Ruth and Sister Helen from New York had arrived and taken up their posts at Canfield.

Eliza shuttled between the pantry, where there was never enough to go around and where every day those who came looked thinner and more exhausted and less hopeful, and Canfield, where the older children knew they ought to be grateful to be alive but were destitute and bereft, so gratitude was a far stretch. The littler ones cried themselves to stillness, realizing at last that familiar arms were not coming no matter the pitch of their travails.

At the end of the fourth day, Eliza closed the pantry and prayed that an early-morning train would bring needed goods before hundreds of people would arrive at the church once again seeking what no one else seemed to have. She pulled the door closed behind her just as Sister Clare, another of the New York nurses, came into the Sisters House and folded in on herself on a bench.

"Sister Clare! Are you unwell?"

Sister Clare raised her head and wiped tears off both cheeks with the back of her hand. "We cannot get there fast enough. We try, but there are too many."

Eliza sat beside Sister Clare, a hand on her shoulder.

"We get there only to find that everyone inside the house has died," Sister Clare said. "The worst cases are the ones where I can lay my hand on a forehead and know only moments earlier I would have found someone alive."

Eliza's chest clenched. "Surely in those cases death would have come anyway."

"Yes, but they might not have died alone. They might have died knowing that someone cared. I might at least have offered comfort. I am a nurse, after all."

Eliza made circles with her fingertips on Sister Clare's back. "Thank you so much for coming to Memphis. We love our city, of course, but for people to come to us from other places means a great deal."

"We serve a great God together," Sister Clare said. "When you have that call on your heart, you cannot say no, not for your own convenience, not for any reason. One must keep one's vows."

"We are so grateful. I'm sure Mrs. Bullock has

kept some food for you. Shall I get your plate?"

"Are the others all back?"

"I believe Sister Hughetta is still out."

Sister Clare stood. "Perhaps I will wait for her so she will not have to eat alone."

Eliza nodded.

"You must have missed your dinner by now as well."

"Callie has gotten used to my erratic hours," Eliza said. "She simply plans for me to be late now."

"You should not have to walk alone at this hour."

"I am not alone," Eliza said. "The Lord God is with me." And the streets were not dark. They were lit by barrels burning infected clothing and household goods, heaps of fiery mattresses unfit for anyone ever to rest upon again, patrols laying down another coat of lime.

Still, she hastened her steps home.

The house was dark. Callie should have lit the lamps by now, one in the front hall to guide Eliza's path into the house and one in the dining room where her evening meal would be served no matter what hour she arrived home. Eliza fumbled with a seldom-used key to the front door in the dark and then with matches to light a kerosene lamp on an entry table.

"Callie!"

She carried the lamp through the front parlor,

through the dining room, into the kitchen, and into the narrow maid's room Callie had occupied the last couple of weeks, panicked with every step that Callie had succumbed to fever and was suffering alone.

But the house was empty, and there was no sign of an evening meal in progress. Eliza lit another lamp—her mother would be aghast that she was not lighting the gas lamps on the walls, but Eliza found the kerosene lamps faster in this moment—and looked for clues for what might have happened to Callie.

There on the dining room table was a torn scrap of paper with four words scribbled on it. *Sister sick. Gone there.*

Eliza laid the note back on the table. In all the conversations she and Callie had about her family, she'd learned how miraculous it was that Callie and her sister had found each other again following the war after being sold apart when they weren't much older than her sister's girls were now. She learned her sister had married a good man. She learned that the little boy had been a surprise when her sister had thought the hope of another child was long past. She knew Callie lived with her sister's family. What Eliza didn't know was the street where the family lived. She only knew the general part of town where many of the former slave families lived if they chose not to take live-in employment.

"Oh Callie," she said to the empty house.

Eliza left her lamp on the table and went to the front porch. Though her neighborhood was sparsely populated now, it was not exempt from the nightly ritual of fires to extinguish the fever from the streets of Memphis. Lucent flashes of orange and yellow discharged against blackness and spiraled into smoke the desperate hope that this effort would move the city closer to the end of the siege. Somewhere a cannon fired ammunition against the enemy of disease.

She was on her own now.

CHAPTER SIXTEEN

S he's gone. Jillian, she's gone!"
Jillian was operating on insufficient sleep for the third night in a row and was only halfway through her first cup of coffee in a pale yellow mug that held an inadequate quantity and featured a thin handle useless for anything more than adornment, making it destined for the collection of nonrepeaters before she filled it a second time.

"Who's gone?" she said into the phone.

"Meri, of course," Nia said. "Who else would I be calling about?"

Jillian rubbed one eye. A sick friend listed on the prayer chain at church? Nia's elderly mother-in-law? Carlotta's infirm mother?

"Where did she go?"

"Wake up, Jillian," Nia snapped. "I am not kidding around. "I can't find Meri, and this time she took her car."

Jillian gulped coffee before setting down the mug. "But my dad said she seemed fine when he walked her home last time. He was going to talk to you last night."

"Well, even the great Nolan Duffy gets it wrong sometimes, I guess."

"Nia, that's not fair."

"I'm sorry. I'm just feeling frantic. Meri did seem fine last night. She told me she had a nice time with the two of you, and she insisted on wiping down the kitchen for me, even though I told her twice she didn't have to. She even volunteered to get up early and preheat the oven for the breakfast casseroles and set up the coffee urn. I said that would be a great help."

"And did she?"

"Yes," Nia said. "But then she was nowhere to be found. Nowhere to actually help serve breakfast to our guests—I have half a dozen out there today—and nowhere to help with the washing up so we could get an early start."

"That's right. Antiquing."

"I thought she might enjoy it. I was offering an olive branch. If she saw something she liked, I might even have bought it and found a spot for it just to show I didn't hate her."

"Or get her not to hate you."

"Whatever. Stay on topic. I've looked everywhere for her, all around the Inn, even in the basement where I've never even asked her to go. She left. In a car."

"She's got to be around," Jillian said. "A quick personal errand, perhaps?"

Nia's exhale rasped with irritation. "We were supposed to leave Leo in charge at the Inn as soon as we cleaned up. I made it clear that even though she wouldn't be working at the Inn, I still considered it work, and would of course pay her. She didn't have to count it as time off, so there was no reason for her not to go. Unless she didn't want to have anything to do with me and just didn't want to tell me, any more than she doesn't want to tell her own parents the truth."

"Let's not go there." Jillian poured more coffee down her throat. "Are her things still in her room?"

"You can't honestly ask me to go look," Nia said.

"If she's gone, what difference can it make?"

"If she comes home and finds me there?"

Nia had a point. If Meri showed up, this fret frenzy would be over, but it would be replaced by War of the Worlds—and Meri really would leave. "You're sure she's not in the room?"

"Who else would drive away in her car, Jillian? She doesn't exactly leave her keys on a hook in the kitchen. I can't leave until the last of the guests finishes eating, but then we'll go."

"Go where?"

"To look for Meri. Jillian, what's wrong with you? Keep up."

What's wrong with me? Jillian clamped her lips against the retort forming in her mind and said instead, "But we have no idea where she is."

"Be here in thirty minutes. She'll have gotten a head start, but we might still catch her." Nia clicked off.

Jillian stared at the phone. If Meri truly had a head start, it was much more than thirty minutes. Hours, maybe. And if she had decided to refuse their offers of help and leave—even without her paycheck—what were the chances they would find her now?

She freshened up, filled her travel mug with another round of fortifying caffeine, and prepared to leave the house. Nia shouldn't be driving in her state of mind. Jillian would take her seldom-used small SUV out of the garage, and if Meri didn't turn up in the next few minutes, she would insist on being behind the wheel.

Her phone rang again when she had one step out the back door. Sure it was Nia calling off the search, she had a smart remark ready, but a St. Louis area code displayed.

"Jillian Parisi-Duffy."

"This is Suzanne Plank. I got your message."

"Oh! Thanks for calling back." Jillian dropped her keys on the counter and picked up a pen.

"I did know Annabel Rosario from a couple of classes," Suzanne said, "but I haven't spoken to her in months. Probably close to a year. I was sorry when I heard she might be dropping out of premed."

Premed? "Do you have a phone number or an email address—even if it's old? She's not in trouble. I'm not a collection agency or any-thing."

"How can I be sure?"

"It would be illegal for me to lie to you about that. I actually want to help her."

Silence, while Suzanne Plank considered what to do.

"I guess it would be all right," Suzanne said. "I'm really not sure if she's in classes anymore. The email I have is a Yahoo address, not a university one, so maybe she still has it. I don't know about the phone."

"Whatever you can give me will be a great help," Jillian said. Finally she was speaking to someone at least mildly sympathetic toward Annabel Rosario.

She ran back into her office, where she had an introductory email prepared on her computer, and sent a message to the Yahoo address. While she backed her car out of the driveway and pointed it toward the Inn, she called the phone number Suzanne provided, but a robotic voice informed her it was no longer in service.

Come on, Yahoo. Come through for me.

Nia came flying out the front door of the Inn and jumped into Jillian's car before Jillian even had a chance to put it in PARK and turn off the engine.

"I still think you should check to see if she took her things before we go on a wild-goose chase," Jillian said.

"I am not crossing that line again." Nia's jaw

was set with babysitter authority. "Are you saying you want to?"

"It's not my house."

"See. You don't want to either."

Jillian puffed her cheeks and whiffed resignation. "We're jumping to some pretty big conclusions here."

"So go ahead. Go inside. You be the one to open her door. Open her closet. Snoop in her drawers."

Jillian opened her car door. Nia glared, dared. Jillian pulled the door closed. She'd made Nia confess her transgression. She didn't want to have to do the same.

"We should just wait," Jillian said.

"That's not what my gut says. This is the first time she's even started her car since she moved it to the parking space back here almost a week ago. This is not nothing."

Nia had a point. Again. If Meri had bolted, no matter what she'd said last night and the seeming peace treaty with Nia, the behavior would be consistent with her overall emotional state and rising anxiety. "Did she give you her cell number?"

Nia banged her head on the headrest twice. "Jillian."

"I know, I know," Jillian said. "Even if she did, she doesn't answer it. So where are we going?"

"I've been racking my brain, and I'm coming up with nothing."

"Nia, we need a plan."

"I don't know where she goes," Nia said. "She's only been here a week, and she hasn't had that much free time. Who does she know besides you and me and your dad? She spends a lot of time in her room or out on the patio on her laptop. She doesn't actually *go* anywhere unless I send her on an errand."

"Then maybe she hasn't actually gone anywhere now," Jillian said. "Everybody needs to, I don't know, go to the drugstore every now and then. Makeup. Hair spray. Shampoo. Whatever."

"And exactly why would she do that in the precise window when she was supposed to be helping me so we could go to the antique stores in Leadville?"

"Fine. We'll drive around town and look for her car. If you spot it, let me know, and I'll park."

"Maybe Digger's Delight," Nia said. "She and Carolyn seemed to connect the other day."

"It's a little early for Carolyn to be open, but we can try." Meri at least had been interested in the building's history the day she visited the shop. Jillian swung around the block and headed toward the candy store.

"There's a note on the door," Nia said.

"You know how Carolyn is. She closes at her convenience."

"Stop. I want to read it."

"It won't be about Meri."

"You don't know that."

"Look, Nia," Jillian said, "if Meri left, there's nothing we can do. If she didn't, she's going to turn up at the Inn wondering where *you* are."

"I thought you wanted to help her."

"I did. I do. But you can't always help people who don't want to be helped."

"Just park the car."

They got out to read Carolyn's note. *Closed until further notice.* Her usual notes said something like *Back soon* or *Grabbing lunch.*

"Something's wrong with Carolyn." Jillian could see yesterday's leftover candy in the displays but no additions from this morning and no sign Carolyn had been on the premises. She strode next door and knocked on Kris Bryant's ice cream parlor. It was also too early for Kris to be open, but she'd be inside preparing for the day.

"What's going on?" Kris answered the door waving a long metal ladle.

"Have you seen Meri?" Nia asked.

"And where's Carolyn?" Jillian asked.

"No, and with her daughter." Kris pointed to each inquirer in turn. "Carolyn got a call that her daughter was in bad shape, so she went down to Golden. You know it's been a rough pregnancy. No, I don't know when she'll be back."

"If you see Meri, call me," Nia said.

"Have you misplaced your new Carlotta in only a week?" Kris said.

"Not in the mood." Nia marched away.

They circled through downtown Canyon Mines three times before agreeing they could be positive Meri's car was not parked in front of any of the shops or in any of the rear lots. Jillian headed back to the Inn.

No sign of Meri's car there either.

"Should we check with Leo?" Jillian asked. "Maybe he's heard from her."

"He was up and out early with his truck to get a load of wood. Some big project."

"So no one has been minding the Inn?"

"Technically, no. But don't lecture me. He'll be back soon. That was always the plan. Leo goes early. We feed the guests. He comes back. Meri and I leave."

"I could leave you here and look on my own," Jillian said. The mound of work on her desk multiplied mentally every time she thought of it. Even if Meri left her personal things at the Inn, it was possible she just needed some space. Shouldn't they let her have it? If Nia wanted to be hard-nosed and dock her pay later, she could.

"Not a chance," Nia said. "Drive west, on the old highway out of town."

"Toward the old mine?"

"Yes."

"Wouldn't she just take the interstate if she was actually leaving?"

"Not if she was trying to stay out of sight."

"Okay. There are some good hiking trails out there. Maybe she just wanted to clear her mind."

They drove out toward the mine. In a couple of hours it would open to tours every two hours, but for now there wasn't much traffic.

And there was no sign of Meri's tan Camry.

Jillian glanced over at Nia. Meri could have turned on the oven to preheat hours before breakfast and be anywhere in Clear Creek County by now—or across the state line into Wyoming. Nia picking random destinations and saying, "Go there," made no sense.

"Nia, I really think we should just go back to the Inn."

"We're here now. We might as well have a look around."

"Her car is not here."

"There are trailheads all along this area with little parking lots."

"Then we'll keep driving."

"I want to get out."

"Nia."

"Jillian, I did this. I have to do something to fix it."

Jillian parked the car and turned toward Nia. "Fine. We'll get out and look around—for a few minutes. But for the record, you didn't do this. Meri arrived with a burden as deep as this canyon. Your heart is just as big, but that doesn't mean you can fix whatever went wrong in her family and chased her a thousand miles from home."

They got out and walked down the trail that circled around the old mine, occasionally calling Meri's name and peering through trees at clearings just off the road where someone might leave a car whether or not they were legally designated parking areas. Jillian let Nia push ahead of her. Burning off some energy might put Nia in a more reasonable frame of mind. But this was going to be a time-limited effort because it just didn't make sense beyond Nia's grasping for redemption. Slowing her own gait, Jillian pulled out her phone to check her emails and voice messages. She wouldn't out-and-out return calls in front of Nia, but if she at least knew what was waiting for her once she got back to her desk, she might be able to manage her own frame of mind.

When she looked up from her phone, Nia was nowhere in sight.

"Nia!" Jillian picked up speed, scanned the path, and called again. "Nia!"

"Here."

"Where?" Jillian spun around and still didn't see Nia.

"Down here."

Jillian followed the sound of Nia's voice and found her sprawled on the slope just off the trail twenty yards ahead.

"What happened?"

192

"I don't know. One minute I was up and the next I was down."

"Are you hurt?"

"My knee."

Jillian reached to examine the injury.

"Don't even think about touching it!"

Jillian backed off.

"It's not broken," Nia said. "I'm sure of that. But you can take my word that it's a bad twist. This is not one of those situations where you have to examine the data for yourself."

"I believe you. But how are we going to get you back to the car?"

Jillian's phone rang, and she looked at the ID. "My dad."

"Hey Silly Jilly," he said. "Just checking in to make sure you're not drinking too much coffee."

"I can honestly say I've had hardly any today."

"That doesn't sound like you at all," Nolan said. "In fact, it doesn't sound like you're in your office."

"I'm not."

Nia moaned as she gripped Jillian's shoulder with one hand and pulled herself upright.

"Who's that?" Nolan said. "Where are you?"

"Nia and I are out by the old mine."

"Um, what? That's never been your favorite excursion."

"Meri's missing. Nia wanted to look for her."

"At the mine?"

"That's right."

"Random. Was that a reasonable decision?"

"Doubtful." Jillian kept her responses cryptic. At least Nia couldn't hear Nolan's skeptical end of the conversation.

"Why the groaning?" he asked.

"Twisted knee."

"I see. I take it Meri's car is missing as well."

"You got it."

Nia grunted as she tested the damage on her injured leg. Jillian dug a heel into the slope to brace them both.

"Wish I could come home to join the search party, but I just barely got here," Nolan said.

"I know. It's all right." If Meri was taking a breather, she'd show up. If she had taken her stuff and left, even Nolan couldn't catch her now. At some point logic would prevail.

"My last meeting is not until midafternoon, down at the Anschutz campus of the university. I'll try to head home right after that. If she hasn't turned up by then . . . well, we'll get our heads together about what makes sense."

"Thanks, Dad." Jillian ended the call and returned the phone to a pocket.

Still leaning on Jillian, Nia pointed. "I think we should go that way."

"You're kidding, right?"

"I'm not giving up now."

"I dare you to let go of me and try to walk."

Nia glowered.

"If we're lucky, we'll make it back to the car before we become dinner for coyotes." Jillian shifted her weight to better support Nia's and put an arm around Nia's waist. "Your knee needs some attention, even if it's just ice and elevating."

"But Meri."

"Meri is a big girl. When she's ready for help, she'll get help. Now prepare to hop."

CHAPTER SEVENTEEN

Nolan had long ago made peace with the reality that his chosen profession required billable hours, or at least justifiable flat fees for set services. Helping someone out of the latitude of his heart was not frowned upon as long as he generated his share of the firm's income. Today's final meeting was a happy blend of those priorities—an old friend who steadfastly refused any legal favors Nolan offered over the years and called to inquire where his invoice was if he didn't receive one within ten days. After two mediation meetings earlier in the day—one that brought understanding and fairness and one still fraught with hostility—Nolan was glad to see his old college buddy, now an academician and hospital administrator, about updating his will to provide a trust for a suddenly disabled grandchild. They could have met in Nolan's office, but he didn't mind the ten-mile drive in the Colorado sunshine and a peek into what his friend's daily life was now. He arrived with a standard set of questions to ask about the purpose and parameters of the trust and left with the answers necessary to generate the document for signature and a promise to meet again within the next couple of weeks.

Nolan stepped out of the building and squinted into the late-afternoon sunlight to reorient himself to where he had left his car. Far away. He remembered that much. The university had two campuses, the downtown one nearer his office, where Jillian had studied, and this one in a medical complex. The presence of a large teaching hospital complicated parking, but Nolan never minded parking in what felt like the far reaches of civilization to many people. A walk was always welcome. He pointed himself toward his reliable truck that withstood winter in the mountains and stretched his long legs in a pace he didn't have to worry about anyone else matching.

Then he stopped. He hadn't checked for a message from Jillian in more than an hour. Shielding his phone from the glare, he woke the screen.

Nothing. With a sigh, Nolan dropped the phone back in a pocket and blew out his cheeks. He'd have to go straight home, and those ten miles of goodwill in the wrong direction for his friend's convenience now meant recovering them in the opposite direction bogged down in rush hour traffic.

He glanced both directions to cross a lane that wound through the campus tying its buildings together.

And blinked. And looked again. He tried not to stare, but how could he not?

197

A young woman emerging from an exit fifty yards from him looked strikingly like Meri. The same build. The same hair. The same glasses. This woman wore a straight light blue skirt and stylish short gray jacket, rather than the jeans and cargo pants Meri sported with her long-sleeved tees, and carried a small red leather briefcase. Like Nolan had, she took a moment to get her bearings. She had the look of someone slightly lost, not someone leaving a normal day's work in a familiar building.

When she tilted her head at that certain angle, to the left with jaw forward, he knew.

It *was* Meri.

Nolan fished his phone out of his pocket and opened a text message to Jillian.

I HAVE HER.

WHAT DO YOU MEAN YOU HAVE HER?

MERI. WALKING TOWARD HER NOW.

WHAT'S SHE DOING IN DENVER?

HOPING TO FIND OUT.

Nolan pivoted away from the direction of his own car and strode toward Meri, who was walking away from him but not with great speed. When he was close enough not to have to shout, he spoke. "Meri."

She turned, startled. "Is this where you work?"

"I just finished a meeting with a client who works here." Nolan moved his briefcase to the other hand. "Meri, everyone is looking for you."

"Why? I'm not lost. I got slightly disoriented finding this place because of construction that GPS apparently didn't factor in, but I figured it out."

"Have you been here all day?"

"Not *here* here. I allowed extra time to find my way," Meri said, "and I sat in a coffee shop for a long time trying to think through the questions they might ask and how I should answer them."

Nolan fixed his gaze on her dark, uncertain eyes.

"Meri, this is a well-known regional medical campus. People wait for months to get appointments here. Are you—"

"What?"

"Ill? Are you ill? Did you come to Colorado because you're ill? Nia thought you were spending the day together."

Meri tilted her head in that way. "Didn't Leo tell anyone?"

"Leo?"

"I told him this morning before I left. This came up at the last minute, and I wanted to leave early to make sure I didn't get caught in traffic, since I didn't know how bad it might get."

"Pretty bad. I do the same thing sometimes."

"He was the only one up. So I asked him to tell Nia I was really sorry, and I would explain everything later, but something came up that was really important and I needed the day off."

"Leo must not have given Nia the message. She's been frantic with worry."

Meri's shoulders sank. "I never meant to do that to her."

"Traffic will be a bear in the reverse direction right now," Nolan said. "Why don't we go somewhere and have coffee—or an early dinner?"

Meri laughed. "You are always trying to ply me with food and beverage."

"Is it working?"

"Yes. I admit I haven't actually eaten any real food today. Too nervous."

She still hadn't said what she was doing on the medical campus, but Nolan let that go for the moment. "Is it all right if I let Jillian know you're okay?"

Meri nodded.

Nolan sent a quick text and said, "I know a place near here. I can drive and then bring you back for your car."

Twelve minutes later they settled into a booth.

"There won't be any opera-singing chefs," Nolan said, "but they make a decent risotto."

"I wouldn't expect anyone to match your talents." Meri opened a menu and pushed her glasses up her nose.

"I used to offer to sing for Jillian in restaurants, but she never much cared for the idea."

"That might be a bit over the line even for you."

Nolan feigned offense. "Even for me?"

"What else do you recommend?"

"The vegetarian stuffed mushroom, if you insist on knowing. They use a caramelized onion that pairs nicely with the naturally occurring creaminess of the short-grain rice of the risotto."

Meri closed the menu. "I don't really know what you're talking about, but it sounds good to me."

When the waiter came, Nolan placed identical orders.

"Now," he said, leaning back in the bench, "perhaps we can start at the very beginning of this day. Are you here because you're ill?"

"No! Nothing like that."

Nolan breathed out relief. "Glad to have that cleared up."

"I only found out late last night that there was an opening for an interview today," Meri said. "I feel so stupid. I wasted so much energy being angry with Nia and stomping around. Then she tried to smooth things over with a day of antiquing. How could I say no? Last night, after I came home from your place, I never even checked my email until nearly midnight, and that changed everything."

"An interview?"

"They had someone drop out of the schedule at the end of the business day yesterday, so they offered me the spot because they knew I wasn't too far away and might be able to get there on short notice. Of course I said yes—hoping they'd see my response first thing this morning."

"An interview for what, Meri?"

She took a deep breath. "Graduate school. I applied to enter a program for a master's of public administration in nonprofit organization."

"Wow." Nolan leaned forward, elbows on the table. "Two days ago—even yesterday—you seemed very eager to get out of Dodge and drop off the grid."

"I know." Her eyes, muddy liquid pools now, met his gaze with reluctance. "Ninety-five percent of the fibers of my being still want to do that."

"But the other five percent are fighting back."

"Really hard." Meri picked up her water glass, and the ice cubes clinked in her shaking hand.

"You don't have to fight alone."

"So you keep saying."

"Because I mean it. We all do."

Meri swallowed water. "People always say to just do the next right thing. That's not always as easy as it sounds."

The waiter arrived and set plates in front of them. Nolan waited for Meri to arrange her napkin and utensils and fuss with the contents of the bread basket.

"You only arrived in Canyon Mines a week ago," Nolan said. "Were you in Denver before that?"

She shook her head.

"Then how did this happen so fast?"

"I've been looking at programs like this one. Dreaming mostly. I knew I couldn't . . . well, you know. I had to go to med school."

"I'd love to hear about your dream."

"Before we eat, will you say that blessing your mother used to say?" Meri said.

"Of course." He offered her a hand, and she took it. "May you always find nourishment for your body at the table. May sustenance for your spirit rise and fill you with each dawn. And may life always feed you with the light of joy along the way."

"That's my dream. I thought about that a lot last night, especially after I read the email. Sustenance for my spirit. The light of joy along the way."

"Those words have carried me through many dark hours as well as happy ones." Nolan handed Meri the bread basket.

"Do you believe in calling? Choosing your path because your path chooses you, or because God puts it before you so plainly you can't walk any other way?"

"Meri Davies, we are wading in pretty deep waters."

She squeezed the cloudiness from her eyes and looked at him again with the clearest, non-secretive eyes Nolan had yet seen in her face. "Do you? Please tell me."

"I do. Absolutely."

"The work you do is a calling?"

"A gift and a calling. A redemption of sorts. On my best days, I help people make peace with themselves through the law, and I find great satisfaction in that."

"I've looked at these programs for a long time, but this is the first time I took the next right step," Meri said. "When it looked like I might actually be able to start in the spring term, I applied online. I worked on my essay in every spare moment for days."

"And the evenings when you holed up in your room at the Inn right after supper?"

She nodded. "It was a long shot. I knew that. Who knows what the process really was—deadlines, review committees, and all that? And I only submitted an unofficial transcript, which is all I had. There was no time to get an official one from Sewanee. Certainly it showed nothing that suggested a good fit for nonprofit public administration. Double-majoring in two sciences doesn't leave a lot of time for exploring other people-related subjects."

"You're not eating," Nolan said. "At least try."

She picked up her fork and slid it under the risotto.

"You were always headed for medical school," Nolan said.

"Right. And it was just a couple of days ago

when I sent it in. It was crazy. I have hardly any money I can really call my own, and I spent a good chunk of it on an application fee for a program I probably won't get into."

Nolan raised his eyebrows. "Yet you got a very improbable interview under a most improbable time frame."

Meri turned her empty palms up. "I don't know what to say about that."

"Perhaps that you do understand calling after all, and perhaps that you are right about not belonging in medical school."

She pinched her nose under her glasses. "That was awkward! During the interview, I had to account for the time since I graduated from college. Obviously I haven't been working."

"What did you say?"

"I had five different angles prepared, but I went with the truth. No fluff. I don't want to go back to med school. I never wanted to be there in the first place."

"You could be a doctor in the nonprofit world."

"I suppose so. I want to help children, and my parents would say I could be a pediatrician. A pediatric surgeon. A pediatric oncologist. A pediatric neurologist or something or other. But that's not what I mean."

"What do you mean?" Now that he had Meri talking steadily, Nolan could relax and enjoy his own meal.

"I got lucky. My ancestors were slaves, but through the generations, my family became one where everyone gets an education and a good job. It happens to be in medicine, but does it have to be?" She took a bite of food, closed her eyes, and swayed a bit.

"Meri, are you all right?"

"You were right about the mushroom. This is incredible."

He chuckled. "Back to your graduate work plans. What do you have in mind?"

"Underprivileged children. True community development that makes their lives better now and changes the future for them."

"That's quite a vision, Meri. Impressive."

"But to be a leader in the field requires graduate work—at least a master's, probably a PhD."

"Any parent would be proud of such ambition."

She shook her head. "Not any parent. Not mine. They'll say first get an MD and finish a residency. Get board certified. Then if I still want to play around with these other things . . ."

"I'm sorry, Meri."

"There is truth in the speech I grew up with— that privilege comes with responsibility. But for me that's not everything."

"What else?"

"I also grew up going to church. And I paid attention. To the idea that the suffering of the

Lord should mean something in how I use my life for other people. And to what Jesus said about the least of these."

"Which brings us back to the children," Nolan said.

Meri nodded. "Let the little children come. Shouldn't we help them come? Shouldn't we help them see that they matter to God?"

"I believe we should."

"I don't have much time." Meri twisted her napkin in her lap. "I know that. But after today, at least if I get in I can say I have a plan. That will count for something."

"So you'll stay?"

Meri turned her head and gazed across the restaurant. "Ninety-five percent of me still says to go—and not to wait until Tuesday."

"But five percent."

She nodded.

"That's not statistically insignificant."

She allowed a half smile.

"How much time do you have, Meri?"

"I'm not sure. I haven't been using my phone because I don't want to read or hear the gazillion messages they're leaving me. I set up a brand-new email account to use for my application and suspended the one my family uses. But it can't be long. They'll know where I am by now, and it's just a matter of time until they clear their busy schedules and descend."

"We're not the easiest place to get to," Nolan said.

"But not the hardest either. They know where it is. They've all been to Canyon Mines before. Once upon a time even my brother liked exploring mine country. The tunnels were his thing."

"So here's the plan," Nolan said. "You have to drive your own car back tonight, obviously. But after that, you don't have to be alone. Not at the Inn, not on errands. We can make sure that if your family shows up unannounced, someone is there to have your back."

"You would do that?"

"Of course we would."

"What's the catch?"

"I wouldn't call it a catch. Just your part in helping everyone be prepared."

Meri waited in silence.

"Turn on your phone. You don't have to answer it. But listen to messages. Minimize the surprise factor."

More silence.

Then, "I'll think about it."

"Besides," Nolan said, "Nia's going to need you to stick close. Something about injuring her knee."

CHAPTER EIGHTEEN

Memphis, September 5, 1878

"Must you go out, Sister Constance?" Eliza didn't like the way the nun looked. Even disguised beneath the bulk of her habit, Sister Constance's frame was growing thin. When had she last slept through the night?

"There are more calls to make than ever." As she did every morning, Sister Constance tucked a linen cloth soaked in disinfecting carbolic acid beneath her apron. "And now we have fewer nurses than ever to make them. We give thanks that Sister Frances has recovered from her illness, but she is overwhelmed with the number of orphans and how many have been sick. I cannot ask more of her, and you have seen for yourself the load Sister Ruth bears at Canfield. The Howards have nothing more to offer us either."

"But Sister Constance, you are exhausted," Eliza said. "And there is endless correspondence work. Can you not stay in and attend to that and be doing work that is needful but less demanding?"

"Every moment matters, Eliza. Every day we find people who die for no reason other than they lacked basic nursing to be sure they do not become dehydrated or simply starve to death because they are alone when they fall ill."

"Then let me go," Eliza said.

"We need you here. How many come to the church every day?"

"I lose count. Hundreds."

"And who will help them?"

"Mrs. Haskins will come. And Mrs. Bullock is here."

Sister Constance looked at Eliza with narrowed eyes.

"I beg your forgiveness," Eliza said. "I know Mrs. Bullock is not at my beck and call, and she is as busy as anyone keeping up with the deluge of work. But Sister, you are about to drop."

"And you come earlier every morning and stay later every evening, and do every errand I ask of you," Sister Constance said.

"There is nothing for me at home, and the need is so great here."

"No word from Callie? Not even a message?"

Eliza shook her head. "It's only been two days. If she's caring for family with fever, sending a message is the last thing she has time for. I understand that."

"Still, you would like to know."

Eliza shook a finger at Sister Constance. "Do not change the subject."

"I will not relent, Eliza. Do not delay me further. The others have already gone with their jars of tea and broth. I have calls all up and down Alabama Street."

Eliza gave a half sigh. "Of course, Sister. I will open the pantry early."

Mrs. Bullock came into the hall and handed Sister Constance a worn leather case packed with tea and broth to administer. "There will be more by midmorning."

"Thank you, Mrs. Bullock." Sister Constance left without another look back.

"I do not know how she can keep going," Eliza said to the housekeeper.

"Only by the grace of God."

"May she find it in abundance today."

"We all know she's exhausted," Mrs. Bullock said. "But she won't stop. It's a wonder she accomplishes half of what she does in the condition she's in."

"The accounts, the supplies, the correspondence—it's too much."

"What choice does she have? Her heart is breaking with sorrow."

"Here comes Mrs. Haskins." Mrs. Bullock pointed through a window at a stout figure coming up the front walk.

"What would I do without her?"

"You would be no better off than Sister Constance."

Eliza greeted her stalwart volunteer. She worried at first when the older woman had turned up to work in the pantry and dispense food, clothing, tea, and broth, but Mrs. Haskins insisted she'd had yellow fever five years earlier and wouldn't get it again. Besides, she was old enough that she gave no more thought to her life when she saw the stacks of coffins in the streets and the unending lines outside St. Mary's every day. It was nearly impossible now to hear of a block within the city limits where no home had been infected. Yellow pieces of cardboard marked the homes of the ill. When someone within passed, yellow changed to black, with a scrawled note, *Coffin needed.* A wagon left an empty coffin. The plague cheated the families of parting rituals or comforting ceremonies as they simply cleaned the bodies of their loved ones and placed them in pine boxes with mixtures of tar and acid and held vigil for the next wagon and the shout of, "Bring out your dead."

"Are we ready?" Mrs. Haskins unpinned her hat and hung it on a hook. "No point in trying to organize, now is there? We just have to give out what we have for as long as it lasts."

"Right," Eliza said, "and then tea and broth after that for as long as the jars last."

"If the able-bodied would just bring back the empties more often. We can disinfect them properly and replenish more quickly." Mrs. Bullock turned and shuffled toward the kitchen.

The morning was bustling. Eliza's mind shifted

between the unabating stream of requests coming through the door—today they had bread, rice, grits, sugar, dried peas, onions, coffee, and soap to offer—and the scene awaiting at Canfield if she could manage to get away from the cathedral complex. With just a couple of volunteers to help them care for fifty children, young Sister Ruth and Sister Helen were nearly vanquished by the challenge. The woman who lived there, according to Sister Ruth, offered little help beyond looking after the six orphans who had been her charge before the crisis. Sister Ruth's orphans never had enough clean clothes. Each one who arrived required a carbolic bath and fresh clothes, but no one had time to wash the ones they arrived in. The cook did his best, but he never knew what he would have to work with to prepare meals for more than sixty people. He conscripted some of the older orphans to help, but keeping everyone fed was a daybreak-to-sundown endeavor.

And Canfield was no longer exempt from the fever. A Canfield child had fallen ill and become the first patient of a new infirmary opened on Market Street—Church Home and the Sisters House infirmary were too full to take the child. If Eliza's house belonged to her, rather than her parents, she would gladly throw open the doors and convert its empty rooms to wards for the sick. She had not quite worked out how to manage her mother's response if she did so.

Eliza eyed a sack of flour and fifty pounds of potatoes in the corner of the pantry. If she could not go herself, perhaps she could send the St. Mary's cart with someone else to drive it.

Ned had fallen ill. Sister Thecla did not think he would survive.

Doors opened and closed, but Eliza could not leave the pantry to see which of the sisters were coming and going from their calls. Probably they were returning only for more tea and broth, not stopping even long enough to eat whatever meager lunch Mrs. Bullock had cobbled together between the duties she had assumed on behalf of the sick. Eliza's stomach growled. Without Callie, she was leaving her home in the mornings with a far less fortifying breakfast, but she would not say anything. She had crackers from her own cupboard in her bag.

"Eliza! Mrs. Bullock!"

The shout came from the parlor.

"Go," Mrs. Haskins said before calmly turning to the next person in line.

Eliza hustled through the house to the parlor to find Sister Clare and Mrs. Bullock bending over Sister Constance on a sofa.

"She is very ill," Sister Clare said.

"It is only a slight headache," Sister Constance said. "I just needed a moment of rest."

"It's one o'clock," Eliza said. "Have you eaten at all today?"

"I don't care to eat anything just now." Sister Constance started to push herself upright on the sofa, but her weakness was clear to all.

"I will bring a plate all the same," Mrs. Bullock said.

"No thank you, Mrs. Bullock," Sister Constance said. "But I do have some correspondence to attend to. I wonder if you can take some dictation. I would like to acknowledge some generous offerings we have received."

"Sister Constance," Mrs. Bullock said, "I do think you should rest."

"Yes. You should go to bed for a true rest," Sister Clare said.

"I agree." Eliza sat on the sofa and put a hand under Sister Constance's elbow.

Sister Constance shook off the touch, and this time her effort to sit up was successful. "A glass of water will be welcome. That is all I need for the headache. Then I will make more calls later."

Eliza caught Sister Clare's eyes. Sister Constance was flushed with fever.

"Might we bring you a pillow?" Sister Clare said. "You might as well be comfortable as you work on your correspondence."

"I suppose there is no harm in that, if you insist," Sister Constance said. "You are all fussing too much."

Mrs. Bullock left briefly and returned with a glass of water and writing materials. Sister

Clare fetched a pillow. When they had made Sister Constance as comfortable as she would allow, Eliza had in mind her own effort for Sister Constance's good.

Dr. Armstrong.

He lived nearby, and he was treating hundreds of patients in the neighborhood around the church. She would find him.

Outside, Eliza batted a mosquito away from her face. Fever had been sweeping down Alabama Street. Unless he was off to Canfield, the doctor wouldn't have gone far. If Eliza stood on the street and waited, he was likely to emerge from one of the houses within view sooner or later. She covered her nose and mouth with a handkerchief and paced up Alabama.

"Help!"

Eliza rotated toward the cry.

A woman leaned on a half-rotted porch railing. "We need the undertaker. It's been two days, and no one has brought us coffins."

Coffins. More than one.

Eliza swallowed. "How many?"

The woman pointed to the black sign. "Two adults. One child."

"How many are sick now?"

"My other boy." The woman's voice, dispassionate until now, caught. "And me."

"Have you anyone to nurse you?"

She shook her head.

Eliza took note of the house. "I will let the sisters at St. Mary's know. They have soup and tea."

"I've heard. But I cannot leave."

"And you should not."

"The coffins . . ."

"I'll remember."

The woman withdrew, and Eliza stood for a moment, eyes closed and stomach revolting at the thought of two days inside that closed-up house in the heat with three corpses. Then she pushed out her breath and opened her eyes.

There was Dr. Armstrong, four houses down but walking in Eliza's direction. She hustled toward him.

"I will come," he said when she explained. "I was headed near there. I need to restock my medicine bag."

Sister Constance waved him off as soon as he darkened the door. "I have not the fever. It is only a headache. It will go off at sunset." She lounged on the sofa but held correspondence in her hands.

Eliza looked at Mrs. Bullock, who sat with her dictation pad and pencil and shrugged.

Dr. Armstrong picked up Sister Constance's wrist to count her pulse and scrutinized her face. "Perhaps you are right. But you should go to bed and rest."

"And on a comfortable mattress," Mrs. Bullock said. "We have one that is not being used."

"I will not hear of it," Sister Constance said.

"You must rest." Dr. Armstrong was firm.

"Perhaps. But not on a mattress. I have taken a pledge of poverty, and I will not forsake it for a headache." Sister Constance paused and looked away. "And if it should be yellow jack, the mattress would have to be burned, and that would be a waste."

Mrs. Bullock stood up. "Then I think we have finished today's correspondence, and I will help you to your bed."

"Thank you, Mrs. Bullock," Dr. Armstrong said.

"Yes," Eliza said, "thank you."

When Sister Constance wobbled, Mrs. Bullock held steady and led her from the room.

"I will check on her this evening," Dr. Armstrong said. "I must get some more quinine and arsenic. Miz Eliza, have you any extra handkerchiefs in your supply pantry?"

"I believe so."

Eliza sent the doctor on his way with her contribution to his supplies. She'd barely closed the door behind him and was mentally organizing herself to return to Mrs. Haskins's side and the afternoon throng in the pantry when the main door opened—weakly—again.

"Sister Thecla!"

Eliza caught the nun in her arms.

"Sister Clare!" Eliza called.

For the second time in an hour, footsteps came from around the house.

"The poor woman I have just seen," Sister Thecla said. "I could do nothing for her but ease her death."

"That is not nothing," Eliza said.

"I'm sorry, but I have the fever," Sister Thecla said. "Give me a cup of tea, and then I shall go to bed."

"You will have the mattress," Mrs. Bullock said. "I will put a fresh sheet on it."

"I will have neither," Sister Thecla said, "for you would have to burn them both."

Sister Clare led Sister Thecla away.

The hours in the pantry passed swiftly because of the immensity of need. But they passed without pleasure. Those who came cried out with heartbreaking circumstances two or three women in the pantry could not change. Whenever Eliza crept out for a moment, hoping for news of the sisters who had fallen ill, she only found Sister Clare trying to manage in the kitchen without Mrs. Bullock, who was the only one nursing Sisters Constance and Thecla.

After the pantry closed for the day and Mrs. Haskins went home, Eliza faced the task of sorting the crates delivered to the back door that afternoon. They'd already begun rummaging through the contents to meet the day's needs. Now she inventoried what remained and arranged contents on the shelves for tomorrow.

And waited for Dr. Armstrong, who had promised to return.

At eight o'clock, he pronounced both sisters ill with yellow fever. Though his diagnosis was no surprise, the certainty rent the hearts of the household.

"Let me stay and help care for them," Eliza said. "There's nothing for me at home."

Mrs. Bullock shook her head. "They wouldn't have it. Mrs. Vaughan is coming. I've already sent word. She's one of the best nurses, and Sister Thecla has asked for her."

"Of course." Eliza sucked in her disappointment. The sisters should have a trained and experienced nurse. "But I want to do something for them."

"Pray," Mrs. Bullock said. "That would mean the most to them."

CHAPTER NINETEEN

Coffee. Check. Definitely. The mug was a pleasing enough shade of blue, and wide enough to hold a full-fledged latte with a thick layer of frothed milk and optional whipped cream. But it felt like the pottery mixture included a secret ingredient of cement, and Jillian couldn't see herself filling and lifting it multiple times every day indefinitely.

Breakfast. Check. Well, sort of. Jillian had eaten leftover beef and snow peas zapped in the microwave, a perfectly nutritious choice.

To-do list. Check. Quite detailed, in fact.

Files. Check. Organized in order of priority and time commitment.

This was Friday. If Jillian was to have any hope of a real weekend, she would have to plow through the work today. Last night she'd stayed up late catching up on the half day lost to looking for someone who didn't need finding after all. She was ready to quote on two out of three proposals, Mrs. Answald's project was ready to take to the FedEx store for careful packaging—a day later than Jillian planned—and she had at least rough notes about how else to go about locating Annabel Rosario in St. Louis, so she didn't have to duck Raúl's next call. With a bit of luck, her day would also include uncovering where Meri's first name came from.

Her mother's antique clock, sitting on the bookcase in Jillian's office, still ran as long as it received twice-yearly checkups at the Hands-On Clock Repair Shop. The hands ticked toward the opening hour of the FedEx office, and Jillian dropped a fresh thumb drive, with only the one project on it, into her favorite canvas bag before sliding pages printed in well-saturated color on her best-quality paper into a clear plastic envelope and fastened it closed. A standard business envelope with her final invoice went on top.

"Well, top of the morning to you."

Try as she might, Jillian could never master lifting only one eyebrow at her father the way he could at her. "The morning is half-gone, Dad."

"It's eight o'clock."

"You're taking advantage of the privilege of working from home."

"Where on earth did you get such a slavish work ethic?" Nolan dropped into the upholstered chair across from her desk.

"Just trying to keep up. First on the list, be able to tell Mrs. Answald that FedEx is in possession of her project in the manner she specified."

"Perfect," Nolan said. "On your way back, you can stop by the Inn."

"You're home today. Why don't you stop by the Inn?"

"Because I found Meri in the big city yesterday." Nolan grinned. "A single young woman among a ten-county metropolitan statistical area population of nearly three million people. Tag, you're it."

"Dad. Some people might suggest there was divine intervention involved."

"I concede the point, counselor." Nolan raised his coffee mug. "Seriously, Jillian. You're the genealogist. I think she needs to hear from you what you know about who the Canfields were. And while you're at it, reinforce that I'm not the only one on Team Meri."

"But you're the affable team captain with the indomitable spirit."

"I wear the title proudly."

"Fine." Jillian gathered up her canvas bag, phone, and keys. "I'm in full agreement with the plan to have someone with her as much as we can, but you have to take your turn."

He saluted her. "Yes, Deputy Captain."

"You're impossible."

"What happened to affable?"

"Out the window."

Jillian's computer sounded the arrival of an email, and she leaned toward the screen—and squealed.

"Jillian Siobhan! What got into you?"

"My lost heir in St. Louis answered my email." Jillian clicked the message open. "It's really her, Dad. I found her!"

"What about Mrs. Answald?"

"You're right." Jillian pulled her fingers from the keyboard. "Annabel gave me a number. FedEx first, and then I can call her."

"Don't forget Meri."

"I won't."

After the FedEx stop, Jillian phoned Annabel Rosario but got a voice mail box. She left a message, but promised herself she would keep calling until she got through, and moved on to the Inn.

She parked in front and went in through the main doors. Meri whizzed across the broad hallway between the library on one side and the parlor on the other. Nia limped slowly from the kitchen through the dining room on Leo's arm.

Meri whizzed back in the other direction. "I can't get her to sit down," she said in Jillian's direction. "I told her I'll take care of everything."

"It's not that bad." Nia allowed Leo to pull out a chair in the dining room. "It's been two days. I can do more than these control freaks allow."

Jillian was dubious but saw no reason to pick a fight.

"It's my fault," Leo said. "Meri gave me the message. She even offered to write a note to Nia, and I said that wasn't necessary because I would see her before I left to get my load of wood. I'm the one who forgot."

"Meri is safe," Jillian said. "Let's focus on that."

"Agreed," Nia said.

Meri pulled another chair from under the table and a pillow from a small rocker under the window. "Elevate your leg. It's swelling again. I'll get you some ice."

"I'll get the ice." Leo ducked back into the kitchen.

Jillian sucked in the corners of her mouth to keep from laughing. Nia did need looking after, but two people constantly hovering would fracture her tolerance into more pieces than crunching fall leaves outside.

"Can you spare Meri for a few minutes?" Jillian said.

"Please," Nia said.

"But we're booked full up for the entire week-end," Meri said. "There's still a lot to do to be ready."

"If Jillian wants to see you, I'm sure she has a reason," Nia said. "Go. Use the library."

"I can dust while we talk," Meri said.

"Or you can just talk while you talk," Nia said. "It's all right."

In the library, a room Jillian admired but rarely sat in during her visits to the Inn, they settled into

225

opposite matching champagne-colored Victorian spoon-back tufted armchairs with a round mahogany side table between them.

"I thought you might want to know something about the name Canfield," she said.

"You found something?" Meri's head tilted.

"I haven't yet tied it specifically to your family, but there is some interesting backdrop." Jillian explained the basic history of Martha Canfield's philanthropic work in the South, particularly Memphis.

"She was a white woman?" Meri asked.

Jillian nodded. "The orphanage was established for black children, though there was a brief time during the 1878 yellow fever epidemic when it served children of all races and denominations. It closed in 1885. If the name came into your family because of an association with the orphanage, and stayed through the generations, it must have been a positive association."

"I'm pretty sure Canny would just as soon the memory of it had faded away before it reached him," Meri said.

"Well, I'm glad it didn't," Jillian said. "The fact that it has lasted this long means something, and that will help us get to the root of your family tree—at least if it's connected to Canfield Asylum in Memphis."

"So that's where you're going to look?"

"I'm going to try. I'm sure I can't find direct

records just floating around on the internet, but if I work my way back through your family tree with the information you've provided, and perhaps use some of my networks with other genealogists, it might well lead us there."

"Wow. An orphanage. Wouldn't that mean an adoption at some point?"

"Not necessarily. And birth and marriage certificates, and even adoptions, were not as standard as they are now."

"I'm still confused about how this is going to help with my parents," Meri said.

"It might not," Jillian admitted. "But it might, depending on what we find."

Meri scratched her hairline. "I don't know. It seems . . . interesting but far-fetched."

Jillian took three slow breaths, waiting for Meri's thoughts to further congeal. She hadn't noticed the line in Meri's forehead before, a worry line if ever she'd seen one.

Jillian leaned toward Meri. "Is there no one in your family who would stand with you?"

Meri ran a tongue across her bottom lip. "Maybe Pru."

"Pru?"

"My sister."

"Is she a doctor?"

"A resident. OB-GYN."

"What kind of doctor is your brother?"

"Neurologist. Two years into his own practice."

"Does your sister like medicine?"

"I've never asked her."

Right. Not a relevant question in the Davies family.

"Do you think she's a safe person for you to talk to?" Jillian asked.

Meri nodded slowly. "She would tell me the truth."

Jillian stood up. "Call her. Soon. If for no other reason than to let someone in your family know you're all right and what's really going on."

Meri blew out a slender shard of a breath. "I'll try." The response sounded politely noncommittal to Jillian.

"We can touch base later in the day." Jillian couldn't force Meri to call Pru, but maybe Meri would surprise her.

Jillian called Annabel Rosario three more times before getting an answer. Finally, a weary alto voice carried across the miles.

Yes, she could confirm the name of her father, though she hadn't known him well. She hadn't even seen him since she was three, and he died when she was nine. All the information matched Jillian's findings.

No, she knew next to nothing about his family. After her parents split up, she only knew her mother's relatives. She'd run out of money, had to drop out of college except for a class here and there, and was working as a teacher's aide in a day care center. At least she got to be around children. It wasn't the same as being a pediatrician, but it was something.

The pounding on Jillian's front door disturbed the endorphins flooding her brain at the thought of how Annabel's life was about to change.

"Hold on," she told Annabel. "Someone's at my door. But I have more to tell you. Please don't hang up."

She ran down the hall and opened the door. Meri fell in.

"I called Pru." Meri spoke with a breathlessness Jillian did not attribute simply to the walk—or run—from the Inn. It was the winded gulping of distress.

Jillian held up a finger and pointed to her phone. "Let me just finish this call." She took Meri's elbow and guided her into the living room, to the comfortable purple chair with the ottoman. With her eyes on Meri, she resumed her conversation with Annabel.

"I imagine you'd go back to school if you could."

"It would take a miracle. I'm trying to get some loans. Then there will be medical school to think of, and the astronomical debt that comes with that. Maybe I should just be a teacher. But that's not why you called. I don't understand why you tracked me down."

"Are your grades pretty good?" Jillian said.

"Very. Ms. Parisi-Duffy, this is feeling a little weird."

Jillian took a breath. "You might want to be sitting down."

"Is this bad news?"

"I don't think so, no. But it might make your knees wobble."

In front of Jillian, Meri's head was in her hands. But Jillian couldn't hang up on Annabel now. Neither could she let Meri out of her sight.

"Your father had a great-uncle," she said. "His grandfather's brother. He was quite elderly and passed away recently, leaving a house and a life insurance policy. There are no other living heirs. That's why we were looking for you."

"I don't understand," Annabel said.

"You are the heir."

Silence.

"This is a scam."

"No! It's not." Jillian gave the name of the law firm handling the deceased's estate along with a website and phone number. "I'm a genealogist who was hired to find the next of kin. Once I report that I have made contact with you, you can expect a call, followed by a registered letter, from the law firm about settling the estate."

"The estate?" Annabel echoed.

"You can go back to school," Jillian said. "If you have the grades to get into medical school, you can be a pediatrician."

More silence.

Then tears. "Is this for real?"

"Absolutely. The packet from the law firm will include a family tree. You can at least know something about where your father came from."

Now Meri was crying. Tears in stereo. Jillian made sure Annabel had taken down the law firm's information before ending the call.

"I'm a horrible person," Meri said.

"No, you're not." Jillian sat on the ottoman and put a hand on Meri's leg.

"I don't know who you were talking to, but I heard enough to know you just gave that person a future as a doctor."

"I gave her news of an inheritance. If she chooses to use it to become a doctor, and really does have the ability, that's up to her."

"Meanwhile, I've been trying my best *not* to have to be a doctor."

"It's not your calling. It might be hers. You're trying to find your own future. What you do have in common is you both want to help children. I know that for a fact, and I haven't even met Annabel Rosario."

Meri threw her head against the back of the chair. "Pru said that if I don't want to be a doctor, then don't."

"That's good. I'm glad you called her."

"She also said the rest of them are closing in. That's what she said. Closing in."

"What exactly did she mean?"

"They're almost here, Jillian! Our phones are all on the same family plan, so I figured they were using the location feature to find where my phone was. Even if I ditched my phone somewhere, they would go to the last place they found it."

"But you haven't ditched it."

"No. And they know that, because I've turned it on a few times. Pru said they're booking flights."

"All of them?"

"I'm not sure. Not Pru. I know she's not coming. Even if residents could get time off for a family crisis, she wouldn't think this merits an intervention."

Jillian wondered why Nolan had not yet responded to the commotion and come down from his second-story office. He would know what to say to Meri before she completely fell apart.

"Meri, you could have gone anywhere," Jillian said. "You could have driven anywhere in the US. But you came to a little mountain town in Colorado that you've been to before when you were a child."

Meri squeezed her eyes closed.

"Why here, Meri?"

Tears leaked down Meri's face in a slow trail from behind closed eyelids. "Because this is the last place I remember being happy. I was eleven that summer. When I was twelve they started sending me to camps to make sure I would excel at all the sciences necessary to be a doctor. I just wanted to feel that again before it all came crashing in."

CHAPTER TWENTY

Memphis, September 9, 1878

Eliza jumped from the straight-back chair where she had been keeping vigil outside Sister Constance's room.

"Has she wakened?" Eliza peered through the crack in the doorway at Mrs. Bullock, who had relieved Mrs. Vaughan for the night in nursing Sister Constance. In the next room, Sister Thecla lingered in her own illness with her own nurse.

Mrs. Bullock laid a cool cloth on the nun's forehead and glanced over her forehead at Eliza. "No. I believe we must let her wake on heaven's shores."

On the bed, Sister Constance moaned. Her pitch rose and fell slightly, but it did not approximate words.

"I must come in, Mrs. Bullock," Eliza said. "If this is truly to be the end, let me say goodbye."

Mrs. Bullock crossed the room and put a hand on the door. "Dr. Armstrong does not think that wise. It was my mistake not to be sure the door was closed. You have not slept properly in four days. At least go to the parlor and rest."

The door closed, and Eliza's chest seized.

Heaven's shores. As a good Christian, she ought to take comfort that Sister Constance—and probably Sister Thecla as well—would soon see their blessed Savior. But what a grievous hollow their absence would leave in this world.

Already St. Mary's was spinning in the loss of Father Harris, dean of the cathedral, in the Savior's arms three days now.

And now the sisters.

Eliza shuffled toward the kitchen. Someone was always there these days, if only to brew a fresh pot of coffee or sit in bewildered shock between chores or calls. Every moment close to the failing sisters, rather than down the street or blocks away wondering what was happening, was prized. Every sound from their rooms made the house inhabitants lurch.

Sister Clare sat at the table, bleary eyed, a tin mug in front of her. "There's plenty."

"I thought you might have gone to bed." Eliza took another tin mug from the cupboard and filled it.

"How does anyone sleep with a broken heart?"

"Exhaustion?"

"I am beyond that point."

"You must guard your own health."

"You as well."

"Did I hear Sister Frances's voice?" Eliza raised tepid coffee to her lips.

"She came and went quickly," Sister Clare said.

"She wants so much to be here while the sisters are ill and would gladly take longer shifts to nurse them, but most of the children at Church Home are ill. Dying, truth be told. We may have to help her get the undertaker to respond to her pleas. Do they really think she can just leave their little bodies wrapped in blankets on the porch for the flies and maggots to feast on?"

Eliza put her head in her hands. "It is only the ninth of September, but we need the miracle of an early frost to bring an end to this madness."

"Perhaps we should ask Father Dalzell to lead us in prayer."

The priest from Louisiana had arrived Saturday, determined that St. Mary's should not be without a pastor for even one Sunday, though there was barely anyone to attend services. Father Schuyler had arrived from New York the day before as well.

Eliza blew out breath. "I cannot help wondering if it is wise for anyone else new to enter Memphis."

"We must come," Sister Clare said. "People are dying—hundreds every day now. I have no regret that I came, just as you have no regret for staying when you could have left."

Eliza could not dispute this assessment. Her telegram to her mother had been making just this argument. So far Sisters Ruth, Helen, and Clare had remained healthy, but many others who arrived from northern states to serve as nurses and doctors in the Memphis epidemic had dropped ill within days after arrival and themselves required care—ultimately adding to the burden of the exhausted medical system rather than relieving it. Where the balance lay, Eliza did not know.

"Will Sister Constance make it through the night?" Eliza asked.

Sister Clare shrugged. "I have often judged these things wrong."

"You should rest."

"So we are back to that, are we?"

"Why don't we both go to the parlor?" Eliza stood. "We can freshen our coffee cups first. At least it will be a comfortable place to hold vigil."

Sister Clare nodded. In the parlor they found Sister Hughetta sitting, pale and still, with Miss Murdock. No one had been to bed and, it seemed, no one had any intention of going to bed as long as Sisters Constance and Thecla were on the brink of death. Eliza had been home only for the briefest of times in the last few days, her greatest motivation to be sure she did not miss communication from Callie or indication that she might have been in the house—some sign that she was well.

But there was none. Eliza left a note in the kitchen that the sisters were ill. If Callie came home, she would know where to find Eliza.

She would not allow herself to picture Callie writhing feverish in damp sheets. Except of course she had. Eliza blinked and did what she'd been doing for days—replaced that image with one of Callie whole and upright and nursing her sister back to health. Many were sick. Not everyone perished.

The wick in the single lamp lit in the parlor burned down, and no one rose to adjust it as the gathered women absorbed the moans of Sister Constance that filled the house, though in decreasing volume, and the hours wore toward daylight.

The knock on the front door roused Eliza, and she realized she had dozed off on the sofa across from where Sister Constance had conceded to her illness. No one sat on the infected piece of furniture, covered in a sheet, which would likely be hauled out for burning. Everyone startled at the sound of someone at the door. Miss Murdock was first to jump up, while the others rubbed their eyes. Eliza focused on the clock. It was barely six in the morning.

Miss Murdock was back in a moment with a priest. "Father Dalzell."

"Good morning," he said. "I met some of you when I arrived. I greet you all in the peace of Christ and the love of many in Louisiana who are praying for our brothers and sisters here in Memphis."

"Thank you, Father." Sister Clare stood. "May we offer you some refreshment?"

"It is I who have come to offer the refreshment of Christ's body to Sister Constance," he said, "if she would like to commune."

Eliza stifled a gasp with the realization she had not heard moaning for quite some time. Surely Mrs. Bullock would have come to the parlor if the sister had passed.

"I will go inquire," Sister Hughetta said.

Both nuns left the parlor together. When she saw that the priest meant to go as well, Eliza joined the entourage.

Mrs. Bullock allowed admittance for the priest but cautioned the sisters to keep their distance and left the door ajar.

Eliza put three fingers to her lips. *Surely he has come too late for this.*

"Dear Sister," Father Dalzell said, "I have come to bring you the Blessed Sacrament of our dear Lord. Do you desire to receive it?"

"Oh, so very much!"

Eliza grabbed Sister Hughetta's hand. How was it possible that Sister Constance's voice was so clear and her countenance so bright after a night of moaning? Yet it was so. As she received communion, she gave every response the liturgy required.

Miss Murdock announced that she had prepared breakfast, and Mrs. Bullock shooed everyone toward the kitchen, including Father Dalzell, with the certainty that Father Schuyler would soon arrive as well. And Eliza knew Mrs. Haskins would turn up as soon as she'd had her own breakfast. The pantry must open even while the Sisters House cared for their own and held a vigil of prayer in their hearts.

Sisters Clare and Hughetta did their best to set the importance of the calls that must be made, with only the two of them to make them now. When Mrs. Vaughan arrived for her daytime duties, moving between the two sickrooms, Mrs. Bullock took the advice she had been dispensing to everyone else and retired to her room for a few hours of rest, leaving Miss Murdock to manage in the kitchen. Father Dalzell and Father Schuyler plunged in for their first full week of work in Memphis. Eliza admired their commitment to provide pastoral care and be hands for whatever task was needed—filling jars of broth in the kitchen, distributing food in the pantry, sorting the correspondence and financial records that Sister Constance had to abandon. The day was as unrelenting as all the days had become. Intermittent reports came of how the ill sisters were, but with no encouragement. Sister Constance asked for one book and then another but sent them both back because she could not read. Then she fell into unconsciousness. Right from the start both sisters had been too ill to be told that the other was sick as well.

Eliza handed out one packet of relief goods after another, hour after hour. Father Dalzell agreed to find his way to Church Home and see what he might do to relieve the dire situation there. Father Schuyler had the greater challenge of organizing goods to transport out to Canfield. The horse and carriage could be made available during a certain window of the afternoon. A wagon would be better, but there was not one to be had. Eliza caught Father Schuyler standing stunned on the street corner in front of the cathedral as wagons of coffins, both empty and full, rumbled by and the magnitude of what he had volunteered for sank in.

"I knew what I read in the newspapers," he said, "and in Sister Constance's letters to us in New York. But to see it with my own eyes—to *smell* it in the street—it is difficult to explain."

"Yet the love of Christ compels us," Eliza said.

"Yes. Yes. I cannot find a wagon. The carriage will have to do."

And this was the day. And this was the heart-ache. And this was the grief.

Eliza refused to go home. And she would not be banished to the parlor. She took up her post in the straight-back chair between the rooms of Sister Constance and Sister Thecla.

"Alleluia! Osanna!"

The cry came at midnight, and Eliza knew these

were Sister Constance's final words. After this came only another night of moaning. By seven in the morning, the bells began to ring for Sister Constance.

Mrs. Haskins turned up with her daughter-in-law in tow.

"I heard the bells," she said. "I know you will want to be with the sisters today."

"You are a dear." Eliza's voice caught.

"How is she?"

"They won't let me see her, but the end is close."

"They are protecting you, Miz Eliza."

"Soon there will be no one left in this city to protect."

"Go be with the sisters."

Sister Constance drew her last breath at ten. So many would have liked to give her the farewell she deserved, but in the midst of an epidemic she could have little more recognition than any of the others who perished. Mrs. Bullock insisted on cleaning her body, and Sister Clare helped robe her in her habit. Sister Ruth came from Canfield as soon as she got word. The little group of nuns carried her to their small chapel, roses resting on her bosom, and Father Dalzell read the brief commendatory prayer.

"Sister Hughetta, are you all right?" Eliza caught the nun's elbow at the close of the service.

"I feel faint."

"Sit down."

Sister Hughetta did faint. And though she roused, she fainted again before the nuns had organized a wagon to carry Sister Constance's coffin to Elmwood Cemetery, and she had to stay behind. It was only Sisters Frances, Clare, and Ruth, along with Mrs. Bullock and Eliza who followed to the hastily dug grave.

Two days later the bells rang again, this time for Sister Thecla, who had lingered and suffered longer. She had never even known of her Mother Superior's illness and loss. On this same day, Father Schuyler fell ill. And Dr. Armstrong was too ill to see patients. With proper nursing, many did recover, but Sister Clare did not believe Dr. Armstrong would be one of them, nor Father Schuyler.

Mrs. Bullock, for all her love and devotion to the sisters, paid the price and fell ill.

Sister Ruth, perhaps because she had come into town from the safety of Canfield, fell ill. She was only twenty-six and had served well and kindly but could serve no more.

Sister Hughetta's fainting was not heartbreak but fever.

Sister Clare was down.

The death toll at St. Mary's became a daily horror.

Yet the lines at the pantry continued, and the illness sweeping through the streets was unforgiving of the grief and loss within the walls of the cathedral or the Sisters House. Miss Murdock kept making broth and tea. Mrs. Haskins kept arriving at the pantry. Nursing volunteers kept asking where they should make their calls.

Someone had to make decisions.

CHAPTER TWENTY-ONE

Memphis, September 20, 1878

Eliza paid dearly for Harry's agreement to transport her trunk to the Sisters House, and even then she had to wait until he circled back through her nearly empty neighborhood after picking up three coffins and had to consent to having her trunk wedged in among the deceased in the wagon while she rode on the bench beside Harry.

"I heard you had the fever, Harry." Eliza pulled the front door of her house closed tight and checked that it locked. She would not be back anytime soon.

"Yes, ma'am." Harry hefted the trunk toward the wagon.

Was it possible he'd gone grayer in the last month? Certainly he was thinner.

"And your wife?"

He said nothing but only shoved the trunk into a space where it barely fit, even though Eliza had packed her smallest trunk with only a few dresses and personal items.

"I'm sorry, Harry," she said softly when he offered his hand to assist her up to the bench. "I hadn't heard."

"A week ago." He picked up the reins and nudged the horse forward.

Eliza raised her handkerchief to her face as she did now whenever she was out. The sight of coffins stacked on corners or rolling through streets on wagons might be common, but her stomach had not acclimated to the stench of the epidemic, nor her lungs to the constant dust of lime and gunpowder in the air.

"You are doing valuable work," Eliza said. "You are a brave soul to carry on as you have."

"Still got rent to pay. Ain't exactly too many of my usual customers around anymore."

"They'll be back when this is all over."

"Mebbe. The ones that left and ain't dead. But Memphis won't never be the same."

"Never is a long time, Harry."

"Longer than I got left." Harry reached under his hat and scratched the left side of his head. "Dang mosquitos. All the livelong day."

"I know what you mean. Some days I do believe my only salvation is I don't see the light of day."

"Worse after sunset."

"Some days I don't see the night sky either."

Harry scratched another mosquito bite. Eliza quelled another rebellious roll of her stomach. They fell into silence for the remaining blocks to the St. Mary's complex. Harry offered assistance as Eliza gathered her skirts to climb out of the wagon.

"Thank you for the detour," she said.

"Dese folks ain't in no hurry."

Harry carried the trunk inside the Sisters House and looked at her, his face a question.

"I've chosen a small room at the back," Eliza said. "Straight down that hall."

It was convenient to the main activity. She would hear the cries from the infirmary if one of the nurses there called her name. No one else had used the room to infect it with illness. It seemed too much trouble to ask Harry to bring a mattress from home, and she would not use the only one in the entire Sisters House when one after another the nuns refused to use it when stricken. It might still go to a patient. Eliza would sleep on a wooden bed the way the nuns had, with a thin pallet of hay the only comfort.

Harry carried the trunk through and tipped his hat before leaving.

In the kitchen, three vats of broth simmered and two of tea. Miss Murdock was keeping up. How, Eliza did not know. Nearly every day in the last week Eliza had sent Miss Murdock to the Howard Association offices at the Peabody Hotel to plead for nurses. The sisters had always been doing too much, and now with all of them gone or ill, it was impossible to keep up.

On the table, a telegram leaned against the saltshaker. Last week Eliza had instructed the telegraph office to simply deliver her messages here. She had no time to write proper letters to her mother. She had no time to even craft replies and send a messenger down to the telegraph office. There was no messenger to send.

Eliza opened the telegram.

FRIGHTENED FOR YOU *Stop* EVERY DAY NEWS IS WORSE *Stop* I PRAY CALLIE IS CARING FOR YOUR EVERY NEED *Stop* IF YOU WILL NOT COME SEND WORD OF YOUR HEALTH *Stop* LOVE MOTHER

Eliza dropped the message on the table. If she could scrounge up a spare moment and a message, she could assure her mother she was well. She would say nothing of Callie. She'd heard nothing for three weeks, and her mother would only be distressed at the thought of losing a favored house servant. The greater question was, how much longer could she truthfully say she was only running the pantry and not caring for the sick?

Miss Murdock entered the room. "I have not overboiled the broth, have I?"

"Peacefully simmering." Eliza hadn't looked, but she'd heard no alarming noises from the stove. "The others should be here soon for the meeting."

"I made some sweet tea last night, and we have plenty of extra ice."

"You precious dear. Such a treat in all this sweltering weather."

Miss Murdock opened the icebox and removed two glass pitchers.

"I'll take one of those." Eliza led the way to the modest dining room, which on this morning would also serve as a meeting room assembling Father Dalzell, who was the only priest on hand, a pair of volunteer nurses not on duty—and no doubt exhausted—and with God's favor a representative of the Howard Association who might be persuaded of the need to cease making them waste time sending someone with daily pleas.

Faces around the table a few minutes later were drawn. Though they met at the Sisters House, no nun was present. Sister Ruth had died only three days ago. Sister Frances could not be spared from Church Home, where orphans passed every day despite her efforts, and while Sister Hughetta was going to recover, she was far too frail to attend a meeting.

After Father Dalzell prayed to acknowledge God's presence and invite the Holy Spirit's wisdom, a few hands reached for sweet tea but all faces turned toward Eliza.

"We are in a wretched state," she said. "We all know this. We have lost some of the dearest people God has ever fashioned from the dust of this earth, and I don't believe I shall ever understand why He has called them home when they were serving Him so faithfully and selflessly. But they are gone from us, and we wish to carry on and honor them as well as God by serving just as they did. We fumble to know how, and that is why we are here together. Perhaps reports from the nurses among us will help us chart our way forward. Miss Beeson, may I ask you to begin?"

"I could tell so many stories." Miss Beeson straightened her shoulders. "Only this week I found three children in a small cottage with their mother. I was passing by and thought to see how she was doing and found her dead. The children are so young. They thought she was only sleeping. I had to send one of them to the infirmary on Market Street and the others to Canfield. I don't know if they shall ever see one another again. But with no family to ready the mother, the undertaker refused to pick her up. It took me another day before I could get the police to insist someone take her away."

"The police department have very few officers still on their feet." Mr. Skorman from the Howard Association spoke. "Perhaps eight or ten for all of Memphis."

"We are not without sympathy," Eliza said, "and we realize you are not unaware. Nevertheless, we must hear the stories lest we simply throw up our hands against the immensity of the need."

Father Dalzell spoke. "I have been here but ten days, and in my endeavors to provide pastoral care to those who are clearly dying, I see that they pass away or fall into unconsciousness before we reach them. I drove out to a family where a father and two daughters were all sick. As I arrived, they were bringing out the remains of one child and inside the other was gone as well and the father was breathing his last. It is a heartsickness like no other to see such a scene and know that you have come too late to offer comfort or spiritual care even when there can be no cure. Yet I understand why the sisters have made such a valiant effort to reach as many as they could. In each sick and dying person, every sister beheld her suffering Lord. How could they turn away?"

"Thank you, Father." Eliza swallowed hard. How indeed? It was for this reason that the sisters had made more promises than they could keep and worked themselves to death. "Miss Newell, have you a word for us?"

"Yesterday I had to persuade a devoted husband to leave the sofa in the room where his wife lay ill and go to the bed in the next room," Miss Newell said. "While another nurse I was training attended him—for he was also ill—I put their little girl to bed in her own crib. I believe we reached them in time in this case. We arranged someone to stay and care for them. If we can get there in time, we *can* save some people. But we *must* have more nurses, Mr. Skorman."

"I well understand this," Mr. Skorman said. "We are indeed in a wretched state, because we can obtain no more nurses for any amount of money. We do our best to raise money and increase our offer of payment for those who come, but there is also rising fear that doctors and nurses are taking trains into a death trap. It is difficult to make an argument otherwise."

A pall cast across the room with this truth. Eliza caught Father Dalzell's eye.

"Mr. Skorman," Eliza said, "by Father Dalzell's gracious kindness, we have some pastoral care, despite great personal risk. However, St. Mary's has lost its Mother Superior and all but two nuns. One of the remaining nuns is bedridden still, and I cannot advocate sending her out on calls among the sick until we are certain she is healthy. The other has survived an illness but is working herself to the bone at Church Home with orphans dying from the fever every single day—and a struggle to get coffins or an undertaker on some of those days. I fear for her well-being. At the request of the relief committee, St. Mary's undertook to care for dozens of orphans at the Canfield Asylum, and now we have lost Sister Ruth, on loan from New York. Sister Clare, also on loan, is down. Sister Helen, on loan, is doing all she can to fill in the gaps and thus is not with us this morning. Surely you can see that St. Mary's is stretched far beyond the limited resources it had even a few weeks ago."

"I do see this," Mr. Skorman said. "I also see

that we have in our midst someone quite capable to be the individual with whom the Howards should continue to communicate."

"May I have this person's name, please?"

"You bear the name."

"Do you mean me?" Eliza said.

"I do."

"Father Dalzell would be appropriate," Eliza said. "I am only here to assist as a member of St. Mary's Church."

"Father Dalzell is doing the needful work of many priests, and you have proven yourself a fine administrator. If I promise to bear down on trying to find you more nurses to assign to your calls, will you promise to administer their assignments out of St. Mary's?"

"We need a doctor, as well. We lost Dr. Armstrong. We are running an infirmary and two orphanages, remember."

"I remember. Do we have an agreement?"

Eliza gave a slow nod. "I too behold my suffering Lord."

CHAPTER TWENTY-TWO

"If I go to the Inn now," Nolan said, "I'm pretty sure I can score some leftover breakfast french toast cream cheese casserole."

"Possibly. That's what Nia makes on Saturdays." Jillian didn't look up from her computer. "I'm only going to work a few hours this morning, Dad. There were quite a few interruptions this week."

"Right. I could stay and whisk you up some pancakes."

"Nope. Go check on Meri while I wrap up these client reports."

"Maybe Nia can spare her this afternoon and we can do something."

Jillian nodded and kept clicking the keyboard.

Nolan grabbed a light flannel-lined jacket off the hook in the kitchen and went out the back door. It was late enough that he didn't expect to find breakfast still under way with guests at the polished long oak dining room table, and he would roll up his sleeves to help clean up the kitchen sooner than be underfoot. All that mattered was getting a read on Meri. At the last minute, Nolan strode around the side of the Inn to the rear parking area.

Meri's car was there. Her five percent was still fighting back.

On the back porch, Nolan raised his knuckles to rap on the back door, but voices stilled the arc of his hand. Thick walls of the Victorian house and the more modern double-pane windows the Dunstons had installed for energy efficiency muffled the words, but the tone was indisputably irritable, bordering on angry.

Nolan knocked, reinforced his movement with a convivial "Hello!" and pressed the brass handle to poke his head into the kitchen.

The exchange stopped, mid-dispute. Sitting at the round table, Nia aimed her scowl in Nolan's direction, though he was certain it had ensconced itself on her face before his arrival. Meri's shoulders slumped, and she twisted away from him toward a pile of dishes stacked beside the sink. Leo hustled through from the dining room, his features scrunched in confusion that matched Nolan's.

"Sounds like the team needs to come together in here," Leo said.

"Then I've arrived just in time." Nolan closed the door behind him.

"Don't patronize me." Nia planted her hands on the table on either side of her open laptop and pushed her weight upward. "There's too much work to do."

Leo lurched toward her. "Sweetheart, we've

talked about this. You're not ready to be standing up on your own as much as you're used to. Meri is right here to help you, and I closed my workshop for the day. You just have to tell us what you need."

At the counter, Meri dropped a mixing bowl, and it clattered around the industrial-size stainless cavern.

"Hey!"

Leo's hand on Nia's shoulder held her down.

"Sorry," Meri muttered, picking up the bowl and a sponge to scrub it with.

"Nia, do you need some ice for your leg?" Leo said.

"No, I do not need some ice for my leg. I can walk just fine, if a bit slowly."

"Your knee swells when you stand for too long."

"Meri," Nia snapped, "make sure you get everything scrubbed out of that bowl. It should never have sat all night without being cleaned. Now everything is dried on."

"That was my fault," Leo said. "Don't take it out on Meri. She's doing her job."

"She didn't this morning." Nia glared at Nolan. "What do you need?"

He hesitated to answer.

"I'm very sorry about this morning." Meri spoke as she scrubbed dried egg mixture without turning around.

"I don't understand," Nia said. "You made the

french toast casseroles perfectly last night, doing everything I said. They looked as good as any I've put together. Leo got them in the oven this morning right on time."

"She said she was sorry," Leo said. "Do you want some coffee? I'm sure Nolan does."

"Coffee would be grand." Nolan nodded. His choice was to walk away from whatever the morning's disaster had been or stay and see what it had to do with Meri. He would stay.

"Burning french toast casserole," Nia muttered. "You both promised me you could handle the morning. All she had to do was take them out on time and set them on the sidebar with fresh fruit and pastries."

"It wasn't as bad as all that," Leo said. "The guests hardly knew the difference."

Nia scoffed. "You say that because you don't read Yelp reviews. This is a bed-and-*breakfast*. We have a reputation to maintain. You think people don't notice when the bottom layer of breakfast is burned to the pan?"

Meri put the cleaned bowl in the rack to dry and started in on the stack of dishes to rinse and load in the dishwasher. Beside the plates, soapy water filled two large glass rectangular baking dishes. If Meri's shoulders sloped any further, they'd be hanging at her waist. Nolan had known Nia when she was a teenager, when her moody spells had been at their height. An independent personality running a business sidelined by even a minor injury wasn't a great mix, but if she chased Meri off now with her bad mood, she'd be undoing a lot of painstaking work accomplished over the last few days.

"I'll clean up," Nolan said. "The three of you could use a breather."

"No thanks." Meri increased the strength of stream coming from the faucet.

Nolan reached around her, stopped the water, and gently guided her shoulders toward the table. "Coffee coming right up. Any extra pastries?"

"On the counter." Nia tilted her head toward a stoneware platter covered in plastic wrap.

"Mugs still in this cupboard?" Nolan asked.

"I can get them," Leo said.

"Sit." Nolan filled three mugs, looked around until his eyes settled on the sugar and creamer, and pulled the plastic wrap off the pastries. He delivered everything to the table. "A royal feast for Canyon Mines' royal family."

Nia crossed her eyes. "Puleeze."

Nolan had dishes to clear up and counters to wipe down. He couldn't make Nia and Meri speak amicably to each other, or even eat turnovers, but sitting across the table might make them less likely to speak irritably for a few minutes. Even silence would be healing space, and when the temperature in the room came down a few degrees he would put on his mediator's hat.

Nia was staring at her laptop even as she sipped coffee and nibbled around the edges of a pastry. Leo picked up the Denver newspaper. Meri pulled her phone from a pocket. At least she had taken his advice not to cut herself off from her family completely by refusing to look at her phone.

"These bookings don't look right," Nia said.

Nolan glanced over his shoulder. "I'm sure you can straighten it out after you've had a break. Just enjoy your coffee and turnover for now."

Nia pushed her pastry away. "Meri, you did these bookings last night, didn't you?"

Meri's dull eyes went darker. "Yes."

"They're incomplete. And the information we have is conflicting. They don't make the least bit of sense." Nia turned the laptop for Meri to see for herself.

"I'm sorry."

"Now I don't know how to prepare for guests for the weekend after next. When they're coming, how many, payment method."

"It's two weeks away," Nolan said. "Plenty of time to sort things out."

"I'll call everyone and confirm the information," Meri said. "I'll make it right this afternoon."

"It's not that hard to get right in the first place. It's all basic to the job."

"Nia!" Leo's intonation took on a spiked contour.

She pressed her lips together.

Meri stood up. "Nolan, I'll finish cleaning up."

"I've got it in hand. Just the casserole dishes left."

"Which are burned," Meri said. "I'm the one who let them burn. I'll clean them."

"I don't mind at all."

"I want to do it." Meri picked up the pastry platter, which still held three options, determined in her penance.

Nolan surrendered and glanced around for a dish towel to dry his hands. He didn't see the platter slide out of Meri's hands, but the clangor of it shattering on the geometric black and gray floor tiles spun him around in time to see Meri drop to her knees.

In tears.

Full-on wrenching sobs.

In the range of emotions Nolan had seen in Meri over the last ten days, occasionally he'd seen glimpses of the lifetime of tears welled up in her. But she hadn't cried like this.

He met her on the floor and took her in his arms. Around them, Leo quietly swept up the remains of the shattered platter. Gradually Meri's shaking stilled.

"Thank you, Meri," Nia said.

The unexpected calm in Nia's voice drew everyone's eyes.

"I never much liked that platter. I've always

regretted buying it in a secondhand shop. I only used it because I paid too much for it not to, and the colors suited the dining room. The truth is I thought it was ugly, and I've resented it for years."

Nolan burst out laughing, and Meri raised a hand to swipe at her tears.

"I'm so sorry." Still on the floor, Meri shifted her weight to her heels. "I'm a nervous wreck. I haven't had a straight thought since last night. I should have told you all."

Nolan helped Meri to her feet. "Told us what?"

"I've been tracking my family's locations by following where their phones are. We have that family app where you can do that. That's how they know where I am. And they're getting close."

"Close to Canyon Mines?" Nia tried to stand. Leo pulled her down again.

Meri nodded. "They'll be here today. In a few hours."

"Five percent," Nolan said.

"Five percent of what?" Nia said.

"Meri knows."

Meri nodded. "It may be more like three percent. Or two and a half. This is not going to be pretty."

CHAPTER TWENTY-THREE

Memphis, September 25, 1878

W ill the Howards let us keep the new nurses, do you think?" Sister Hughetta was upright at the dining table, lingering over her tea.

Eliza looked up from the never-ending lists she had spread on the table. "I do hope so. It was like pulling teeth to get them."

"I am ready for calls." Sister Hughetta pushed her empty teacup away.

Eliza eyed her. "Just yesterday the doctor advised at least one more day of rest."

"I disagree. I have seen enough of yellow jack to know that it has run its course in my case."

"One more day, Sister Hughetta." Eliza shuffled her lists. She would have to manage somehow.

Miss Beeson rushed into the room and threw herself into a chair across from Eliza.

"What is it?" Eliza stood. This was not good news.

"Miss Newell. Her landlady found her this morning on the floor of her room. She'd probably been there all night in her own vomit. Quite ill. I've just come from there."

"Heavens." Eliza sank back into her seat. "Will she be cared for there?"

Miss Beeson shook her head. "The landlady will have none of it. She insists she is not running an infirmary. I was able to make arrangements to move Miss Newell to Market Street."

Eliza nodded and recorded the information. She would pray the young nurse had been found before this ruinous disease would take her.

Miss Murdock slipped into the room with a stack of papers.

"More calls?" Eliza said.

Miss Murdock nodded and left.

Eliza flipped through the slips of paper. Names and addresses, or sometimes just brief descriptions of where the houses were and who might be in them. Children. Young mothers. Elderly people with no one to look after them. Scribbles about who had already passed in the household.

For the moment, Eliza set the new names aside and picked up a list she had already prepared and handed it to Miss Beeson.

"Without Miss Newell I will have to think again about the plan for the morning, but we can begin here."

Miss Beeson nodded and took the list. "Will Father Dalzell be making calls?"

"I believe so."

"And the doctor?"

"In the afternoon. Make sure you bring back word of the most serious cases."

The other nurses filed through the room in the next few minutes, and Eliza disbursed assignments. Each time she considered adding at least one of the new names, but the lists already were unreasonably long.

"I will be taking some calls today," Eliza said to Sister Hughetta.

"What about the correspondence?"

"I will do it this evening. That is what Sister Constance did."

"Sister Constance also said that you were to be caring for the poor and not the sick."

Eliza pushed back her chair. "It is true that I am not a trained nurse, but many people who make calls are not trained nurses. I have watched the nurses caring for those in our infirmary and the children at the orphanage, even if I was not allowed across the threshold. I can make sure people have water, broth, and tea. I can make sure there is food. I can make sure there are no corpses in the house, and that the sick are not alone. I can see who are the sickest and need the doctor most. I can judge who requires a nurse to remain with them and who can manage if a nurse checks in every day."

Sister Hughetta's eyebrows went up. "You have been thinking about this for some time, haven't you?"

"Yes, I have. And the moment has come."

"Can I at least help you put some things in a cart?" Sister Hughetta said. "I can carry jars of tea from the kitchen, and you'll want some clean linens and tins of meat."

To this Eliza was agreeable. The old horse who had served St. Mary's well for so long stood by as they loaded a small cart. When they tried to hitch the cart to the horse, however, he resisted.

"He's lame," Sister Hughetta said.

"Lame?"

"Look at how he's walking." Sister Hughetta leaned into the side of the horse and lifted one of his legs. "His shoes are completely worn. It would be cruel to take him out on the streets."

The fortitude that had buoyed Eliza escaped like hissing steam. "There is no blacksmith left in the entirety of Memphis. I have heard of others who inquired and found no one."

"We can fit you out with one of our large bags and you can carry what you are able," Sister Hughetta said. "You'll just have to come back and forth. Many of the nurses work that way. We don't always have a cart to use."

"I know this to be true," Eliza said, "but I am going to do something I should have done long ago."

"What is that?"

"Find another horse. Two horses. And a carriage." It would be something else to explain

265

to her parents later. But she was a grown woman of nearly forty, not a twelve-year-old. Was there nothing of the family's belongings she might control? "Father Dalzell has been using the deanery rig. Help me find him—if you are not finding this too tiring."

"Quite the opposite." Sister Hughetta's cheeks pinked up, and she strutted toward the deanery. Eliza reconsidered defying the doctor's order that Sister Hughetta needed one more day before resuming full duties.

They found Father Dalzell three blocks away. Eliza offered thanks to God that it was not three miles and explained her plan. She knew the livery where her father had boarded the family horses when he left for Wisconsin. The epidemic meant that her parents' stay was extended, but she was prepared to talk the livery owner into releasing the horses to her even in the absence of her father's permission. She required Father Dalzell for his cart to drive her but also for the authority his clerical garb would lend.

Eliza wound herself up for full bluster at the livery.

The head groomsman waved her off. "The owner died two weeks ago. His wife wants to stay open, but a groom and the exercise boy are gone as well. You'll do me a favor if you take your horses for now."

Father Dalzell tied the two brown mares to the

back of his own cart and gently led them through the streets to Eliza's family home, where they hitched one to the family carriage.

"I learned to drive at St. Mary's," Eliza assured him. Almost a whole month ago. She left out the fact that she'd driven a horse and cart fewer than a dozen times since. "If you wouldn't mind leading the other horse to the Sisters House, I would deeply appreciate it. Someone can use it with the spare cart there."

She'd lost most of the morning fetching the two horses and the carriage, but she ought to have done it days ago. Weeks ago. At least she was doing it now. She had the rest of the day to think about where the two horses could board now and who might look after them. Perhaps the Heard boys would like to do it. Getting the feel of the reins, she sat in the familiar carriage, with her mother's scent embedded in the upholstery, and guided it back to the Sisters House to load with supplies.

Day one. She would put herself on the list every day now, just as Sister Constance had done.

In the first home, a mother and child were both down with the fever, but an aunt was there to care for them. What they lacked was clean bedding and dressing gowns—and food. The tins lying open around the small rooms were scraped clean, not a morsel left behind, but the open shelves above the stove had nothing left on them. Eliza helped to change the beds, and she left two jars of soup and a loaf of bread, along with a bag of rice, dried peas, and canned tomatoes.

"Keep them covered," Eliza said to the aunt. "They must sweat out the fever. Sponge baths are important. Small sips of tea throughout the day. I will have you on the list for someone to check in tomorrow, but if things get worse, you *must* send word to the Sisters House."

Eliza moved on to her next call. The note she'd received that morning said the nurse had not come for two days. Inside the second house, no one was upright but a twelve-year-old boy who ought not to be responsible for a house full of sick family members. This yellow fever outbreak brought enough *ought nots* to make the head spin. It seemed to Eliza that delirium had overtaken the boy's mother, who thrashed against her tangled sweat-drenched bedding, mumbling nonsense.

"How long has she been like this?"

"Since yesterday," he said. "That's why I ran down with a note this morning."

"I will put her on the list for the doctor's rounds." Eliza took a folded sheet of stationery from her bag. "In the meantime, let's sponge her off and see if we can bring the fever down. We must try to get her to lie quietly. And we'll try to get a bit of tea or broth into everyone else. Does the stove work?"

He nodded and showed her where the matches were. She found pots, and while they waited for tea and broth to warm, she broke off chunks of ice into a bowl of water and bathed the mother, speaking in soothing tones all the while and hoping this would calm her enough to encourage her to lie still. The results were mixed. The sponge bath was complete, and Eliza tucked a fresh top sheet around the woman, but she still spoke in sentences that made no sense.

"You will have to keep trying to cool her," Eliza said, "while I do my best to find a nurse who can properly sit with her and the doctor can get here."

The boy nodded his blanched face once again and took a big, brave breath.

In the third house everyone—all adults, as far as she could see—were stricken, but in her judgment, compared with what she had seen in the infirmary and at the Church Home orphanage, they had weathered the worst. What they required now was nourishment. Broths and rice, primarily. Perhaps they would be the rare household in which everyone survived.

It would be impossible to have too many infirmaries in Memphis. Eliza's family home, with all its space, was shuttered and useless at the moment. It could well serve as an infirmary. But it would need beds and staff and supplies and

269

food and medicine, and Eliza had no assurance she would be able to organize these necessities.

Yet yellow fever knew no limits, neither race nor income nor vocation nor neighborhood.

CHAPTER TWENTY-FOUR

"So she's going to keep you updated?" Jillian poured steamed, frothy milk on top of a base of Brazilian coffee and a hint of hazelnut syrup. The mug was a simple, classic white, with an almost squarish shape at the base but rounded just enough at the top to keep from dumping hot liquid down her shirt. But something about it was still not quite right.

"It didn't seem right to suggest Meri leave the Inn," Nolan said, "when Leo wants to keep Nia off her feet and Meri's family is going to descend."

Jillian sipped coffee and grinned at her father over the foaming mug. "I'd like to be a fly on the wall if they show up at the Inn to face Nia without Meri, especially after the mood you described this morning."

"Be that as it may in the world of fine entertainment," Nolan said, "our job is to support Meri, not take over. Besides, Nia backed off once she realized why Meri was rattled beyond the point of functioning. Now what about you?"

"What about me?"

"When you planned your day, we didn't know the Davieses were coming. We need answers only you can give us."

Jillian gulped too much hot coffee in one mouthful and struggled to swallow it before inhaling air to cool her mouth.

"Dad, I'm not a magician."

"Just a minute. Incoming text." Nolan glanced at his phone. "Pru has verified that she's not coming. It's only the parents and the brother."

"What does Meri think is going to happen?"

"Three against one, Jilly. What does it sound like to you?"

"They're not coming just to see if she's all right."

Nolan shook his head. "She's going to need us."

"I thought we weren't taking over."

"Just to level the playing field. My guess is they need to understand their own family just as much as Meri does."

"It's been a crunch of a week, Dad. I haven't gotten all that far with the family tree."

"You have the Canfield piece."

"Which I haven't tied to the Davies family." Not by a long shot.

"Then I guess you have your marching orders."

Jillian buzzed her lips. Raúl's formal report was going to be late, but at least she'd already passed on everything he needed to know to close out legal matters with Annabel Rosario's life-changing news.

"I'd better get on it, then," Jillian said.

"I'll bring you lunch in a while."

"Thanks."

"You know, there's another mug just like mine around here somewhere."

Jillian made a face. "Next you'll be trying to get me to drink black coffee."

Jillian withdrew to her office, where she stacked and cross-stacked papers from the active projects she'd hoped to wind up today and moved the pile to the corner of the desk. A clear desktop and a fresh yellow legal pad gave her a clean start on the question in front of her as she minimized the open windows on her computer and opened the notes she'd begun on the genealogy of Meriwether Eliza Davies. Both of her parents were well known in their fields with biographical information attached to publications. It didn't take long to gather enough information on them to push back another generation, particularly on the Davies side.

C. Michael Davies was the son of Thomas Davies, MD. Conflicting records showed him born in Atlanta and Meriwether County, Georgia.

Meriwether.

"They must have just landed at DIA." Nolan stepped into her office with a grilled sandwich made with three kinds of cheese and avocado slices. "Suddenly all three phones are on the move again."

"Dad, look." Jillian put a finger on her screen, moving it from left to right under the information.

"I knew you'd find something."

"He'd be old enough to be in the last census that's public information."

"You'd better hurry. They're probably getting a rental car at DIA."

"There's certainly no other way to get to Canyon Mines."

"Eat," Nolan said. "You'll need fortification when we go over there."

Her eyes darted up at him. "You don't mean today."

"Of course." His phone sounded an alert, and he scanned it. "Yep, definitely leaving DIA. Phones on the move and heading west. We'll want to be at the Inn no later than ninety minutes from now. Sooner is better."

Jillian picked up one piece of her sandwich, which her father had cut into quarter triangles just as he had all her life, and bit into it. Thomas Davies should be in the 1940 census. An address would make it easier to find the right enumeration district to be sure she was on the correct trail, but she didn't have that tidbit of information. She kept poking around.

Jillian's sandwich had gone cold, but she ate it anyway. Cold food was an occupational hazard—at least the way she practiced her occupation.

"Jilly, we have to go."

She looked up at her father. "I just have a few more things I want to check out in the 1940 census."

"I wish you had time, but you don't. My phone is blowing up with messages from Meri. And Nia. And Leo. She's a mess, and they're afraid she's going to decide she can't be there when her family arrives."

"Maybe she shouldn't be," Jillian said.

"She should be." Nolan left no room for discussion. "She just shouldn't be alone. And Nia. Well."

"It's all right, Dad. She's my friend and I love her, but she's Nia."

He waved his hand in four quick, tight circles. "So do that thing where you spiff up in three minutes flat and let's get out of here."

Meri was pacing the back patio when they arrived. "Is there some way I can be unconscious while this transpires?"

"Five percent." Nolan pointed to himself. "Five percent more." Then to Jillian. "Five percent more. Inside is another ten percent in your corner. You're up to twenty-five percent strong and fighting. And that's simple addition. I happen to think it works by multiplication. Five times five times five times five times five."

Meri squeezed her head between her hands. "I'll bet you played college sports. You know all the pep talks. But I am in serious trouble here, Nolan. I flunked out of med school and ran away."

"And within a week you got yourself an interview with a top-notch graduate program in public administration."

"By the way," Jillian said, "I want to see that essay one of these days. It must have been incredibly persuasive."

Meri's phone pinged.

"Is it them?" Nolan asked.

"Pru," Meri said, reading the screen. " 'You can do this. I'm here for you.' "

"Sounds like another five percent to multiply by," Nolan said. "The math is getting astronomical in your favor."

The back door of the Inn opened, and Leo stepped out. "I think they're pulling up now."

Jillian fixed her eyes on Meri, wondering if she had her car keys in her pocket and if somebody should shift position to be between Meri and her car.

Meri's hand went to her jeans pocket.

Jillian took a step toward the car.

"I'm just going to text my sister," Meri said. "She still prays. This seems like a good time to ask her to do it, if she's not in the middle of surgery or something."

"Good call," Jillian said.

Meri's steps were unhurried but direct. Flanked by Jillian and Nolan, she walked through the Inn and waited on the wide, welcoming porch while the engine of a black Lexus SUV shut off and three doors opened simultaneously.

"That's Canny who was driving?" Jillian whispered.

Meri nodded.

Canny made no bones about who was in charge, beading his eyes on his sister while coming around the car and waiting for his parents to emerge from the passenger side.

Meri took a few steps forward as her family ascended the steps. "Welcome to the Inn at Hidden Run."

Canny laughed. "An ironic name, don't you think?"

"There's some local history to it." Meri kept her cool. "There was an old ski run near here years ago. The exact location was lost for a long time, but documents in the local heritage museum revealed it."

"Thanks for the tourism lesson," Canny said. "You can run, but you can't hide."

"These are my friends, Jillian and her father, Nolan."

Good job. Don't let him rattle you.

"My brother, Canny," Meri said, "and my parents, Michael and Juliette."

"Nice to meet you." Jillian made a point to shake all three hands firmly and look into three sets of eyes without inhibition or intimidation.

"We're so pleased to meet you," Nolan said when it was his turn to shake hands. "Come on inside and meet the owners of the Inn."

Nia and Leo were in the parlor and offered the same gracious welcome they extended to every guest who came through their doors.

"I'll show you the ground level," Meri said. "Dad, I think you'll really like the library in particular."

Nia, Leo, Jillian, and Nolan looked at each other with wide eyes while Meri took her family into the broad hall and across to the library and dining room before ducking into the kitchen and circling back to the parlor.

"You have a lovely inn," Juliette said. "You've taken great care with the restorations."

"We remember this building before the renovations, of course," Michael said. "We had only ever seen it from the outside, and it was in disrepair in those days, but even then we couldn't help wondering what it could become with the right attention. Quite impressive."

"Yes, it was lovely to see," Juliette said, "especially since our visit will be so short. Whatever Meri owes for her stay here, of course we will settle up before she leaves."

"Mom, you misunderstand," Meri said.

"Meri has been an exceptional employee," Nia said. "I was at a loss on my own, and she turned up at just the right time and jumped right in."

"Employee?"

"That's right," Meri said. "I have a job."

Juliette's gaze remained on Nia. "In that case,

I'm sorry that my daughter's shortsighted actions will leave you shorthanded."

"There was no need for you to come." Meri set her timbre sedate and tight.

"You weren't taking our calls," Canny said. "What choice did we have?"

"I would have talked to you when I was ready."

Nia pushed herself upright on the arm of her chair. Leo jumped to assist.

"Why don't I bring us all some refreshments?" Nia said. "Jillian?"

"Coming to help."

Nolan said nothing but also stood. Jillian looked back to see him flashing five fingers at Meri, then closing his fist and repeating the gesture four more times. Five times five times five times five times five. Jillian flashed another five fingers on behalf of Pru, the latest member of Team Meri.

Leo put a fresh pot of coffee on to brew. Nia pointed Jillian to a tub of freshly baked scones and strawberry jam.

"Well, there you have it," Nia said.

"I know it's a big house," Jillian said, "but is it my imagination or are their voices already rising?"

"Not your imagination," Leo said.

"What do you think is going to happen out there?" Nia asked.

"They're either going to talk it out or duke it

279

out," Leo said. "Surely now that they're face-to-face, they can figure things out."

"I don't know," Nia said, "considering this is exactly the scenario Meri drove halfway across the country to avoid."

"Maybe, maybe not," Nolan said. "Whether she chose this place when she left Memphis or somewhere in the middle of Kansas, she didn't just get off the highway randomly in Canyon Mines. Given some time, her family might figure that out."

"Might," Jillian said.

"We have to keep working all the angles," Nolan said. "And we can't leave Meri on her own, especially now."

The door from the dining room swung open, and Meri entered. "They're going to find someplace to stay."

Reprieve rode out on Jillian's breath. At least they weren't snatching Meri this afternoon.

"How long are they planning to be in town?" Nia asked.

Meri sighed. "I'm not sure."

"We came in here to get refreshments," Nia said, "so let's take some refreshments. Meri, take the coffee. Leo, the plates. Nolan, matching cups. Jillian, you have the scones."

In the parlor, the Davieses had their genteel party faces on again.

CHAPTER TWENTY-FIVE

Nolan made sure to select a seat close to Meri's parents and within reach of the refreshment.

"I explained that the Inn is fully booked tonight." Meri set the carafe on the coffee table. Her relief devoured the empty spaces of the room.

In the absence of her movement to pour coffee, Nolan filled a cup and offered it to Meri's father. "Do you require accoutrements?"

"Straight-up black is the only way to drink coffee," Michael said.

"A man after my own heart." Nolan looked at Juliette and wagged one eyebrow.

"None for me, thank you," she said.

"My mother has a strict rule about no caffeine after two o'clock." Meri placed a scone on a plate and handed it to Juliette. As an apparent afterthought, she offered a napkin.

"I'm a surgeon," Juliette said, "with a habit of early-morning calls. I can't afford caffeine-induced insomnia when people's lives are in my hands."

"Just the surgeon I'd want to have," Nolan said. Nolan pegged Canny as someone who would pour his own coffee and help himself to two scones, which is just what happened in under sixty seconds.

"I'm sorry about not being able to offer you rooms," Nia said, once Leo settled her in a chair. "There are two chain motels at the east end of town and another to the west. They have many more rooms than we do."

"And they don't usually fill up except during high ski season," Nolan said.

"I'd be happy to call around for you," Nia said.

"I don't think so," Meri said.

Nolan poured his own coffee and considered Meri's agitation as he settled in his chair. She hadn't even chosen a seat in a pretense of manners, instead moving around to position herself behind the sofa her parents occupied, where she wouldn't have to look them in the eye.

"What I mean is," Meri said, "I don't think my parents—or my brother—would be comfortable in those motels."

"They're not fancy," Nia said, "but they're clean and well kept. And very convenient."

"I think they'd be happier in the long run if they drove a little farther to find something with more amenities."

"I could call my friend in Genesee," Nia said. "She has a nice lodge-style bed-and-breakfast. Maybe she has space."

"It's only a half an hour to Denver," Meri said,

"and they'd have their choice of hotels they're used to. Canny likes things just so."

Canny polished off his first scone. "There must be a nice place around here to go to an early dinner. We'll get things settled, and there's a good chance all four of us can still head back to Denver for a late flight."

"Canny." Meri barely opened her teeth to speak. "We had an agreement, and this wasn't it."

"Meri is right." Juliette held her scone politely but didn't actually bite into it. "We agreed to sleep on things and talk again tomorrow in a reasonable manner when we haven't been traveling all day."

Nolan set his coffee cup down on the table, planted his hands on his knees, and leaned forward.

"Then I know just the thing to do," he said. "Jillian and I have lots of space at our house. Plenty of bedrooms and baths, and I'm a pretty good cook, if I do say so myself, and Jillian is a masterful barista no matter what time of day you like your caffeine."

He avoided Jillian's eyes, which would be full of shock. And scolding. And more shock. *You can't be serious,* they would say. But he was.

"It's not officially a bed-and-breakfast," he continued, "but it's another old Victorian, and if you like this place, I think you'd enjoy seeing the way ours is restored as well—with some tasteful upgrades for modern living. Isn't that right, Jillian?"

Her mother would have kicked him under the table for laying a trap like this. He turned and met his mirror green eyes in his daughter's face, which otherwise looked so much like her mother's. A stunned flicker gave way to assent.

"Of course," Jillian said. "There's no point in doing all that driving back and forth when we have the space."

That's my girl. We can't abandon Meri now that events have come to this.

"Give us a quick head start," Nolan said, "to knock the cobwebs out of a couple of spare rooms. It's been a while since we had overnight guests. Meri knows the way. She can bring you over later and stay for dinner—if Nia can spare her."

"That sounds perfect!" Nia said. "You're welcome to enjoy the parlor as long as you like, or wander across the hall to the library or the dining room. Leo will keep the coffee coming— or herbal tea, if you prefer, Juliette."

Over her parents' heads, Meri eyed Nolan with wide, dark, confused orbs.

"Let me just clear away some of these things before I go." Nolan picked up the empty scones plate and his own drained coffee cup.

"I'll make Mom's tea," Meri said.

Nolan followed her into the kitchen.

"What are you doing?" Meri filled the kettle and rummaged in a canister for herbal tea options. "All this coffee and tea and pastry and dinner business. Do you spend day and night thinking about eating?"

"It's going to be okay," Nolan said. "Team Meri, remember?"

"I almost had them out of here. Three doctors practicing in specialized fields. The odds are good that one of them would get a call that required getting back to Tennessee. That would at least break down this united front they have going on."

"But you haven't settled anything." Nolan gently set down the dishes beside the sink. "You were just chasing them away. What happened to five times five times five times five times five?"

"Canny makes me crazy, that's what."

"I can see that."

"You didn't hear what he said as soon as you all left the room."

"At my house, he'll be on my turf."

"He thinks the world is his turf."

"I've met a few people like your brother in my career. I can handle Canny."

"My mother will want honey. Two spoonfuls." Meri opened a cabinet and removed a honey jar.

"At a fancy hotel in Denver, she won't have a daughter who knows just how she likes her tea."

Meri braced herself against the counter and

tilted her head up toward the ceiling. "I told them I don't want to go home. As far as I'm concerned, my brother can go back to DIA for his precious red-eye."

"Your mother seems to think you had a different agreement."

Meri blew out heavy breath. "Can't I just go with you now? I can make up their beds or something."

Nolan covered Meri's hand on the counter. "Ninety-five percent of me wants to say yes."

"But that stupid five percent makes you determined that I'm going to talk to my parents."

"It's the *right* five percent."

"What if I decided I don't want to?"

"You're strong, Meri. They're here, and so are you. That in itself is an accomplishment."

"It feels like a punishment."

"But you're coming to my house for dinner!"

"Plying me with food again. Are you going to sing?"

"Would you like me to?"

"I haven't decided."

"Text me! I'll review my repertoire."

Meri's phone sounded an alert. "Pru. She says call if I want to talk. She's off tonight."

"Then take her up on it," Nolan said.

The kitchen door swung open, and Leo carried in the empty coffee carafe. "Everything okay in here?"

Nolan shook a finger at him. "You, my friend, must be on your very best behavior. None of this business where you start in on one of those stories that trap people with their own manners and then bore everyone to death."

"Who, me?"

"Quintessential innkeeper, Leo. This is important. And Nia can't have a bad afternoon either. Not today. She cannot let the Davieses get under her skin."

Leo saluted. "I think she's doing rather well."

The kettle whistled. Meri snatched it off the stove and filled the mug.

"It's a nice afternoon for a walk," Leo said. "Maybe your family would like to wander downtown to stretch their legs after traveling so long."

"Good idea," Nolan said. "A little distraction from mission impossible can't hurt—as long as you go along. Remember, someone is always with Meri."

Nolan set a spirited pace home, which Jillian matched.

"You start on getting a couple of rooms ready," he said, "while I go to the grocery store for fixings for a fancy dinner. And breakfast. Surely they can manage sharing the hall bath, don't you think?"

"I suppose," Jillian said, "but you have things backward. You do the rooms and I'll shop."

"But I'm cooking."

"But you never shop. You don't know how to shop. I know it's a disparate skill set to cook but not shop, but do we really have to have this particular conversation on this particular day? There's no telling what you'll come home with. I don't mind eating your inventive concoctions, but I'm not sure Meri would appreciate your experimenting on her parents."

"Okay, Silly Jilly, you've made your point."

"So come up with actual recipes and make me an actual list while I try to come up with actual matching clean linens."

"There's a reason you're in charge of things like this."

"For sure."

"I've been thinking about some new sushi combinations I'd like to try."

"Dad."

"Nepali cuisine?"

"Try again."

"You're saying stick to something I know I can do well."

"Bingo."

"Italian or Irish it is."

"Something nice but not outrageous. Right down the center lane, please."

"How about Italian sausage with an orecchiette pasta in a garlic wine sauce with spinach and grape tomatoes swimming in lemon butter and a baked crust of parmesan cheese."

"Something like that, yes. I'll set a fancy table with all Mom's best stuff."

"We'll have to buy a cheesecake. No time to make one."

"I'll swing by Ben's and see what he has."

"Then get the bread while you're there. And fixings for salad—an interesting one."

"A list, Dad."

"Right." Nolan pushed his key into the back door and set to his assigned task while Jillian scampered up the stairs to the linen closet. Her footsteps told him she was leaving clean sheets in the two bedrooms that spanned the front of the house. His master suite and office were on one side, and Jillian's room and bath were on the other.

Ten minutes later, she flew out the back door with a list, and Nolan set the oven to preheat and arranged his pots and mixing bowls in the kitchen before going upstairs to do the beds.

Forty minutes after that, Jillian was back with groceries, baked goods, and cheesecake. Nolan set to work in the kitchen while she spiffed up the hall bath and started on the dining room table.

Twenty minutes after that, Nolan's phone sounded an alert, a text from Nia.

GETTING CLOSE? BACK FROM THEIR WALK. THE BROTHER IS A PIECE OF WORK. MERI IS ANTSY.

Nolan punched a button to answer.

NEED 30 MINUTES. THEN SEND THEM OVER.

Either Nia or Meri couldn't wait that long. Twenty-two minutes later, the doorbell rang. The dining room table looked fabulous. Jillian was upstairs putting herself together. Nolan checked his shirt to be sure he hadn't spattered it with sauce, raked a hand through his hair without benefit of a mirror, and answered the front door.

He intended his smile to be real even if the Davieses had plastered theirs on.

CHAPTER TWENTY-SIX

Memphis, October 6, 1878

The boat's in, and they've started unloading." Sister Hughetta's voice showed no hint of her weeks of illness even at barely seven in the morning.

"I have the wagon nearly hitched." Eliza drew the back of her hand across her forehead and resisted the urge to wipe the perspiration on her skirt. The temperature was not yet beastly, but the effort of uniting two horses and the largest wagon she could barter for the day still taxed her skills.

"You should have asked for help." Sister Hughetta reached in and grasped the hitch with both hands. Between the two of them, they made sure it was secure. The wagon would be far heavier on the return journey. "I keep telling you that I can go down to the dock."

"I know." Eliza brushed dust off her skirt. "I wish we could both go. I wish we could take two wagons. But . . ."

"It's not fair." Sister Hughetta's voice cracked. "Sister Frances was already sick. She got well. She took care of so many children. Wasn't it enough that she saw so many of them carted away in coffins—in wagons just like this one? Did she have to have the fever after all?"

Eliza squeezed the nun's hand, silent. Sister Frances's death two days ago had stunned them all. She had never truly regained her strength after her first illness. None of this was fair. Eliza had given up expecting an epidemic to conform to any predictability beyond spreading wildly, much less that it should strike only those who in some manner deserved it.

No one deserved it.

"I can manage at the dock," Eliza said. "You are much more knowledgeable and experienced with the patients. If one of us is to stay behind and manage what the morning will bring when the notes start coming in and the nurses report, it should be you."

"Do not bring back any more double-lined gloves donated by well-meaning souls in Minnesota," Sister Hughetta said.

"I shall do my best to refuse unsorted barrels rolled in my direction." Eliza reached into the wagon bed and lifted an iron rod with a flattened end.

Sister Hughetta gasped. "You plan to open them?"

"If I must."

"Can you manage it?"

"I have hired the Heard boys. Fifteen and sixteen years old."

"During the war they would have been considered men of age to fight."

Eliza nodded. "They've done well looking after the horses. I am certain they can pry open a sealed barrel and lift only the goods I select into the wagon."

"They are good boys," Sister Hughetta said. "Church every Sunday all their lives, even after their mother died in the last epidemic."

"Thanks be to God their father recovered in this one." Eliza moved toward the wagon bench. "I must go."

"But you haven't had breakfast."

"No time." Eliza hiked up her skirt and climbed to the bench to take up the reins. There was little traffic in the streets of Memphis these days. It wouldn't matter that she had never before guided a wagon of this size.

Gerald and Buntyn Heard were waiting for her outside the narrow house where they lived with their father.

"Would you like me to drive, Miz Eliza?" Gerald said.

For a fraction of a second Eliza considered surrendering the reins. It would be a relief not to be physically responsible, in this moment, for the ragged clatter and sway of the wagon.

"Nonsense," she said. "Just climb in and let's get going."

Buntyn jumped into the empty bed. Perhaps still unpersuaded of Eliza's abilities, Gerald sat beside her on the bench.

"Do you know the way?" Gerald asked.

"Yes, of course." Not precisely, but close enough. The river was only in one direction, after all. Not many ships were in the harbor these days, and the *John M. Chambers* from St. Louis would be flying a yellow flag as dismal warning of its mission. It would be the only one where anyone was lined up to collect supplies.

Eliza's fruitless search for Hank and Robert had taught her something of the streets between her more familiar neighborhood, which she saw little of now, and the docks. Now her eyes roamed for Callie. How was it that she knew nothing more about where Callie lived than Hank and Robert? Callie hadn't been one of the family's slaves before the war, but she'd been the first to hire on for paid domestic service afterward, when Eliza's parents finally reconciled their past with what the future demanded of them and offered a wage. Callie served faithfully ever since, thirteen years, with a half day off each week and her turn for a brief leave in the summer, which was more generous than most households offered.

Yet Eliza didn't know where to look for Callie

now. It simply hadn't been information suitable to know. At least that is what her mother would say. One did not cross that line, not after the war, not with servants who chose to live out. Whatever regard you might develop for them, or they for you, they did not owe you explanations.

That was before this despicable epidemic. Eliza yanked on the reins, making the most slovenly left turn since the day she first handled a team.

"Miz Eliza?" Gerald gripped the bench.

"Pa says don't ask questions," Buntyn said from behind them.

"It's all right," Eliza said. "I'm looking for someone and thought we might be in the right neighborhood."

"What about the ship?" Gerald said.

"They'll be unloading for hours."

"Isn't this where the colored folks live?"

Buntyn punched his brother's shoulder.

Eliza set her jaw and swallowed. "I'm looking for my housekeeper."

"Is she sick?"

"That is what I would like to ascertain." *Is she alive?*

"Don't you know where she lives?"

Buntyn punched his brother again. "Pa would not like this."

"You are right," Eliza said. "I only asked his permission to take you with me to the dock."

"I didn't mean like that, Miz Eliza," Buntyn

295

said. "I meant Gerald's questions. It's not polite. Pa's always telling him that. He lowers his voice and says, 'Geraldous.' "

Now it was Gerald's turn to punch. "Don't call me that."

"It's your right Christian name."

Eliza eyed Gerald, who for the moment contained his stream of questions, and reined the rig to a stop and set the brake. "You stay with the wagon. I'll be right back." For good measure, in case the horses decided to resist the brake, she handed Gerald the reins.

She dismounted and stared at the house she'd parked in front of, feeling as though all the sermons she'd ever heard about listening to the promptings of the Holy Spirit were gurgling inside her. Is that what had led her here, to this place in this moment? Is that what had made her choose this street, and this house?

One might never be certain, but one must act nevertheless.

Eliza knocked on the door and made her inquiry. The woman in the threshold only narrowed her eyes and shook her head, not recognizing Callie's name or the description Eliza offered. When the door closed softly and courteously though, Eliza could not shake the sensation that had brought her—or *might* have. She surveyed the neighborhood, praying for direction with each inhalation and exhalation.

Callie. Lord, where is Callie? Show me who knows.

She waved to the Heard boys and chose another house.

"Not far from here," was the response this time.

Eliza's heart leaped.

A few blocks down. One turn, and then another. A small house set back behind another.

After profuse thanks, Eliza hastened back to the rig and took back the reins.

"Miz Eliza?"

"Yes, Gerald?"

"Aren't we going too fast?"

"Not fast enough." Eliza slowed the speed not at all.

A few blocks down. One turn, and then another. She found the house that matched the description exactly and raced toward the door.

"Miz Eliza?"

"No, Gerald," she said without looking over her shoulder, "you can't come. Wait in the wagon."

She could not know what was on the other side of the door when she knocked firmly.

No answer.

Another knock.

No answer. But the stench from within was undeniable.

Eliza raised a sleeve to cover her nose and turned the knob. The door gave and opened to empty, shrouded darkness.

She checked the small room at the back of the house. Empty, the beds stripped. If Callie and her family had ever been there, they had not survived. As Eliza hurried back to outside air, she chose to believe it was the wrong house, that the young woman who gave the directions had the wrong family in mind—anything but that Callie was gone. Her sister. Her sister's husband. The girls. The little boy who was the darling of them all. Callie. Eliza hadn't met the rest of the family, but she'd seen the smiles at the corners of Callie's lips and the shine in her eyes when she spoke of them.

They can't be gone.

She would inquire at the Board of Health. Surely they were keeping a list of the names of the dead—at least the ones they could identify.

"Let's go, boys." Eliza climbed back into the wagon. "We have work to do."

"Miz Eliza?"

"Yes, Gerald." She could not help her sigh.

"What happened in there?"

"It was the wrong house after all."

"Are you sure?"

Buntyn jabbed.

"I'm just trying to help. You look upset."

"Thank you, Gerald," Eliza said. "You will have plenty of opportunity to help in just a few minutes. We're almost to the dock."

As they approached the *John M. Chambers*,

Eliza had only to look for the glut of wagons in order to determine where to try to tie up her rig. She took both boys with her to a makeshift check-in area, where she stood in line to establish her credentials with the Citizens Relief Committee. The committee might have intended a more organized method of distributing goods, perhaps over a period of days rather than hours, but every organization involved in relief efforts seemed represented on the dock and ready to leave with at least some goods. More could come later if necessary, but it was common knowledge that the ship's captain intended to unload quickly and get out of port with minimal exposure to the diseased city. A man in a worn gray suit with matching worn gray eyes pointed to two dozen barrels already off-loaded and turned a sheet of paper toward Eliza to sign.

The Heard boys moved toward the barrels. Eliza grabbed Buntyn's arm, and they stopped.

"What do these barrels contain?" Eliza asked the man, with no intention of blindly signing for items she could not use.

"Relief goods."

"Might you be more specific?"

"I'm afraid not."

"Are the barrels not marked?"

The man cocked his head. "I was not responsible for the state of the ship's goods at the point of departure."

Eliza said, "I have a list of what we need most." Mattresses, pillows, grits, potatoes, soap, blankets, sheeting, clothing, sugar, coffee, bacon, canned beef.

"We have what we have," the man said. "We've hardly had time to see what it is ourselves before the deluge began."

"There must be a ship's manifest. Some sort of inventory."

"We are very busy. Surely anything will be helpful."

"No matter. We'll find what we need," Eliza said. "Gerald, we are going to need the tools from the back of the wagon to open these barrels."

"Is that allowed, Miz Eliza?"

"I am allowing it," Eliza said. She turned to the man at the desk. "I will be sure to inform you what we leave with so you can update your own records accordingly."

"That is not our system."

"Today it is my system. Gerald, go."

Gerald dashed off toward the wagon, and Eliza and Buntyn circled the barrels. For most of her life, her experience with barrels was limited to watching them go by in the back of a wagon on the way to a mercantile or grocer's. She never thought much about what was in them. When she shopped, the goods were already sorted and on the shelves. Eliza shoved one of the barrels for a sense of its weight and what the boys would be up against in transporting them to the wagon—should she decide to accept the contents. It was unforgiving. But the boys were strong, and the barrels would roll.

What was taking Geraldous so long? Eliza glanced up.

A willowy dark form in a blue calico dress slid into a slit in the crowd.

Callie.

"Wait right here," she said to Buntyn. "When your brother is back, do not move. Do you understand?"

Buntyn nodded. He was the one she could trust to follow instructions without questions.

Eliza raised her hem enough to free her steps and chased the blue calico, diving into the throng of goods seekers and dodging dockworkers and rising mountains of crates and barrels.

"Callie!" she called. But the woman did not turn.

Her quest demanded Eliza abandon usual measures of courtesy as she pushed through without apologies to the people whose shoulders she knocked or toes she pinched under her steps.

Finally she had the woman's elbow in her grasp. "Callie."

The figure turned. The face was not Callie's. The form and dress were so similar, even the hair and hat, but the features were nothing like Callie's.

"My deepest apologies," Eliza muttered. "I was mistaken."

She allowed herself to close her eyes in disappointment for the four seconds it took to inhale deeply, exhale sharply, and reset her mind to the purpose of this outing.

The boys. The barrels. The goods for St. Mary's.

She spotted a crate of mattresses and insisted that they must have some. Pillows were in heavy demand, and she did not get many. She did indeed open the unmarked barrels and choose what she believed would be helpful. Two were full of potatoes, and she directed the boys to roll them directly to the wagon. In the end she accepted four barrels of unsorted clothing, knowing some of it would be frivolous or useless to the climate. But she returned to St. Mary's with most of the items on her list and a few she had not expected.

But no Callie.

CHAPTER TWENTY-SEVEN

It worked.

At least, sort of. Every minute was awkward, in Jillian's opinion, but her father was unflappable. The fine china and candlelight conjured an elegant atmosphere where voices did not rise and manners were observed. If Saturday's dinner conversation strayed into territory deemed in the off-limits "sleep on it agreement" zone, Nolan deftly raised another topic.

Cuisine.

Travel.

Music.

Books.

Architecture.

There was plenty to talk about that did not violate the Davies Family Peace Accord. After dinner, Nolan led the guests through a full tour of the home, complete with a running narrative of its history as two joined cottages with mirroring floor plans and answering questions amiably to the best of his ability. By the time he walked Meri back to the Inn, leaving Jillian to settle the guests into their rooms, the mood was civil if not genuinely calm.

Jillian waited for Nolan on the front porch.

"Well?" He sat on the double-wide wicker chair beside her. "Do you think they got a taste of being in the same room without railroading each other?"

"What happens tomorrow, Dad?"

"I make omelets to order, and you play the role of barista."

"And Meri?"

"She's not coming for breakfast. The Inn is full up, remember?"

"Ah, sneaky. She's working."

"My take is the Davieses will not storm over there and make a scene in front of guests over breakfast. We can invite them to church or suggest a half-day outing they might enjoy. Then we'll do a late lunch."

"Here?"

Nolan nodded.

"And you will officially go into mediator mode."

"Perhaps more clandestinely than officially, but yes."

Jillian stood up. "I've got some things to do in my office."

"Still determined to finish that report today?"

"No. I want to look into some census records before I call in some genealogical reinforcements. Canny is a loose cannon. We're running out of time."

Jillian returned to the yellow legal pad she'd

left in front of her computer hours ago and logged into the 1940 census. A useful feature of the 1940 census was that, because of mobility during the Great Depression, the questions asked also included where people resided in 1935. That might tell her where to go in the 1930 census, and she would work backward from there. Unlike Dr. Juliette Mathers, she had no rule against late-night caffeine, especially when she expected to be at this task for several hours. Her hunch said she was going to end up in Memphis at Canfield Asylum, but she needed a more solid trail before prevailing on someone in Memphis to get eyes on the real evidence—if it even existed anymore.

She flipped the yellow legal sheets as she filled them with notes deep into the night.

In the morning when Jillian dragged down the back stairs after a few hours of sleep, she heard her dad's rattling preparations before she reached the bottom step. Nolan had omelet ingredients lined up on the breakfast bar: a bowl of beaten eggs, chopped onions, green and red peppers, mushrooms, black olives, fresh spinach, swiss and cheddar cheese, and crumbled bacon. The omelet pans were warmed, buttered, and ready to go. Honey-wheat bread from Ben's Bakery was sliced and ready to toast. The kitchen nook table was set with stoneware, and the bright color of a clear glass pitcher of orange juice beckoned guests. Wiping sleep from her eyes, Jillian took up her position beside her barista machines before the first of the Davieses turned up in the kitchen.

"You've changed your clothes and done your hair differently," Nolan said, "so I assume you didn't spend the entire night in your office."

"I'll never get that sleep back," Jillian said, "but it was worth it. I found Meri's grandfather—and the 'Canfield' of his generation. It's a sad story."

Juliette's heels clicked against the hardwood floor of the hall as she came through the open door. "Good morning. Michael and Canny will be down soon. How gracious of you to plan another feast for us this morning."

"I hope you're hungry." Nolan gestured to the omelet bar options.

"My goodness. And that looks like more than an ordinary coffeepot."

Jillian picked up a large empty stoneware mug matching the table dishes. "It would be my pleasure to serve as your barista this morning."

Juliette glanced over her shoulder. "Quick, before Michael comes down with his speech about black coffee! I'd love a creamy latte, extra hot if possible."

"Whipped cream?"

"You can do that?"

"But of course. Perhaps a hint of semisweet chocolate shavings to top it off?"

"That does sound magnificent."

"And how would madam like her omelet?" Nolan picked up the bowl of beaten eggs.

Breakfast went smoothly—with no mention of Meri. *Weird,* Jillian thought, *but perhaps for the best.* Canny passed on going to church, claiming he had a hundred emails to answer, and went straight up to his room, but Michael and Juliette accepted the invitation—again without asking if Meri might be there. Perhaps not mentioning her was part of the "sleep on it" agreement. Nia and Leo were there, which meant it was Meri's turn to stay on duty at the Inn. After church, Nolan dropped Juliette and Michael about a mile and a half down Main Street with the assurance that most of the shops would be open on Sunday afternoon, and people were known to get lost in the Victorium Emporium or go into sugar comas in the candy store or ice cream parlor. Lunch, and Meri, would be waiting for them when they made their way back to the house, whenever that was.

Lunch was a hearty Irish lamb stew, with carrots and potatoes and garnished with chives, parsley, thyme, and bay leaf. They were in the dining room again, eating from a collection of eclectic shallow bowls Jillian's mother had enjoyed collecting over the years, some as long ago as before Jillian was born and some only weeks before her death. For a man who couldn't understand how the aisles of a grocery store were organized and filled a cart strictly on the impulse method, her father certainly had discovered his flair for cooking out of the necessity of feeding his motherless child.

Jillian and her father sat at opposite ends of the table. Michael and Juliette were beside each other on one side, and their son and daughter across from them.

"Nolan has a family blessing he says at meals," Meri said. "Let me see if I get it right."

"You want to say my Irish blessing?" Nolan raised that free-spirited eyebrow.

"I want to try."

"Go for it."

"May you always find nourishment for your body at the table," Meri said. "May sustenance for your spirit rise and fill you with each dawn. And may life always feed you with the light of joy along the way."

"Well done!" Nolan clapped three times. "You shall have the first of the stew."

"I've never heard that one," Juliette said.

"His grandmother made it up," Meri said.

"That's the best kind," Michael said. "My grandfather used to be full of pithy wisdom. I remember hanging on his every word."

Nolan filled bowls with stew, and the bread basket made its way around the table.

"My father used to send me to spend summers

with my grandfather, out in sharecropping rural Georgia," Michael said.

"But Grandpa Thomas was from Chattanooga." Meri's head tilted.

"Later on he was. But he started out in practice with his father, in Meriwether County, Georgia."

Meri's head dropped forward. "I'm named for a county?"

"You're named for my happy childhood," Michael said, "and for the summers I spent at my grandfather's side learning the art of medicine long before proving myself worthy for the white man's world of medical school and making sure my children could go to any medical school they chose."

Jillian scanned the table for reactions.

Meri froze.

Juliette pushed food around in her bowl.

Canny nodded approvingly and helped himself to more bread.

Michael met Nolan's affable gaze with a challenge. Enough of playing around Canyon Mines. Enough of avoiding the real reason they were gathered around this table.

Nolan was unfazed. "Meri tells us there is a Canfield in every generation of your family. Did you know Jillian is a genealogist? She finds these things fascinating."

"That's true," Jillian said. "A name and a birth date can uncover a wealth of information in a family tree. I understand you are the Canfield in your generation. Your father must have had a brother?"

Michael nodded. "Died in infancy though."

Jillian already knew this. Thomas's eldest brother, bearing the legacy name, was listed in the 1930 census—just barely—and then disappeared.

"My brother Seamus got the family name," Nolan said. "He wasn't fond of it as a kid. People don't always know how to pronounce it when they see it or spell it when they hear it. But now I think he's glad to have it, because it was my father's name as well."

Jillian stifled a smile as Canny flashed Nolan a look that said he couldn't possibly understand the weight of a difficult name. Would he have a less overbearing personality if he were called Rob or Steve or Trevor? And how about Pru, the sister in between Canny and Meri? Was her residency schedule the only reason that kept her out of this family confrontation, or did the middle child simply have less of a penchant for family drama?

"My grandfather was the first Canfield Davies," Michael said. "I'm sure it broke his heart to lose his son, but he would be so delighted that my son both bears his name and the profession he gave his life to."

"Was he the first doctor in your family?" Jillian asked.

"His father was also a physician, Dr. Samuel

Davies, no small accomplishment for a child born to former slaves."

Jillian debated whether to bring up Canfield Asylum. If Meri mentioned it, she would elaborate. Otherwise, she'd prefer to have more evidence of a connection. So many African Americans hit a wall when they researched their family lines precisely because slave records were incomplete or last names were absent or shifted or birth dates were unknown. Martha Canfield of Ohio wasn't a slave owner, but she couldn't have been the only Canfield in the South after the Civil War. Jillian needed more to substantiate her theory.

Canny was finished wolfing down his meal and pushed his bowl toward the center of the table.

"We slept on it," he said, "and you all had a nice stroll down memory lane. It's time we dealt with the matter at hand."

"What Canny means," Juliette said, "is that we so appreciate your hospitality, but the weekend is coming to a close, so we should be making our plans for returning to Denver, and Meri will need some time to gather her things before we go."

Meri clinked her spoon in her bowl, reached for her water glass, and swallowed half its contents. "I understand that you all have responsibilities to get back to, but I won't be leaving with you."

Juliette and Michael exchanged glances.

"We can make some calls," Michael said. "Your

311

mother doesn't have any surgeries tomorrow, and we understand you may feel you need another day to make arrangements with your employer."

"Nia," Meri said. "Nia and Leo."

"Yes, of course." Juliette gestured toward Nolan. "If we can prevail on our generous hosts, we can stay another night and arrange to go home tomorrow."

"Of course you can stay," Nolan said.

"The dean has agreed to take you back, Meriwether," Michael said. "On probation, of course. There is no getting around that. But he recognizes your potential and is confident a student of your caliber can make up the work you missed the last two weeks. But if the absence becomes prolonged, you may have to wait and begin the entire year again next fall."

"That would be a shame," Juliette said, "considering that it's only October. Losing an entire academic year is quite a setback."

"And totally unnecessary," Canny said.

Jillian looked from Meri to Nolan, who flashed five fingers before deftly starting the bread basket on another cycle around the table.

"So this is the reasonable manner in which we agreed we were going to talk?" Meri pushed her chair back. "You all very sweetly—well, Canny doesn't know how to be sweet to save his life—you all tell me what arrangements and decisions you've already made about my life and offer the gracious concession that I might want one more day to get on board?"

"Now, Meriwether," Michael said, "we have your best interest at heart. We don't want you to be rash and make a mistake you'll regret."

Meri stood up and replaced her chair neatly under the table. "I don't intend to do that either, Dad. But I'm not going back to med school. In fact, I'm not going back to Tennessee. Nolan, thank you for another lovely meal. I'm sorry I can't stay to help clean up."

CHAPTER TWENTY-EIGHT

"I'll go." Nolan held up both hands, momentarily paralyzing the three members of the Davies family.

"What gives you the right?" Canny demanded, on his feet.

"I've earned her trust. And frankly, you're not helping matters."

"Excuse me?"

"Meri needs her family to hear her. I'd like to try again to make that happen. So I'm going after her, and I suggest the three of you help Jillian clear the dishes and clean up the kitchen."

Juliette tucked a stray gray hair back where it belonged. "If you think that will be helpful, of course we will wait for you to bring Meri back. Then we'll see."

"I didn't say I would bring her back," Nolan said. "I'm going to talk with her, and then I'll come back and talk with you."

"You can't believe she's serious about dropping out of medical school," Canny said.

"It's not my job to speak for Meri," Nolan said. "But I have some experience in these things, and I do know when parties at the table are talking past one another, and I want to help you with that."

"This is a family matter," Michael said.

"I suggest you all make the necessary phone calls to extend your stay in Canyon Mines."

"Impossible," Canny said.

"Imperative," Nolan said.

"You're over the line."

Nolan headed toward the front door.

Jillian followed him out to the porch. "Dad!"

"I'll be back as soon as I can," he said.

She followed him down the steps. "What am I supposed to do?"

"Well, you can do the dishes, or I'll do them when I get back."

"I mean about *them,* Dad." Jillian trailed him a few strides along the sidewalk.

"Jilly, I'll be back as soon as I can. I want to do what I can to make sure Meri will still be in town in the morning." Meri remained within sight but was moving fast, and Nolan wasn't about to lose her.

Jillian stopped. "You're right. Go."

Seven minutes racing behind Meri to the Inn, twelve minutes calming her, seven minutes extracting a strategy from Nia and Leo to do their best to keep her engaged and away from her car, and ten minutes power walking back home at a less breathless pace.

Thirty-six minutes during which the Davieses could have done who knows what.

But the black SUV was still parked in front.

Canny was out of sight, probably in his room. Michael was at the cleared dining room table with a lone mug of coffee. Juliette sat at the breakfast bar watching Jillian wipe down the kitchen counters while the dishwasher hummed at the beginning of its cycle.

He caught Jillian's eye and let out a slow, soundless sigh. "I didn't get my afternoon coffee."

"I'll fix it." Jillian moved toward the coffee machines.

"How is she?" Juliette twisted toward him on her stool.

"She's all right." Nolan put a hand on Juliette's shoulder. "If she were here, she'd make you a cup of herbal tea with honey."

"I don't know what to do."

"Then I'll put the kettle on."

Juliette Mathers was a thoracic surgeon, adjunct medical faculty, and published scholar. And a mother who honestly did not know the next right thing to do. At least one person in the family who could admit this was a place to start.

At dinnertime—late, after a late lunch and upsetting afternoon—Canny said he wanted to go out, and Nolan made several restaurant recommendations. As soon as they were out the door, he pulled out his phone.

"Nia? Meri needs to not be home for the next couple of hours."

"We've already eaten, but I'll get her out."

"Someplace out of town. Right now."

"I'm on it."

"Tell Leo this is a good time for one of his distracting tall tales if the opportunity arises. The complete history of American woodworking legends would do nicely."

Nia's laughter rang so loud Nolan had to hold the phone at arm's length.

Nolan and Jillian ate leftovers of last night's pasta and Italian sausage and connived for the morning.

"I have to find Samuel Davies," Jillian said. "Overnight. It will be practically impossible, Dad."

"Practically."

"It's a figure of speech. You never know what you'll stumble onto, but I'd have to get really lucky. Maybe he would turn up in a 1900 census, but where do I start looking? I have to at least have a county, if not an enumeration district."

"Memphis. Aren't you looking for Canfield Asylum there?"

"They closed in 1885. The biggest population Canfield ever had was during the 1878 yellow fever outbreak when dozens of children were orphaned and sent there. I can't imagine I can find records of the children from so long ago. Adoptions weren't always formal, especially placing black children. They just needed someplace to

317

live because their families were deceased. And if he was at Canfield and was later formally adopted, his name would have changed at some point."

"Jilly, we may not have past the morning."

"She's not going to go home with them."

Nolan shook his head. "But if there's any hope of healing the wound in their family, this is where they will find safe haven together."

Jillian put her plate in the sink. "Then I'm going to need more coffee. And don't give me any of your baloney about decaf."

A moment later, one of Jillian's machines whirred and she carried a large mug into her office. Nolan went into the living room and crossed to the far end the family had always used as a cozy TV corner. But he didn't turn on the television. He needed to hear every approaching sound. He picked up a book and settled in, and the Davieses found him there when they came in from their dinner. A long dinner. Long enough that they might have gone looking for Meri and run into Leo's history lesson or long enough that they'd spent it strategizing what their next move would be. Or both. Nolan didn't ask.

They exchanged pleasantries, Nolan locked up, said good night to Jillian in her office, and trailed up the stairs that ran through the center of the house, beginning from both the front and the back and meeting on a landing halfway up. He took the time for one short text.

CLEAR TO BRING MERI HOME.

Nolan listened for the sounds that the house-guests had settled in and allowed himself to drift to sleep.

He woke to find Jillian hovering over him. Startled, he said, "What time is it?"

"Late enough that I hoped you'd be up," she said. "I couldn't wait any longer."

He sat up and glanced at the clock. "Breakfast. And I have to cancel my whole day in Denver."

"Dad, I have something."

He swung his feet over the side of the bed and rubbed his eyes. "Did you sleep at all?"

"A nap between three and four. But I got into some black holes of the internet about midnight and ended up waking up a contact in Memphis in the middle of the night."

"How to win friends and influence people."

"She knows she could call me if she needed to."

"She also knows something about Canfield, this contact?"

"She has access to local historical records. Scraps of records, really."

"And?"

"She has a key to the building where she works, and she went in at four in the morning for me."

"And?"

"Pretty sure I know something I doubt the Davieses do."

"Then get ready to tell it." Nolan was on his feet and headed toward the closet. "And do *not* let any of them leave the house."

"Where are you going?"

"Based on Meri's mood last night, I think she will require some persuading to return to the negotiating table."

"Because she didn't see any evidence of negotiating yesterday."

"Call Nia and tell her I'm on my way. Make sure Meri is actually still there."

Jillian left the room with her phone already at her ear. Nolan pulled khakis and a polo shirt from his closet, slid his feet into loafers, and grabbed his jacket on his way out the back door. At the Inn, he went straight to the kitchen entrance. Leo saw him and waved him in.

"I don't have anything to say to them." Meri turned to the sink, where a couple of pots awaited washing. "I made myself perfectly clear last night. You wanted me to stand up to them, and I did."

"Yes, you did." Nolan leaned against the counter. "What if I said Jillian found something in your family history that you'll all want to hear?"

Meri's hands in the sink stilled.

"Don't you want to know?" Nia asked. "After all this, don't you want to hear it?"

Meri started scrubbing. "She can tell me after they're gone. I'll still be here."

"Maybe they need to know too," Nia said.

Meri threw her scrubbing pad into soapy water and swatted at the resulting splash. "You people are impossible."

In the kitchen at home, Jillian wilted around the edges at the sight of both Nolan and Meri. He looked over her shoulder. She'd managed a credible batter for buckwheat pancakes—learned from so many Saturday mornings together—and set out a cantaloupe and bananas Nolan didn't know they had.

Jillian let the whisk rest against the side of the batter bowl. "I'm glad you came, Meri."

Meri's arms crossed over her midsection, hands grasping elbows. "I've already had breakfast. I eat before serving the guests."

"Of course you do," Nolan said. "But let Jillian whip you up a fancy coffee."

"I heard movement upstairs," Jillian said. "I have a feeling everyone will be down soon. What kind of coffee would you like? My dad can take over cooking pancakes. Right?"

"A perfect plan." Nolan turned on the griddle in the center of the stove top.

"Shall we eat in the dining room?" Jillian said. "More comfortable for six people."

"An even more perfect plan."

Jillian turned to her barista duties.

"Uh-oh." Meri stiffened.

Three sets of footsteps descended the back stairs, not in a straggling-to-breakfast fashion but a coordinated, united effort that would dump them into the kitchen.

"Good morning." Nolan dropped the first splashes of batter on the hot griddle.

Technically Michael, Juliette, and Canny had broken the boundary and entered the kitchen, but they stopped there.

"Come on in," Nolan said. "Breakfast is almost ready. Jillian has the coffee grounds out."

"Good morning." Canny glanced toward Meri. "Good. You're here. I hope Nolan hasn't gone to too much trouble over breakfast, because we're in a bit of a hurry."

"You're leaving after all?" Meri said.

"You too," Canny said. "I just booked four tickets. We leave DIA in four hours."

Jillian handed Meri her mug of coffee, which she gripped with both hands.

"I think that's for the best," Michael said. "We have prevailed on Nolan and Jillian long enough and staying further will not change the ultimate outcome."

"Dad!" Meri said. "This is not some clinical treatment plan."

Nolan flipped the pancakes.

"This seems harsh right now," Michael said, "but later you will look back on all this as a blip.

No one will ever remember it happened. Your brother understands the pressures of med school. We all do. We're here to help."

The longer Michael spoke, the less Meri looked at him.

"Canny, I hope you can get a refund," Meri said, "because you only need three tickets."

"Actually, you will only need two." Juliette spoke for the first time.

"Mother?" Canny spun on one heel.

"It's time we heard Meri out." Juliette slipped past her son, out of the border zone and into the kitchen. "If she came all these miles to get away from us, after obviously going out of her way to get thrown out of medical school—and to this place of all places—what will it hurt to listen to what she wants to tell us? I, for one, would like to know."

Nolan wanted to throw Juliette a big sloppy kiss clear across the kitchen. For ten seconds, the Davies men stood in stunned silence.

Then Canny erupted. "We talked about this, Mother. The three of us discussed this and agreed that the best way to support Meri is to help her get back on the plan."

Ah. So last night had been a strategy session.

"I'm standing right here, Canny," Meri said. "It's *my* life the three of you are making decisions about."

"If you don't mind, Canfield, I'd like some

breakfast." Juliette eased into the corner seat of the nook. "Meri, why don't you bring your coffee to the table and sit with me."

Nolan grinned and slid the first three pancakes onto a plate and set it in front of Juliette at the kitchen table after all. He stood ready to pour fresh batter onto the griddle.

"Canny, do you want the next batch?"

"None for me, thank you." Canny's civil words answered Nolan's question, but his frigid tone hurled arrows at his mother as she dotted her pancakes with butter.

Jillian handed her a bottle of maple syrup.

"I'm going upstairs to pack," Canny said.

"I'm right behind you," Michael said.

Nolan made more pancakes, and Jillian sliced fruit. But in under fifteen minutes Canfield and Michael thumped back down the front stairs with their bags.

Nolan followed Juliette's gaze. From her corner spot at the kitchen table, Juliette could see straight through the house to the main entryway. Her face twitched. Michael had her bag and briefcase as well as his own. The resolve she'd mustered was already crumbling.

CHAPTER TWENTY-NINE

Memphis, October 17, 1878

When this madness ended and it was safe for her parents to come home, perhaps it would be Eliza who drove them around Memphis. Wherever the household staff had scattered to during their weeks of unexpected extended leave in August, by now any not with her parents in Wisconsin would have sought other work. And who could blame them? They needed wages, and they might not have any surviving reason to return to Memphis, their own friends and family afflicted and buried unceremoniously. Eliza had no way to know how widely the epidemic would affect the household staff social circles.

Eliza had become quite accustomed to driving her own carriage. With the help of the Heard boys, she had learned how to put the top down so that when one of them traveled with her on her rounds to help deliver groceries to households struck by illness they could be in the open air. And keeping the top down made getting everything in and out so much more efficient during multiple trips back to St. Mary's during the day to restock supplies. She was fortunate to have the boys. Their father could not usually spare both of them, but he did his best to have one or the other at the disposal of St. Mary's for at least a few hours each day.

"The least I can do," he said on a daily basis, "for the nuns who saved my life and lost theirs."

The suffering of our Lord. Sister Constance's more theological framing of Mr. Heard's litany was ever in Eliza's mind as she turned the pages of her Bible and murmured prayers throughout the day. Compline in the chapel remained on the daily schedule of the Sisters House, but most evenings it was impossible to guarantee Sister Hughetta—the only surviving nun now—or Father Dalzell would be back from calling on the sick for even the briefest of spoken service.

Eliza stopped in front of her ninth house of the day after freshly reloading the carriage with jars of broth and tea, tins of meat, cans of milk, and sacks of sugar, beans, and potatoes.

"I can help," Gerald said, "if you just let me come in. My mama died, you know."

"I remember." The poor boy had a penchant for reminding her.

"We never had a woman to do for us. I can make tea and warm broth and clean up slop."

"I know you can, Gerald. But this is for your own good—and mine. Where would I be if you got sick and I was deprived of your able assistance with deliveries?"

"Then at least let me drive."

"I'll consider it." Eliza had, in fact, been considering it. If Gerald were driving, she could be looking at plans about the next visit or making notes about the visit just completed while the buggy was in motion. It would save time.

Armed with a basket of tinned meat, broth, tomatoes, and a bag of dried beans, she made her way toward the door of the call at hand. The notes from the nurse who had sat with the family during the worst of it indicated they had lost a grandmother and one small child, but six other household members had survived. They needed looking in on once a day to make sure they were eating and taking enough fluid, in the wake of both illness and heartbreak.

Eliza was relieved to find the windows open and the house reasonably aired out. No matter how many visits she made to homes closed up to contain the sick and dying, her stomach refused the odors that came with the task. The visceral reminder of the devastation itself fueled her compassion through her own exhaustion.

"Hello, Mrs. Fliggin. I'm from St. Mary's. I've come with some provisions and to see how I can make you more comfortable."

Mrs. Fliggin's dark hand let go of the door, and Eliza stepped aside.

From the beginning, St. Mary's was a parish that did not accept donations from members for preferential seating among the pews. It was open to any and all, and many of its worshippers were working-class people who served the same Lord Eliza did—people like Mr. Heard. The area immediately around the church was not home to colored families, but the penetrating dearth of nurses in the city and the augmenting range for which St. Mary's was responsible brought Eliza and her caregivers to homes they might not have visited two months ago.

Eliza reached for the woman's hand. "I am so very sorry for the loved ones you have lost."

"My mama," Mrs. Fliggin said, "and my baby. He would have been three next week."

Eliza did not try to make up words that would bring sense to tragedy. She only squeezed the woman's hand and looked into her eyes.

"My husband—his only son," Mrs. Fliggin said. "I don't know what to say to him."

Nor he to you. Nor I to either one of you.

"I've brought some ingredients that will make a nice hearty stew." Eliza spoke softly. The food would not fill the absences left in the family, but it might help get frail bodies through another day while their love for each other bound up their true wounds. The kitchen had clean water that would suffice both for the stew and for freshening the stair-step sisters. A rickety dresser held frayed but clean clothes, and Eliza swiftly wiped hands and faces and slipped fresh gowns over heads while waiting for the stew to come to a boil.

With meat and tomatoes coming from tins, it was hardly a true homemade stew, but what would Callie think to see Eliza mixing ingredients for a meal to feed a family?

"I kin manage," Mrs. Fliggin said. "With the food. I won't burn the beans, and I make sure the chillun eat."

"Make sure you eat as well."

"I try." Mrs. Fliggin rubbed her forehead. "I be so worried 'bout my friends."

"Have they been ill as well?"

"Mebbe. Dey were. At least Tillie was. I just don't know. Been too sick to pay a call. But I worry. Her lil Sammy is my boy's age. Just a few months older."

"Why don't you tell me how to find where they live," Eliza said. "I'll see if I can discover some information to put your mind at ease."

"You kin do that?"

"I will certainly try." Another slip of paper. Another call to squeeze into an overtaxed schedule. Another nurse to assign.

"Dey church friends, from where our people go. Tillie was sick, and I hear her sister—Callie, that would be—came to look after her. It wasn't the fever at first, but she was poorly. I wondered if it be another child. The fever came later. But I don't know. I ain't heard no more in so long."

Sammy. Tillie. *Callie.*

The names thudded into their slots.

"I would be happy to personally check on Tillie's family," Eliza said. "I can go right now. Where do they live?"

By the time Eliza got back to the carriage, she felt as if someone was using an iron tool to pry the top off the barrel of her head. She put the horse into motion.

"Miz Eliza, where are we going?"

In this moment, Eliza wished it was Buntyn beside her on the bench today rather than Geraldous and his incessant questions.

"Another call, of course."

"Aren't we going to see the Carters?"

"Yes. We will. I just . . . I have become aware of a situation that might be urgent." Eliza reached an intersection and hesitated, trying to remember Mrs. Fliggin's instructions for finding Tillie's home. She started to turn the carriage to the left and then jerked to the right instead—barely missing a coffin wagon lumbering through the corner.

"Miz Eliza!"

"Geraldous!"

He met her glare with a scowl. "You should stop and let me drive."

At least it was not a question. Eliza raised a hand to her splitting head. The day was not even warm, nor the sun bright enough to provoke such a physical complaint. Surely it was only the shock of suddenly having an address for Callie.

She handed the limp reins to Gerald, who ably guided the carriage clear of the intersection.

"I should take you back to the Sisters House, Miz Eliza," Gerald said.

"No." She grasped at the reins. If he was going to do that, she would not let him drive after all.

"Where is it you have a mind to go, Miz Eliza?"

She gave him an address, not certain she hadn't reversed the numbers of the house.

"Weren't we near there a couple of weeks ago?" Gerald said. "The day the ship came in?"

The day she found the empty house full of the stench of death. She pictured the humble structure.

A block away. Had they been only a block away?

They found the house. It was nothing like the one she'd been sent to the last time. At least now she had more reason to believe she was in the right place.

The home was closed up. Though they had not yet had a fall frost, and the daytime hours were pleasant, and the temperatures were dropping. A home might be closed against the fever or simply the changing weather.

"I'm coming in with you," Gerald said.

"You most certainly are not." The boy knew the rules. Eliza exited the carriage. Gerald got out as well, but he stood with the horse and did not follow.

The reek grew more overbearing with every step closer. Knocking on the door was a waste of time. Eliza pushed it open. While her eyes adjusted to the gray hues of the cloistered rooms, she heard only the whimper of a child from an indistinct direction. On a narrow bed in the front room, in nightgowns crusted with vomit, two young women—hardly more than girls—held hands. They did not move, and their eyes stared, unblinking at the ceiling.

Eliza's heart cracked. The dear girls whose mother feared they might fall in with the wrong crowd if they didn't stick together.

Her hand over her nose and mouth, Eliza allowed herself an audible sob. A whimper not her own rose and fell ephemerally, smothered by the sounds from her throat. She stifled herself to listen again.

Silence.

Two half-open doors led deeper into the house. She chose one.

A woman was on the bed and a man—her husband, no doubt—on the floor, collapsed in a posture that suggested his last act had been to reach for her hand.

Tillie. And the good man she'd married.

The cry came again, louder, from the other room.

Eliza held her head between her hands now, every movement threatening to cast her into the

332

abyss of pain. The curtain was open in the second bedroom, allowing in some daylight, and on the bed was the girls' aunt Callie.

Still and stone cold like the others. Who was the first to fall to the fever? The first to expire? The last one to be too weak to even scribble a new message on a bit of cardboard and affix it to the door asking for coffins? All of them gone.

The cry again.

No. Not all.

In the corner, on a small bed, half-hidden under a pile of clothing and damp sheets, was the boy.

The little one whose arrival had been such a surprise to Tillie and brought such joy to all the family. Three. He was three. And alone.

"Come here, Sammy."

The sound of his name brought his head out from under a pillowcase, and he stared at her with wide, dark eyes set in a narrow face not so different from his aunt's.

Eliza plucked the child out of the pile of clothing. His garments betrayed that he hadn't had anyone to take him to the privy in who knows how long, but he had none of the vomit that caked the others, and his skin was cool. His dark eyes mingled terror and hope.

Eliza stumbled out to the carriage, allowing Gerald to meet her halfway up the walk, steady her, and take the boy.

"You are ill, Miz Eliza," he said.

"Yes. Yes, I am."

"The fever?"

She did not answer, instead reaching for the safety of the carriage.

"My mama died from the fever," Gerald said yet again.

"But your daddy did not."

"I am taking you straight home. To the Sisters House, where someone can tend to you."

Eliza would have nodded if she had not feared the pain of the movement.

"You must promise me one thing, Geraldous."

"Miz Eliza?"

"This child shows no sign of illness. As soon as I exit the carriage, you must take him directly to Canfield Asylum."

CHAPTER THIRTY

Meri had set her coffee down and had one hand on the back door. Jillian abandoned her unrequested barista ministrations and crossed the room to stand next to her, wishing the old Victorian was fitted with a modern system that would allow her to say *Alexa, secure the exits* and keep the Davies family inside. She and her dad were outnumbered, but Nolan was already striding toward the front door.

"Well." Juliette dabbed her mouth with a napkin.

"Mom." Meri's decrescendo inflection was rehearsed for a lifetime.

Two small words told the story of a family.

"Jillian has something you'll all be interested to hear." In another few steps, Nolan would be standing between Canny and the main entrance.

He was smooth, that father of hers. Jillian hadn't even had a chance to tell him what her discovery was since waking him that morning. Either he had great faith in her abilities as a genealogist, or he was rolling the dice to bring everyone back to the table to use his skills as a mediator.

Maybe a little of both.

What she had was strong. Jillian shifted her

weight in a way that gently nudged Meri's hand off the doorknob.

Juliette stood up. "Canny has made up his mind."

"Seriously, Mom?"

The exchange involved more words than the previous one, but the plot was unchanged.

"No time." Canny tossed the car keys from one hand to the other and looked down the hall toward the kitchen. "We still have to grab Meri's stuff and get to DIA in time to return the rental."

"I promise it will be worth your while to hear Jillian out." Nolan gestured toward seats in the living room. "Come join us, Juliette. Meri, this is important."

Beside Jillian, Meri huffed but didn't move.

"Don't worry about your car, Meri," Canny said. "I arranged for someone to drive it back to Tennessee. Just leave the keys at the Inn. You'll have it in three days."

"Well done, Canfield," Michael said. "Looking after every detail."

"Except the detail that I'm going to need my car because I'm staying here," Meri muttered.

"If you have something to say," Canny said, "just say it."

"Why?" Meri marched across the kitchen and into the hall. "You won't hear it for all the noise coming out of your own mouth."

"Meri!" Juliette's rebuke was stinging.

"That's right. Take Canny's side, like you always do."

"It's not a matter of sides, Meri." Juliette followed her daughter with the clipped gait Jillian had come to expect from her.

"Isn't it? What happened to hearing me out?"

"Perhaps it would be best after all to just go home and sort all this out in the privacy of the family home. You will have an opportunity to explain why you're unhappy. I still want to hear. Does it really matter if it happens in Colorado or Tennessee?"

Mother and daughter stood halfway between the front and back doors.

Jillian leaned against the back door. Her father obstructed the front. None of the Davieses knew there was a third exit outside her office. That hadn't been part of the house tour. A third way was exactly what they needed, but not a third way out.

"I found some fascinating information about the Davies family history," Jillian said. "It would be such a shame for you all to leave without hearing it."

"Meri is what matters now," Juliette said. "At home we can all work together so she can be successful and things will get back to normal. Her aunt Pru can help, or refer her to someone."

"Refer *me?* Right. I'm the problem here. Sheesh, Mom."

"Ten minutes," Nolan said. "Let's sit down together for ten minutes and hear from Jillian. I really do believe that what she has to say will surprise you and will be part of working together for Meri's good."

Meri tilted her head, as if not sure how to interpret that statement.

"Thank you again for your hospitality." Canny slung a bag over his shoulder and picked up two others with the practice of a seasoned traveler. "But every day that Meri loses, the consequences will only compound."

"I wish you would reconsider," Nolan said.

"We're past that point." Canny sidestepped Nolan, managed to get the front door open unassisted even with his arms full, and lumbered down the walk toward the car.

"Mom, he's got your bag." Meri gestured toward the front door. "Is that really all right with you?"

"Inflaming things further is not likely to bring a good result." Juliette scanned the living room in the manner of someone checking to be sure nothing was forgotten.

"Your mother is right," Michael said.

Meri's eyes begged Jillian to do something. But what?

The front door opened, and Nolan slipped out.

Of one mind and in step, Meri and Jillian raced to the tall front windows.

"What's going on?" Michael asked.

"My dad just wants to talk to Canny." Jillian met Michael's eyes. Together, Michael and Canny were a united front. Separated, she wasn't so sure.

"He doesn't know Canfield," Michael said.

"He's pretty good with people." Jillian shifted her gaze outside again, where her father had his hand on Canny's shoulder and was speaking calmly.

"We're on a schedule," Michael said.

Jillian offered no response. Schedules could be changed. Fifteen hundred flights left Denver's airport every day.

Canny loaded the bags in the back of the SUV and slammed it shut—and then started walking side by side with Nolan down the block.

"What is he doing?" Michael headed for the front door.

"Let him go." Juliette's words stopped Michael's progress.

Jillian knew enough married people to recognize the intonation that caused married people to exchange looks without speaking further and reach an understanding.

"Nolan will handle Canny," Juliette said.

Meri closed her eyes for a second and blew out her breath.

Juliette was flip-flopping like a fish not quite on the hook, and Jillian didn't know if she might actually break free, but every sign of resistance helped Meri's cause.

"You can always get a later flight," Jillian said, "or rebook for the same one tomorrow." Canny had just booked the flight an hour ago. They were probably using a fare with a generous policy for change options. "I'd really like to share with you what I discovered."

"Print it out and put it in a folder. I'll read it on the plane." Michael's eyes followed Canny and Nolan down the street.

Three briefcases still sat in the hall at the bottom of the stairs, and Juliette picked up hers and took it into the living room. Michael did the same and began fussing with papers. Jillian exchanged glances with Meri, who shrugged one shoulder. *This is what they do,* the gesture said.

"Juliette," Jillian said, "I believe I was about to make you some coffee when breakfast was interrupted. I still can."

It sounded feeble. Coffee was not a panacea. Not for a mess like this. But Canny had the car keys and he was down the street, so it seemed a low risk to leave his parents in a room on their own.

"Coffee would be lovely." Juliette glanced up from her open briefcase. "I wonder if you have a to-go cup."

Flip-flopping *again?* What did she think Nolan was handling?

"I think I do," Jillian said. "I'll take a look."

"I'll help." Meri followed Jillian into the kitchen.

"Your mother doesn't really want coffee, does she?" Jillian nevertheless rummaged in a cabinet for a recyclable disposable mug and lid and pushed some buttons on a machine.

"Southern manners," Meri said. "She wants to please you."

"And everybody else, apparently."

"You do know I'm not leaving with them." Meri stilled Jillian's motions and met her eyes.

Jillian nodded. "Trust my dad. What would he say?"

Meri squeezed her eyes closed. "Five percent."

The front door gave its raspy opening protest. Jillian's stomach dropped twelve inches in half a second. The walk wasn't long enough to accomplish anything. Even her father's charms couldn't bend Canny's rigid will. Jillian snapped a lid on Juliette's coffee. Since she'd made it, she might as well go through the motions of offering it.

The latches of Michael's briefcase clicked closed as Jillian handed Juliette the to-go cup.

Nolan pressed his lips together, looked at Jillian, and shook his head about half an inch.

"We've imposed enough." Canny took the to-go cup from his mother's hand and set it down on an end table. "It's time to go."

Really? The woman can't have her coffee?

341

Juliette hadn't really wanted it, but that wasn't the point.

Meri sucked in a breath and pushed it out before kissing her mother's cheek. "Goodbye, Mom. I'll text you. Or something. I know my housing in Memphis is kind of an issue. I'll work on finding a sublet."

"Meri," Canny said.

She flicked her eyes at him. "Canny."

"Get in the car."

"Have a nice trip."

Canny closed the space between them and grabbed Meri's elbow. She yanked away from him, pulled forward to gain some force, and let him have it in the gut with the same elbow.

Definitely one experience Jillian missed out on by not having siblings.

"Meriwether," Michael said.

"Dad." Meri dared him to interfere.

Canny stood with his hand on his stomach.

"Sorry, Canny," Meri said.

"No, you're not."

"Maybe not," she said. "But in case you haven't noticed, I'm a grown-up capable of making my own decisions. You can't just drag me around like I'm some prop in your perfect life."

"Running away was a truly mature decision."

"Canfield," Juliette said.

"Does it ever occur to you maybe I was running toward something, not away?" Meri said.

Canny shook his head. "That wouldn't fit the pattern."

"Fine. You want to see running away?" Meri put her face up against her brother's. "I'll show you running away."

She pushed past everyone in the room.

Out the front door.

Down the porch steps.

Across the street.

Canny shouted after her.

CHAPTER THIRTY-ONE

Canny was halfway down the block before Nolan caught up, passed him, and blocked his path. When Canny tried to push him away, Nolan placed his hands firmly on Canny's shoulders.

He didn't often take physical measures. He was a man of words and diplomacy. A mediator. A negotiator. But in a law practice, mediation was premised upon two parties willingly entering the process even if they were represented by separate counsel. Nolan was fairly certain that Canfield Davies's counsel would have advised him to, well, can it. In this situation, he wasn't sure Canny wouldn't hurt his sister in his insistence to be right—especially after she'd proven she was willing to strike back.

Meri's five percent had sure come roaring out, taking an energy Nolan hadn't seen coming. She deserved her space to get a grip. And she was right. She wasn't a prop in anyone else's life, much less an entire family's structure.

Trailing the sidewalk after Canny and Nolan were Jillian and the rest of the Davieses. He flicked Jillian an eye signal to follow Meri, and she picked up speed while he herded the family back toward the house.

"Please go inside." The last thing he—or Meri—needed was a prolonged spectacle in view of the neighbors. "Now."

Canny glared.

Michael scowled.

Juliette instructed, "Canfield, do as you're told."

What a confusing woman. But her ambiguity was something Nolan could work with. And her tone held more sway with the men than her words. Canny pivoted and marched toward the house.

Inside, Nolan sat the three of them on the sofa and pulled a chair from the opposite side of the room closer so he could lean forward and look them in the eyes.

"This is exactly the kind of scene Meri was trying to avoid when she decided to drive away from Tennessee," Nolan said.

"It's irresponsible." Canny glanced at his father for confirmation.

"I take note of your opinion," Nolan said. "To the contrary, however, I submit that it's incredibly brave of her."

"Brave?" Juliette's gaze lifted.

"The easy thing to do would be to follow the path laid out for her, to please the rest of you. Meri hasn't chosen the easy path."

"It's the best path," Canny said.

Nolan nodded. "Perhaps for you it was, and I

345

can see how that colors what you think is right for your sister. You take pleasure in excelling in what you do as a physician."

"Of course I do."

"I'm not going to speak for Meri," Nolan said, "but my experience as a family lawyer and mediator puts me in a position to say that it's time for you to stop talking and to listen to her—if it's not too late to get her back to the table and make a safe space for her to speak."

The front door creaked, and Jillian entered, shaking her head.

"You lost her?" Nolan said.

"Sorry. It's like that first night. She was just gone."

Juliette threw up her hands. "Meri has been doing this for years. Running off when she doesn't want to face reality. I have tried to be understanding. I really have."

"I have seen your effort," Nolan said.

"And what has it gotten us?" Michael said. "This is why we must be firm with Meri. We know our own daughter."

"I'll go." Nolan stood up and gestured at the three Davieses. "Jillian will make you comfortable, I'm sure."

She nodded her blanched face.

Nolan took his car straight to the Inn. As he suspected, Meri's car was missing from its parking spot.

Leo stuck his head out of his workshop. "You looking for Meri?"

"Yep."

"She slammed in the house, came right back out with her keys, and got in her car."

"No bags?"

"Nope."

That at least was something. "Did you ask where she was going?"

"Tried to. She muttered something about having dug herself a deep, deep hole so she might as well go get in one."

"Thanks, Leo."

"For what?"

"Tell Nia she probably shouldn't expect Meri back today."

"What's going on, Nolan?"

"It's Meri's story to tell." Nolan backed out of the parking lot and turned out on the street and headed west.

"Once upon a time even my brother liked exploring mine country. The tunnels were his thing."

Meri ran from her family to the place where she last had a happy vacation with them. As angry as she was with Canny, giving him an elbow in the gut wasn't what she was after. Not ultimately.

The old highway took Nolan out to the mine, where Tony Rizzo was the current owner of the business giving tours. Nolan plopped a twenty-dollar bill on the counter beside the cash register and glanced up at the clock on the wall.

"Tour just started?" he said to Tony's daughter-in-law.

"Twelve minutes ago. You know we don't let anyone in late."

"Young African American woman, slender, black glasses?"

"Yeah. She bought the last ticket."

"No. I just bought the last ticket." Nolan slid the twenty across the counter and hustled out of the building and across the parking lot toward the tour entrance.

"You can't do this!"

Just watch me.

Nolan had lost count of the number of times he'd taken this tour with out-of-town guests. He could give it in a pinch. The tour began in an equipment shed original to the silver mine's later years in the 1880s, and inside the door would be a rack of hard hats. Much of the opening explanation and safety warnings happened there before a tour group moved into the mine's main tunnel—meaning Meri couldn't be too far ahead of Nolan.

One lone red hard hat hung on a hook. Nolan grabbed it, moved through the shed and out the other end. The last of the tour group was disappearing into the mine's part of the tunnel that had been made safe for modern tour groups with various points of commentary about old equipment and methods. A safety sentry fastened a gate closed.

"I have to get in." Nolan knew this young man. He would give the policy line that it was for everyone's safety that no one could enter late, but Nolan was going into that tunnel. "Where's Tony?"

"Mr. Rizzo?" the young man said.

"Yep."

"I haven't seen him today."

Nolan pulled a business card from his wallet. "If he gives you trouble about letting me in late, you have him call me."

The employee's eyes widened. "A lawyer?"

"That's right. I'm in a hurry, please."

"I don't think I should do this."

"It's imperative that I speak to someone in the tour. I guarantee you won't be in trouble."

"That's not what Mr. Rizzo says."

"I'm not so old and feeble that I can't climb over that gate," Nolan said, "and I will."

The gate swung open.

The tour guide's voice echoed through the tunnel, and Nolan moved swiftly toward it. Twenty people huddled while the guide, a geology graduate from a nearby university dressed in period mining costume, pointed to what had once been an active vein in the rock wall while explaining the first step of breaking into rock with drill bits and hammers and filling them with TNT.

"They'd light the fuses, yell, 'Fire in the hole,' and run," the guide said.

One figure slipped away.

Past the group.

Past an old rusting yellow ore car sitting on the track beneath the modern light that made the mine safe for a tour.

"Excuse me," Nolan whispered several times, threading along the edge of the group.

The tour guide talked about the mucking crew that came in next.

"They said to stay with the group," someone told Nolan.

"Excuse me," Nolan said.

"I'm trying to listen." An older man planted his feet.

"They loaded sixteen tons of ore in a shift," Nolan said, "and hauled it six stories up the shaft in an elevator like that one over there. Excuse me, please."

"Shh," someone else said.

Nolan ignored them. Apparently they hadn't seen Meri slip away—not even the guide. His eyes were on her, moving deeper into the mine. Perhaps she'd been here before, but how much could she remember from when she was eleven?

"Meri," he said, his voice a hoarse whisper.

She burrowed into the tunnel, past the large

blue sign with the signal codes that would save lives if men were six levels beneath the earth. Past the old trammer, the iron donkey engine that eventually replaced live donkeys that went blind working in the darkness hauling ore cars. Past the display of hand tools and headlights the miners wore.

"Meri." He spoke louder, and his voice bounced around the cavern enough to make her turn her head.

"Nolan, what are you doing here?"

"Did you really think I wouldn't come?"

She kept walking, ignoring the group behind them. Eventually, an eight-foot gate would limit her progress, closing off the unsafe areas of the old mine, and only the tour guide would be able to unlock a gate to take the group down a side passage and out the other side of the hill. Apparently she didn't remember that. Nolan slowed his steps and followed until Meri realized no exit was available to her on her own. When she removed her glasses and pushed the heels of her hands into her eyes, he approached.

Meri heaved out a grief-laden breath. "Well, now you've seen it all. The Davies in all their horror."

"They're a tough crowd. I won't disagree with you there."

"I'll bet they're nothing like your brothers."

"You'd be surprised."

Meri looked at him. "Don't you get along with your brothers?"

"It's a work in progress," Nolan said. "Today let's focus on your family."

"I'm not going to Tennessee with them."

"I didn't expect you would. That doesn't remotely resemble what you and I have talked about."

Meri put her glasses back on her face. "Did they leave?"

"I hope not. I asked them not to."

"Nolan, please, it's impossible. Just let them go. I'll deal with it from a distance after all."

The tour group was gaining on them, pausing now for an explanation of the ore cars on display and the underground transport system involved in removing unmilled ore from the mine to the surface. Then they would take a few minutes to look at the old photos from the mine's heyday hung on the rock wall. The guide would nudge them along in about five minutes.

"You asked me a few days ago if I believed in calling," Nolan said.

"I remember."

"Choosing your path because God puts it before you so plainly you can't walk any other way. That's the way you described it."

Meri nodded.

"That's about the best description of calling I've ever heard. Running *toward* something.

Just what you said to your brother. Your family needs to hear that from you when tempers are not flaring."

"Are you planning to stick a sock in Canny's mouth?"

Nolan laughed softly. "I hope it won't come to that. I did give them all a bit of a scolding."

"Really?" She looked up and angled her gaze toward him for the first time.

"Really."

"They're still at the house?"

Nolan nodded.

"With Jillian?"

He nodded again.

"That hardly seems fair to her."

He laughed again. "Come back to the table, Meri. Let's hear what Jillian has to say about your family's history. And then I promise to make space for your family to hear what you have to say."

Meri fingered the car keys dangling from a belt loop. Nolan couldn't be one-hundred-percent sure she wouldn't leave the mine, get in her own car, and drive toward the Wyoming border.

"Five percent still fighting hard?"

CHAPTER THIRTY-TWO

Memphis, August 27, 1909

Eliza's hip hadn't been the same for years. Decades. When one lived to be past seventy, one could not rely on joints gliding as smoothly as they had at forty. She'd never fallen. Nothing had fractured. She had not woken one day of a mind that this was the day that her step was slowing or that it took her ten minutes longer now to walk to church or the shops than it used to. It came an ache here and there, a limp that was slight at first and then undeniable, and then she was alone in the old family home. No one day stuck out in her memory as the day she decided she ought to give up ambulating any distance, yet she had.

Eliza's mother had never quite adjusted to her daughter's habit of driving a carriage, but once Eliza had taken it up during the 1878 epidemic she couldn't go back. She drove only for her own convenience on short errands—not enough to displace the employment of a deserving driver who needed honest work for which her father could well afford to pay. Visiting Canfield Asylum, for instance, was not worth tying up a driver. The dozens of orphans stranded there after the outbreak needed homes, and Eliza would not abandon them, nor the couple who ran the orphanage, simply because the outbreak subsided.

She lost valuable time when she fell ill with the fever. Mrs. Haskins recruited a neighbor who had already survived it to look after Eliza in those days. Later they told her they feared she would not make it, but she had made the turn in the middle of the night and did not relapse into a second, worse, round as so many did.

Dear Mrs. Haskins. Gone more than twenty years ago.

At St. Mary's, Sister Hughetta was the only sister to survive, and a few years later she moved away to start another school in another parish. As far as Eliza knew, the teaching sister had never again been called on for nursing duties.

Eliza adjusted her left hip—the more bother-some one—on the wicker chair on the front porch of her family home. Most of the children at Canfield found homes. With enough patience, which involved a great deal of correspondence and investigation into scant records, she and the others working to place the children found relatives for some of them. News that these relatives would take the orphaned second cousins or children of estranged half-siblings brought rejoicing. If this was not the outcome, they looked for unrelated generous hearts. In the process, a few children grew too old for adoption and had to make their way in the world at tender ages. Others outgrew the adorable younger ages and took longer to place.

Like Sammy. They could find no relatives. His parents' generation had all been born in slavery, and tracing where they had been before the war was nigh impossible, never mind where freedom took them afterward. Eliza had been tempted to keep him. So very tempted. He came willingly to her during her visits to Canfield, tagged along after her as she worked among the children, sat in her lap when she took a moment's respite. She was forty years old then. Even if she met a kindhearted man she could love at that stage of her life, she would likely never have a child. Perhaps God meant for her to have this one. Even now, sitting on her front porch, she could close her eyes and feel the slight weight of him leaning against her.

A letter came from a northern colored family inquiring about adopting one of the children orphaned by the yellow jack. They would like a boy, if one was available, because they had two girls, and a school-age child would fit in well with their household.

Eliza could muster no substantive argument against the placement.

He's mine.

The placement was right for Sammy. A good home. With his own people. In a community that knew and celebrated the traditions his parents would have known. In her neighborhood, a boy with a black face would always be mistaken for and treated like a house servant who had strayed from where he belonged.

He's mine.

But he wasn't hers. He belonged to himself, and to God.

So she hugged him tight and put him on the train going north when he was just past six years old and had already learned to read. Sammy would get a good education in the North. He would be somebody his parents and aunt would have been proud of.

Canfield closed a few years later, after twenty years of serving colored children. Other orphanages did that now. Eliza still made donations when she could.

The first frost came the same day Eliza succumbed, and the epidemic stopped spreading. But it was not as if Memphis snapped back to the city it had been. In fact, it lost its city charter. The shrunken population. The decimated economy. The climate of fear that it could all happen again. It was years of hard-fought strategy to bring it back to an attractive place to live—this time with better sanitation. Not everyone was persuaded of Dr. Walter Reed's theory that mosquitos carried the disease and it was not contact with the sick, after all, that spread the virus, but Eliza thought the notion had merit. He seemed to have gone to a great deal of effort to prove his experiments.

The shaded front porch was Eliza's favorite part of the house now. Every few weeks she toyed with selling and moving to a tidy new bungalow. Someone would have to deal with the house once she was gone anyway. Most of the interior rooms were closed off already. When her hips reached a point of protest about the stairs, though it was not yet severe, she moved downstairs into the room that had once been her father's study. Some days she could still get a whiff of his pipe tobacco, though the walls had been papered over and the furniture exchanged for a bed and sitting area. Eliza lived simply with the help of a companion, Annette, who stayed in the old maid's room because it was the only other room on the ground floor suitable for personal use, and a second woman who came in to do the heavier cleaning once a week. The horses and carriage were gone. If she needed transportation, she or Annette hailed a cab and tried to stay out of the way of those newfangled automobiles whose drivers seemed to believe all former modes of transportation were no longer entitled to occupy space on the roads.

One of them, a practical boxy variety, rather

than the less appealing showy convertible models made for road racing, as Eliza understood it, rolled down the street in a manner suggesting caution although there was no other traffic at this sluggish hour of the afternoon. Eliza fanned herself with an old church bulletin from the side table and peered. The automobile inched forward until it was in front of her home, where it stopped.

Eliza scooted forward in her chair.

A young man emerged and glanced around.

Eliza vaguely remembered being that young. He could not yet be forty, and certainly younger than she was in the days of the yellow jack.

Despite the heat, he wore a gray pinstriped suit and a black hat, and he drove a car, so he was a man of some means though not extravagant. The neighborhood did not receive many colored visitors. Possibly he was a relative of someone who worked on the street in one of the homes that remained more fully staffed than hers. But why had he brought his automobile to rest in front of her house?

The man's eyes settled on Eliza.

Eliza pulled herself upright to call through the screen door to her live-in companion. "Annette? Are you expecting someone?"

The man walked slowly toward the house.

Annette came to the door and looked out. "I don't know him."

"Miz Eliza?" His pitch rose with hope as if to say, *Please be my Miz Eliza.*

Eliza examined his face. She was not so old that her memory was gone, but she did not recall meeting this man.

"I'm Sam," he said, removing his hat. "Sammy."

Her heart rate nearly doubled in the course of the next ten seconds. *Sammy.* Yes, she could see it now. The wide dark eyes, crinkling in the corners of his narrow face. She extended her hands, and he came up onto the porch, where she could reach up and put a palm against his cheek.

"Why, you are nearly as old as I was the last time I saw you," she said.

"Yes, ma'am."

"Ma'am?" Annette still stood in the door.

Without taking her eyes off Sammy, Eliza said, "Annette, we're going to need a pitcher of sweet tea and those apple turnovers you made this morning."

"Be right back." Annette withdrew into the house.

"Sit." Eliza gestured. "August is still unbearably hot in Memphis. At least out here there is shade and a breeze."

Sam took one of the wicker chairs, and Eliza angled another so she could see his face.

"How did you find me?" she said. "You were a child, and you were never at my home back then."

"I couldn't be sure, of course," Sam said, "but I had your family name, and I had a feeling it was an old Memphis family."

"Since 1841."

"And if you didn't leave during the epidemic, like so many, then maybe you never left. I made inquiries, and there you were, sitting on the porch like you were waiting for me."

Perhaps she had been. "Here I am."

Annette came with a tray that held a pitcher, two glasses, and four apple turnovers.

"Annette, this is one of my children," Eliza said. She smiled and leaned forward to tap Sam's knee. "My favorite, actually. The dearest one. You can bring another glass and stay to visit if you like."

"I'll leave you to get reacquainted," Annette said, "but you let me know if you need something."

Eliza filled the glasses with sweet tea and handed one to Sam. Questions barraged her mind. She grappled for a starting point. "What I most want to know is whether you've had a happy life."

He met her eyes. "I have. The family that adopted me was very kind and raised me in the fear and nurture of the Lord. They were frugal and hardworking, and I did not know want a day in my life."

"But did they love you, Sammy?"

"Yes, deeply. They still do. I never had to doubt that."

Eliza sat back in her chair and drew a long draft of tea. The child grew up loved and cared for.

"I went to college, Miz Eliza. My parents did what they could to help, and I worked my way through for the rest."

"Sammy, you're a college man! I'm so proud."

"I'll never forget you were the one who taught me to read."

"You practically taught yourself."

Sam turned his glass in his hand. "When I graduated from college, I talked with my parents about something I wanted to do. I didn't want to hurt them, but it had been on my mind for years by then."

"Goodness, what was that?"

"I wanted to take a surname that connected me to my past."

"Dormer," Eliza said. "We figured out that your family's name was Dormer. I thought it was on the adoption paperwork."

Sam nodded. "It was in the papers. But that wasn't the name I had in mind. That was probably just somebody's plantation master's name, anyway."

He was likely right. Tillie's good man. "Then what?" Eliza said.

"Davies."

Eliza gulped. "You wanted my name?"

"I do remember little bits about my family. The songs my sisters sang to me. The ironing my mother took in to do at night. But I was only three. It's you I remember. Coming out to Canfield nearly every day in the same carriage you rescued me in. Always making time for me. Always making sure I had what I needed. Always patient when I wanted extra attention among the chaos of all those children who lost their families. Answering my questions about everything under the sun. Quelling my fears about going off to a new place with new folks and assuring me I was going to have a wonderful life in a real house with a real family. And it *was* you who taught me to read and set me on a life of learning that I have never taken for granted. I know not many colored children had the opportunities I had."

"Samuel Davies." The knot in Eliza's throat was thick. "I don't know what to say. You honor me."

"Samuel Strickland Davies," he said. "My adoptive parents mean a great deal to me as well. After college I stayed on at Howard University and went to medical school."

"Oh my." The glass in Eliza's hand shook until she set it down. "You are a physician?"

"I am. The Lord blessed me with my wife, Bertha, a nurse, and we moved to Atlanta, where there aren't nearly enough doctors for colored people. Recently we opened a practice in

Meriwether County. We have a little boy, and I hope someday he will go into practice with me and eventually take over."

"A boy of your own! What's his name?"

"Canfield."

"Oh Sam."

"If you hadn't found me and made sure I got to Canfield that afternoon, Miz Eliza, perhaps I would not have lived even another day."

She could not brush away the truth of his statement.

Then he grinned. "We also have a daughter. Brand-new, just six weeks old. We call her Eliza."

"Sammy." Her voice hushed.

"For years I've wanted to see you," Sam said, "and thank you and tell you I've had a good life. I don't take it for granted. I intend to spend it making sure other people get the help they need, the way I got the help I needed. I promise my children will learn that their opportunities come with responsibilities to a cause greater than themselves. And they will know I learned that from you."

Eliza's cheeks were damp. "I only did what the Lord asked of me. 'What doth the Lord require of thee, but to do justly, and to love mercy, and to walk humbly with thy God?'"

"Micah 6:8." Sam sipped his tea. "I wanted to bring the family, but Bertha insisted the baby is too little."

"She sounds like a wise woman. Next time," Eliza said. "Don't wait thirty years, and bring little Miss Eliza Davies of Meriwether County, Georgia, to meet old Miss Eliza Davies of Shelby County, Tennessee."

CHAPTER THIRTY-THREE

Jillian had chosen a seat in the living room that gave her a view of the front door, both of Meri's parents, and her brother. As far as she knew, Canny was the only one with keys to the car, but if he got over the sidewalk confrontation when Nolan interfered with his effort to chase Meri, there was no telling what he'd do. She wasn't taking any chances. Making them comfortable, as her father put it, included keeping them in her line of sight.

Juliette drank her to-go coffee after all. All three of them riffled around in their briefcases. Jillian picked up a genealogy magazine.

"Have you tried calling him?" Michael asked after twenty minutes of this awkward arrangement.

"He'll call me if he has news." Jillian flipped a page. Soon any decent hostess would offer lunch, or at least a snack. She couldn't risk having Canny decide to go out in search of food. And other things. But even cheese and crackers would mean leaving Canny unattended. She could ask Juliette to help her, like keeping a hostage to motivate her son to think twice about how he behaved or any ideas about taking off.

Where would he go? He wouldn't have a clue where to look for Meri, and he was the one most determined not to leave without her.

She glanced at her phone, willing there to be a text from her father.

Nothing. Maybe he didn't have a clue where to look for Meri either. Maybe he'd found her but was unpersuasive. Maybe he was still making the case for her return.

Ring!

Michael slapped a book shut. "She wanted us to go. Maybe we should. If we leave now, we could still catch our plane and get back to our obligations."

"No, sir." Canny set his jaw. "Not without Meri. We came for her, and we'll go home with her."

She's not an antique up for auction. Jillian did well not to drop her head into one hand and shake it. Surely not every big brother was like this.

"We've waited this long." Juliette barely glanced up from the professional journal she was reading through a pair of silver-rimmed glasses. "We should wait for Meri and stay together, even if that means rebooking our flights."

Three people, three opinions. The tension heated from simmering to a low boil.

"I need some air." Canny pushed his briefcase off his lap. "I've got calls to make anyway."

Really? Would he be making calls if he were

driving to Denver right now with his family listening in? Whatever. Maybe he was finally coming to terms with rebooking their flight. Jillian closed her magazine as Canny stepped out to the front porch. At least the curtains were wide open, so she didn't have to be obvious about arranging them in order to keep track of his movements.

Juliette and Michael remained in separate corners of the living room reading separate stacks of printed materials pulled from their separate briefcases. Jillian dropped her magazine on an ottoman and wandered to the end of the hall, ducking around the corner toward her office but close enough to the main hall to keep an eye on Canny. She pulled out her phone and pressed the speed dial number for Kris Bryant.

"Big favor," she said when Kris answered.

"Lucky for you, things are a little slow on Mondays."

"Long story and no time to tell it," Jillian said, "but I need a serious care package. Some of Carolyn's candy, a couple of quarts of ice cream, and a selection of sandwiches from Ben's Bakery. Fancy ones."

"Now I'm a lunch delivery service?" Kris said.

"Did you miss the part about no time to tell the story? Food for six. Urgent."

Jillian clicked off, but before she could stuff her phone back in her pocket and return to the living room, it buzzed.

"Hi, Nia."

"What's going on over there?" Nia said.

"The Big Chill of Chaos. Have you seen my dad?"

"Leo said he was here but was mysterious about where he was going."

"Well, if you see him again, it means everything will come to a head soon."

"And Meri?"

"Wish I could tell you." Canny was wandering closer to the edge of the porch than Jillian would have liked. "Gotta go."

She returned to the living room. "I took the liberty of calling for some lunch to be brought in. I'll just let Canny know."

"We could have gone out," Michael said.

Not a chance. "It's no trouble," Jillian said.

She stepped out onto the porch. "Everything all right?"

"I think you know it's not," Canny said.

At least he wasn't shouting.

"I have a light lunch coming. Thought you might like to know, since you and your dad missed breakfast."

"Thank you." Canny gestured toward the cushioned double-wide wicker chair. "Is it all right if I just sit out here to wait?"

"Of course. I'll keep you company. I have to watch for the food anyway."

No sneaky business. He was entirely too polite,

and the chair he selected wasn't fully visible from inside the living room. Jillian smiled and sat in the rocker. They didn't have to talk, but she wasn't losing another Davies when she hoped her dad would turn up with Meri any minute.

Jillian couldn't remember living anywhere else, other than her college years in Denver, which never truly felt like living away from home. She came home practically every weekend, and met her dad for lunch in Denver a couple of times a month. But this year, at age twenty-eight, marked the halfway point. Half of her life with her mother, and half of her life without being able to tell her mom about her day, or bad dates, or hard decisions, or work triumphs, or secret aspirations.

The rest of her life without her mother present.

She didn't want that for Meri, not when she had a living, breathing mother right there, inside the front door. A mother who had traveled all this way for *some* reason, even if she couldn't quite decide what it was.

Nolan's car turned into the driveway.

"Where's Meri?" Canny demanded.

"She needs some time." Nolan came up the porch steps. "Are the others inside?"

Jillian nodded and moved toward the door.

"What do you mean, she needs some time?" Canny followed Nolan and Jillian inside and announced, "He didn't bring Meri."

370

"Wasn't that the point of going after her?" Michael looked up from his papers.

"She has to come back on her own terms," Nolan said. "I'm hopeful."

Jillian sucked in a corner of her mouth. Hopeful, but not certain.

"Who's that out there?" Juliette nodded out the window.

"Oh, the food!" Jillian returned to the door and slipped out to meet Kris.

"What is going on?" Kris handed her two paper sacks.

"You may have heard Meri's family is in town." Jillian peeked into the bag of bakery sandwiches.

"I did."

"It's complicated. Thanks for doing this. I promise more explanation later, but I have to get back in there."

"Whatever, girlfriend. One of the tubs is chocolate chip cookie dough, and the other is strawberry cream. Meri likes it. Maybe it will help with whatever is going on in there." Kris reached around Jillian's full arms to push open the door before bouncing back down the steps.

"Why don't we have something to eat?" Inside, Jillian caught her father's eye and headed toward the dining room. "It's not my dad's cooking, but it's pretty good."

Nolan took some plates from a cabinet, and Jillian unpacked the bags. Kris had added salads to the sandwiches, a better option than the chips Jillian had expected.

"The ice cream goes into the freezer for later," Jillian said. "I'll grab a pitcher of tea."

The spread was casual but sufficient, and the timing was perfect. Thickly stacked sandwiches—a choice of meats and vegetarian options—and salads created plenty of busy work. Canny's and Michael's lack of breakfast had caught up with them, and their mouths were too occupied to ask the questions dripping in everyone's minds.

Then the door opened with a slow, tentative groan.

Meri stepped in.

The room stilled.

Nolan stood up. "Are you hungry?"

She shook her head.

"Come on in. There's a seat beside Jillian. I'll clear up a little while you settle in. Then we'll talk."

Nolan glanced around the table, his tone and features forbidding anyone to light into Meri.

Under the table, Jillian squeezed Meri's knee in what she hoped felt like reassurance. She may have pinched too hard. The Davies family glanced at each other, occasionally settling a gaze on Meri for a few seconds. When they did, she looked away.

In her lap, Meri turned her phone toward Jillian.

A text from Pru. YOU'VE GOT THIS. AND DON'T FORGET WHO HOLDS YOU.

Nolan returned with bowls and the ice cream. Jillian arranged Carolyn's candy on a couple of small plates.

"We're all here. The first thing I want to say is thank you. This is an important time for your family, and you're all at the table—literally." Nolan met Meri's eyes. "We have strawberry cream. I know you like that. It's a good place to start, right?"

She nodded, and he dished a couple of scoops into a bowl for her. Then he passed the quarts around for the others to make their own selections while he talked. Jillian slipped out to grab a folder from her office with the handwritten notes summarizing her findings and a few other items.

"I'm going to put out a few simple principles to guide us," Nolan said. "First, we are not here for anyone to win. We are here to listen and learn. Second, we will set and maintain a respectful tone. Third, we will work on understanding the varied interests at play. That means no one is forcing anyone to do anything. And fourth, I hope you will all agree that our goal is reconciliation."

Go, Dad. Mr. Mediator.

"So in the interest of listening and learning, we'll start with Jillian explaining her findings about the genealogy of your family."

Jillian sat up straight with her notes on the

table. "I understand that both sides of the family tree have many medical branches, and I would be happy to look further into the Mathers side with a little more time. So far I've explored the Davies side. Michael, in addition to the Canfield name coming down through male members of the family, Meri's middle name, Eliza, is a family name, correct?"

Michael nodded. "I have a sister Eliza, and my father had an aunt Eliza."

"And before that?"

Michael shrugged.

"I think you'll be surprised how that name entered your family. And what do you know about the origin of Canfield?"

"I suppose it meant something in the beginning. Then these things just become tradition in the family. That's how it works in the South."

"I see that a lot," Jillian said. "People name a baby to honor a particular person without knowing the depth of connection to the family line."

"Are you saying you know where these names— Canfield and Eliza—came from?" Meri asked.

"Yes! And they essentially entered your family at the same time."

"Were you right about what you told me about Canfield?" Meri said.

"Wait," Canny said. "Meri already knows what you're going to say?"

Jillian held up one finger. "Not really. I shared a

vague line of investigation with her. But I needed substantiation."

"But you were right," Meri said.

"Yes, but not at all in the way I imagined."

She had everyone's attention now.

"Genealogists often begin with census information. The Canfield who died in infancy appeared in the 1930 census, and then the 1940 census shows all his siblings. Meri, that includes your grandpa Thomas and great-aunt Muriel that you've told me a little about, as well as your great-aunt Eliza."

"She wanted to be a doctor," Michael said, "but it wasn't an easy thing for a black woman in the 1950s. According to my father, when she got pregnant, it seemed like the final obstacle. We gave Meri her name with the hope that Meri would be the one to fulfill that dream."

Meri stirred her melting ice cream. "She used to say it would be so much easier for me now. I was little. I didn't really know what she was talking about."

"Keep going, Jillian," Nolan said.

"I went back to the 1920 census. Michael, when you said that your grandfather had practiced with his father in Meriwether County, that helped a great deal in knowing where to look. I wondered if the same was true the next generation back— that Samuel Davies had been in Meriwether County."

"Was he?" Michael asked. "I don't think I ever really knew."

"He was," Jillian said. "And in addition to his son Canfield—your grandfather—he had a daughter named Eliza. He had two other children, Franklin and Elijah. I haven't found much on Franklin, but it looks like Elijah went north and became a doctor in Chicago."

"I didn't know that," Michael said.

"This is slightly interesting," Canny said, "but I'm not sure what it really has to do with anything. Is there a point?"

"I'm getting there," Jillian said. "Old censuses are not easy to navigate, even with all the paid access I have, without specific information like where the person might have lived at the time the census taker came to do the interview in person. Without that, you have to read a great deal of handwritten notes and abbreviations."

"Jillian was up all night working on this," Nolan said.

"I looked at census data, physicians listings, medical schools listings—such as they were—county records, marriage licenses. Birth records from the late nineteenth century were not standard and give little help."

"The point?" Canny said again.

"I find Samuel Strickland Davies in the 1910 census listed in Meriwether County, married to Bertha Calhoun, with two children, Canfield and

376

Eliza, and practicing medicine. But I don't know where he was in 1900, the time of the previous census. Not in Meriwether County."

"He could have been anywhere," Juliette said.

"Right. Which makes the search really hard without more information. He married Bertha in Atlanta in 1904, but he wasn't in Atlanta in the 1900 census either."

"So where did he come from?" Meri asked.

"I haven't filled in all the gaps yet, but I turned to the best clue I had. Why did he name his son Canfield?" Jillian let the question hang. "My hunch was that he was orphaned during the 1878 outbreak of yellow fever in Memphis and placed in the Canfield Asylum, which took in dozens of children."

"I'm named for an insane asylum?" Canny glanced at Meri. "Pretty sure that's worse than being named for a county."

"You're named for a legacy." Michael's correction was swift. "Both of you are. Let Jillian finish."

"It wasn't an asylum for the mentally ill," Jillian said. "It was an orphanage. You can imagine how much of the record keeping survived. Memphis was a disaster zone. People of means abandoned the city, leaving the poor—mostly the blacks and a lot of Irish immigrants—with a rampant epidemic, a destroyed economy, and a flailing, overwhelmed medical system. When all was said and done and the epidemic was over, people caring for the orphans did their best to find homes for them, but this took some time."

"I have a feeling we're getting to the reason you woke me up so early this morning," Nolan said.

"We are!" Jillian grinned. "Genealogists are a tight bunch. The ones with access to the best information are often on the ground in local places, where historical records are carefully preserved. We network at conferences and in online groups, because we know we need each other. I found an index on the internet of archived documents housed in Memphis. That's not unusual. Lots of museums or universities do that. But I couldn't be sure what they were without seeing them, so I called someone in Memphis basically in the middle of the night. She went into the small historical museum where she works in the archives and got eyes on some correspondence."

All eyes in the room were on Jillian.

"From Dr. Samuel Strickland Davies of Meriwether County, Georgia, to Eliza Davies of Memphis. She was a well-to-do white woman who found him when he was three in the house where the rest of his family had died during the epidemic and sent him to Canfield. It was three years before he was adopted, and she made sure he never wanted for anything while he was there. When he was grown, he took her surname by his own choice."

"And named his daughter for her," Meri said.

Jillian nodded. "They reconnected when he was in his thirties and she was seventy and corresponded for the next eight years until her death. She never had children of her own, but she spent her life looking after other people's."

A sob choked its way up Meri's throat. "She cared for children?"

"It was her vocation," Jillian said. "She believed she should use her privilege in this way, to 'do unto the least of these' and make their lives better."

"She said that?" Meri's shoulders heaved.

"My friend took pictures of the letters and emailed them." Jillian slid several sheets out of the folder and spread them in front of Meri.

Meri leaned forward gingerly, studying the printed pages.

"The letters are not complete," Jillian said. "Some of Samuel's letters were found tucked into various books around the house after Eliza died. Some of them are only pieces, not the entire letters. The personal contents of the house were left to someone locally to dispose of. Even in 1917 someone had the good sense to write to Sam and ask if he still had Eliza's letters, but there'd been a house fire. He only had one left and didn't want to part with it. No one knows what became of it."

"He loved her." Meri's eyes darted along the tight script of Sam's letters. "I wonder if his daughter ever met her."

Jillian shuffled the pages and pointed to a line. "Read this."

" 'Our Eliza cannot stop talking of our visit to your home.' " Meri looked up. "They did meet! In Memphis! There are a lot of old homes. Maybe I've driven by her house."

"Quite possibly. After her parents passed away, Eliza gave away a lot of her money to charitable causes, mostly orphanages and social agencies, and lived very simply. When she died, she left what remained to Samuel, in trust for his children's higher education. It wasn't a great deal by then—primarily the value of the family home in Memphis after it was sold—but it got them started. I have pictures of her will also."

"Dad, you have to see these. Your great-grandfather's handwriting." Meri passed the pages across the table. "His own words about his life and what it meant to him to be a doctor."

The room was hushed, nearly breathless, while Michael and Juliette hunched over fragments of the letters. Even Canny had nothing to say. Jillian smoothed the pages of notes and set down her pen.

Nolan cleared his throat. "I think Meriwether Eliza Davies of Chattanooga, Tennessee, of late of Canyon Mines, Colorado, might be ready to say something about what she is running toward. Am I right?"

Behind her glasses, liquid slithered across Meri's wide eyes, ready to spill down her narrow face. She nodded.

"I got an email just before I came back. I got in."

CHAPTER THIRTY-FOUR

Jillian cradled the mug in both hands the next morning, three fingers through the handle on one side, her palm fitted around the curve of the stoneware on the other. In the last twelve days, she'd tried every mug in the kitchen cupboard. Sizes, weights, color. Vacation logos. Scripture verses. Pithy sayings. Artsy designs. Many she'd forgotten they had. In a few cases she'd seen quickly why the mugs had been relegated to the back of the cabinet. A chip might be tiny, but it was damaging if it hit your lip at the wrong angle. She had them sorted now.

She had her new favorite. This one. Taupe—not beige—with a maroon swirl around the lower portion and large enough to suit the concoctions she liked to create.

And it had been her mother's. Perhaps that was why she hadn't wanted to use it all these years. Now, in this crossover year to the season of living more of her life without her mother than with her, she wanted to hold something her mother often had held. It might stain. It might chip. It might even break. But each time Jillian held it, she would be sharing a moment with her mother. She would take the risk.

Jillian was on the porch, watching Canny load the car. Today it was without urgency or vengeance or authority or any of yesterday's commotion.

Juliette came out. "I'm sorry we didn't get to say goodbye to your father."

"He had a seven o'clock breakfast meeting in Denver," Jillian said. "I didn't see him either."

"Thank him again for us. For everything."

"I will."

"But you're coming to breakfast at the Inn, aren't you?"

Jillian nodded.

"There's room in the car."

"You all go ahead. It's only a ten-minute walk. I'll be right behind you."

Michael came out with both their briefcases. "I've got everything."

"Ready!" Canny closed the rear hatch.

"I'll see you there." Jillian went in the house and breathed in the peace and quiet. This is what she was used to. She'd made it through three days of chaos with the Davies family, an all-nighter piecing together the story behind their family tree, and a long day yesterday witnessing the cathartic result of leading them through information they'd never known and watching what happened when Meri's connection with Eliza Davies fell into place, and her plans for the future transformed her family's understanding of her.

And Memphis. The city was still full of children in need and pockets of community ripe for rebuilding into new, lasting wholeness. It wasn't the place that made Meri feel out of sorts. It was the calling that was wrong. Once she finished her graduate work, she might well go back to Memphis and take up where Eliza Davies left off with the children.

Jillian had missed an entire day of work on Monday and hadn't even kept up with checking email. But all that would have to wait another couple of hours. Breakfast at the Inn with Meri and her family was on the schedule. She left by the main door, pulling it closed, tugging it twice, and double-checking the lock.

At the Inn, amiable bits of conversation wafted from the dining room on the fragrance of one of Nia's egg-and-sausage casseroles. It wasn't the weekend, and on a Tuesday between summer tourism and ski season, there was only one couple at breakfast other than the Davieses. Jillian was here because Meri asked her to be. Perhaps she didn't yet believe her family dynamics had turned a corner, and it was a fair concern. A few hours of bonding—forced bonding, one might say—over long-forgotten family history would not change every ingrained pattern of interaction or temperament.

But it was a start. And there had been no more talk of Meri returning to medical school in Tennessee. Breakfast was easy conversation about the history and architecture of the Inn, Juliette's favorite traditions of southern hospitality, Michael's small but impressive collection of rare books, and Canny shocking Meri with the news that he had a serious girlfriend who wanted to meet his little sister.

"Christmas," Meri said.

"Promise?"

"Promise. I'll stay here, make sure Nia gets someone to replace me, find a place to live in Denver, and come home for a break in December before I start school."

"You're sure about all this?"

"Absolutely. It's a vocation to 'do for the least of these.' "

"All right, then. If any of those kids in your future need doctors, at least you'll know where to find them."

"Count on it."

Canny checked his watch. "We should leave."

"I'll go out with you."

Jillian helped Nia clear the table. "You're walking better."

"The swelling is way down," Nia said. "I have to admit I was a little wild that day, but you have to admit I wasn't completely wrong. Meri did eventually end up at the old mine."

"I'll give you that." Jillian scraped the remains of food off several plates.

"I was also right from day one that something was up with her."

"Right again." Jillian ran some water to rinse dishes.

"Do you think she'll be all right?"

"She's already a lot better than she was. She and her brother had a bona fide conversation just now."

"I've got this," Nia said. "Go say goodbye to your favorite houseguests."

"Ha-ha."

Jillian moved through the Inn to the front porch. Canny and Meri were embracing. Awkwardly, but it was an actual hug. No telling how many years it had been since they did that.

Michael was next, taking his daughter in his arms in a daddy's bear hug that made Jillian believe he'd been wanting to do that for a long time but wasn't sure Meri would welcome it. But she did.

Meri and Juliette stared at each other and took synchronized deep breaths. Then Juliette opened her arms, and Meri fell into them and the tears started.

Mom, I miss you. So much.

The Davieses had a lot to figure out. And they'd have to figure it out one day at a time. One step at a time. One phone call at a time. They'd disappoint each other. Wound each other. Leave holes in each other's lives. Jillian had worked on enough family trees to know these things were true, and sometimes they led to entire branches being lopped off and dropping into obscurity. But they'd also try to graft over their wounds. To nurture buds of new life on the tree. To stand strong against the winds. Because families also did those things.

Jillian descended the porch steps and stood beside Meri as together they waved goodbye to the family inside the SUV pulling away from the curb. Next time Meri would be running toward them. Next time.

AUTHOR'S NOTE

One of my favorite photos of my son is when he is about two, sitting on the front steps of the house we lived in then beside his cousin, my brother's daughter. First cousins who couldn't look less alike. Those two kids share fifty percent of their family heritage, each with a parent whose father was an immigrant from Brazil. But my son was white haired, blue eyed, and fair skinned while his cousin had dark eyes, black hair, and dark skin.

Of course, part of the reason I produced two blond, blue-eyed children despite my Brazilian heritage had to do with marrying someone from a carefully guarded Swedish gene pool until I came along. Or so I'm told.

Genetics is a curious thing.

And lots of people are curious!

But the information we get from spitting in a tube and sending it off for DNA analysis isn't everything. We also need the stories that come through the generations, and so often we miss those. By the time we're old enough to appreciate them, the people who could tell them to us are gone, and with them the cumulative family memories that could help us understand where we came from—and why.

Meri Davies is, of course, fictitious. But the family line I created for her *why* leads back to real events in the history of Memphis. Other cities in the southern states experienced repeated outbreaks of yellow fever as well, particularly those along waterways, which were the commercial highways of the times—and of course breeding ground for mosquitos.

Historians believe yellow fever was imported to the Americans with the West African slave trade and continues to affect the equatorial tropics. While it did spread with the movement of ships carrying cargo from the Caribbean, through Louisiana ports, and up the Mississippi River, *how* individuals became infected was erroneously understood in the late nineteenth century, at the time of "Constance and Her Companions," as the nuns in Memphis are remembered for their sacrificial work. In 1900, US Army physicians James Carroll and Walter Reed proved that mosquitos transmitted the disease, rather than contact with an infected person so feared during the epidemics.

Eliza Davies is fictitious, but the nuns and priests of St. Mary's are not. Many of the scenes in the historical parts of this book are rooted in notes written by one of the nuns about what their daily ministrations were like and the horror of the scenes they encountered. Canfield Asylum is also historical and played a key role in caring for dozens of orphans. Sister Constance really did stand up to men with guns determined she would not bring orphans from the city to Canfield.

On one visit to Memphis I strolled an area known as Victorian Village, toured one of the historic homes that is now a museum, and heard a story of a former occupant. She lived out her last days with her African American companion occupying the bedroom next to hers. It was the only way she could get the care she needed, even if it was scandalous. I couldn't help but make Eliza forward thinking enough that sharing a meal with Callie would have brought her satisfaction—though it never happened—and in the end she was living out her days sharing her home with a companion to look after her, even though real change in race relations was a long way off.

In this first story of the Tree of Life series, my hope is that you will wonder about the *why* and *how* questions of your family. If you have a piece of the saga, be sure to share it with someone younger. If you wonder about decisions or circumstances that shaped your family, ask someone older—or even someone sideways in your family tree. Putting bits and pieces together can make the picture whole, and sometimes as the picture becomes whole, so does the person seeking it.

Olivia Newport
2019

ABOUT THE AUTHOR

Olivia Newport's novels blend the truths of where we find ourselves now with insights into what carried us in the past. Enjoying life with her husband and nearby grown children, she chases joy in stunning Colorado at the foot of Pikes Peak.

Books are produced in the United States using U.S.-based materials

Books are printed using a revolutionary new process called THINKtech™ that lowers energy usage by 70% and increases overall quality

Books are durable and flexible because of Smyth-sewing

Paper is sourced using environmentally responsible foresting methods and the paper is acid-free

Center Point Large Print
600 Brooks Road / PO Box 1
Thorndike, ME 04986-0001 USA

(207) 568-3717

US & Canada:
1 800 929-9108
www.centerpointlargeprint.com